TRINITY

A Novel

LOUISA HALL

corsair

CORSAIR

First published in the US by HarperCollins, 2018
First published in the UK by Corsair, 2018
This edition published in 2019

1 3 5 7 9 10 8 6 4 2

Copyright © 2018 by Louisa Hall

The moral right of the author has been asserted.

This book is a work of fiction. References to real people, events, establishments, organisations, or locales are intended only to provide a sense of authenticity and are used fictitiously. All other characters, and all incident and dialogue, are drawn from the author's imagination and are not to be construed as real.

A CIP catalogue record for this book
is available from the British Library.

ISBN: 978-1-4721-5403-3

Printed and bound by CPI Group (UK) Ltd, Croydon, CR0 4YY

Papers used by Corsair are from well-managed forests
and other responsible sources.

MIX
Paper from
responsible sources
FSC® C104740

Corsair
An imprint of
Little, Brown Book Group
Carmelite House
50 Victoria Embankment
London EC4Y 0DZ

An Hachette UK Company
www.hachette.co.uk

www.littlebrown.co.uk

For William

CONTENTS

PROLOGUE

WHAT I KNOW, FROM EYEWITNESS ACCOUNTS OF THE FINAL
*twenty-four hours, is this: on the afternoon of July 15, 1945,
Robert Oppenheimer drives to the steel shot tower that rises one
hundred feet from the desert.*

*He steps out of the jeep. The wind is blowing harder now, as
Oppenheimer walks to the tower. He climbs one rung at a time,
the warm metal pressing his palms. When he reaches the top,
he pulls himself up to the platform and stands in the shack the
technicians built: a roof and three corrugated metal walls, one
open side facing west.*

*There, he inspects the device. In its cradle, it stands as tall
as his head: a ten-thousand-pound metal capsule, looped and
plugged with detonators. The first nuclear bomb. The work of
the last three years of his life.*

*It's Oppenheimer who managed to persuade General
Groves to run a full-scale test of the weapon. Groves would have
delivered the bombs without testing, on the basis of the theoretical
group's calculations. A test, Groves felt, was a waste of millions of
dollars of plutonium that had taken the army years to extract.*

But Oppenheimer refused. He wouldn't deliver the bombs until they'd run a full test, on the grounds that though the calculations were in all likelihood correct, without an actual experiment, our knowledge of the weapon wasn't complete yet.

Groves finally consented. The test site was chosen, the shot tower erected, and the test bomb, which Oppenheimer now inspects, assembled and hoisted up to the platform.

HOW LONG DOES OPPENHEIMER REMAIN THERE, ONE HUNDRED FEET over the desert, standing beside the assembled device? I can't find any record. I know, however, from photographs, that he's wearing his porkpie hat.

It's the same hat he's worn since he lived in Berkeley, in the small house on Shasta Road, where he later will say he was happy. It's made of brown felt, broad brimmed and battered by use. And if he stands, and faces out the open side of the shack, he looks away from the Oscura mountains toward the Jornada del Muerto basin.

That's what he must see: a vast expanse of cracked, reddish earth spreading toward the mountains on the horizon. Dry shrubs, rocky outcrops, the blades of an occasional yucca, and scattered bones bleached by decades of sunlight.

The wind, according to every account, has only continued to quicken. Now the clouds have grown dark. They pour over the mountains like smoke, and as they cross the sky, they drag their shadows over the snakeweed.

TRINITY

SAM CASAL

San Francisco, 1943

I ONLY FOLLOWED HIM FOR TWO DAYS, IN JUNE OF 1943, SO I CAN'T say that I knew him. Not, at least, in any real sense.

But it's true that I thought about him a lot. Even after he'd gone back to Los Alamos, when I was just tailing that girl. And even after the war had been won, and I'd left G-2 to start my own practice.

Even now, if I'm honest. Every once in a while, when I'm on my way home from the office, I still sometimes think about Opp and that girl having dinner.

On the train, swinging out over the bay, it can start to seem as if there must have been some clue I didn't catch, when I was sitting there at the bar, watching them in the smudged mirror. An exchange between him and the girl. An expression I didn't notice.

It's possible for me to get so caught up in the details of that night that the real world—Joanne and the boys, their football games and the homework—can sometimes start to recede. It's as if I'm on the same train, traveling over the same body of water, but it's almost thirty years ago now, and I'm still with the counterintelligence office, tailing him for Communist contacts.

Then, once again, Opp is sitting a few seats ahead, shaking out the newspaper he bought at the station, and it's my job to stay a few seats behind him.

I've missed my stop a few times. I've had to apologize when I got home, and explain to Joanne that I slept through the station. There she is, folding laundry, or cleaning up after dinner, and I'm running late because all these years later, Opp's still shaking out that old paper.

It's the definition of a cold case. A case I'm not even assigned to, and haven't been for nearly three decades.

But even so, sometimes you can't help reviewing the details. You examine the way she greeted him at the station. You look at the Mexican place where they chose to have dinner. You remember the song they got up to dance to, the run in her stocking, the way she led him into the restaurant.

I know it's all useless. Once I looked long and hard at a girl's face. She was my wife and she was sleeping beside me. In the darkness, I looked at her a long time, but another person is a mystery.

We lived together for nearly a year. In the mornings, I watched her pull on her socks. Her shoes were lined up on the floor of our closet. But I never did know her. I also never knew Opp, or Opp's wife, much less that girl who danced with him at the Mexican restaurant.

It's useless to go back now and try to understand what I couldn't back then. For the most part I resist the temptation, and it only occurs to me in a few specific locations. When I'm on the train, for example. Or if I pass Montgomery Street. If I pause there and try to remember what it was like when Opp had gone back to Los Alamos, and I was just tailing the girl.

I stood in that yard across from her building. Every night, I waited there in the darkness, under that tree. Its leaves smelled bitter and dusty. I could never figure out why. I just waited there, looking up at the lights of that girl's apartment.

By then, I was so tired I started to see things. Like the belly of that plane that passed by so slowly it didn't even seem to be moving. I was sure it wouldn't stay up. I thought it would drop straight out of the sky. I imagined running headfirst into the wreckage.

What a strange time that was. I'm glad it's behind us. Now there's no reason to think of it much. Only if I drive past Montgomery Street, or if I venture back to that Mexican restaurant, and pull open that heavy door, and step into that particular darkness.

Then, sometimes, I can start to suspect once again that maybe the whole series of unsolvable cases started because Opp and that girl went to eat there. Or because they danced to that song. Or because they drove home to her third-story apartment.

That's what it seemed like at the time: that because I couldn't understand Opp, I couldn't trust myself to understand anyone or anything else. Because for reasons I couldn't comprehend in that moment, Opp wasn't content to stay where he was supposed to, at that camp in the desert, sleeping in the house we gave him to share with his wife, waking up early to look after those weapons.

Because he set off on that reckless escape from the mesa,

and fled back to the city, where he took that girl to the Mexican restaurant.

I couldn't understand why he did it. Or why he thought he could do it. He had agents on him at all times. There was a childishness to the whole thing, as though he thought that if he couldn't see us, we couldn't see him and catch what he was doing.

I just didn't get it. It contributed to my sense that we were sliding into a new kind of chaos. As if Opp himself—coming back to the city, spending the night with that girl—had knocked the whole world off its axis.

Now, of course, I can see there were other factors at work. Youth, for example. And stupidity. The fact that we were at war, and the general randomness of existence.

Some planes stay up, some planes go down. Some secrets come out right away, and some of them stay secret forever. I know that as well as I know the back of my own hand, but even now, all these years later, if I step into that restaurant I can start to feel dizzy.

It's as if things might start falling to pieces again, now that the door's been reopened. Then it's as tempting as ever to line up all the facts as they happened.

FOR A MOMENT, FOR INSTANCE, WHEN OPP STEPPED OUT THE BACK door of the Radiation Lab, he stood still and stared out at the bay.

He didn't move. He had the unfocused stare of a blind man, and for a moment I wondered if he needed glasses.

All day, he'd proceeded crisply through his appointments. I assumed he knew that we were behind him. He seemed to be checking off all his preapproved duties, acting in the exaggeratedly purposeful way a person would act if he knew he'd been followed.

From the airport, he headed straight for the Rad Lab, as he'd promised to do. The whole point of the trip, as he'd explained it to Security at Los Alamos, was to go back to Berkeley to interview potential assistants. He spoke only to the graduate students he'd listed. Everything went according to plan. The whole trip was running perfectly smoothly until that strange moment when he stepped out the back door and peered off into the distance, as if he'd been blinded.

Then, abruptly, he headed off toward the station. I followed behind him. He was walking fast, heading down University Avenue. That hadn't been preapproved. I wondered if he thought that he'd lost us, simply by stepping out the back door of the Rad Lab.

It was a sunny afternoon. He was wearing that porkpie hat. One of his hands was stuffed in his pocket. The other hand was curled in a fist, and he refused to look over his shoulder.

Not once, the whole time, did he look back to see me.

That's how I knew he was on his way to do something we would have refused. He wouldn't look back. He stayed on the shady side of the street and shifted his weight side to side if he ever had to stop at a streetlight.

Even when he got to the station, he didn't stop moving. He charged through the front doors and through the main hall as if he planned to sail straight on out again through the opposite exit.

He was still sailing when he glanced up at the departures

list. Overhead, on the board, the slats clacked away briskly, like dominoes falling. Then, for the first time since he left the Rad Lab, he pulled up short. He must have realized his gate wasn't open.

FOR A MINUTE, HE STAYED WHERE HE WAS, LOOKING UP AT THE board. Even then, he refused to glance back.

In his position, another man would have been jumping out of his skin. He'd stepped out of the itinerary given to him by General Groves, carrying top secret nuclear information. He knew that we had evidence of espionage on the mesa. He knew that no matter how firmly General Groves was behind him, his former involvement with Communist groups meant he wasn't above our suspicion.

Another man would've checked for tails every two minutes. But Opp didn't look once. He must have known we were behind him. He just didn't want to admit it.

With one hand still clenched in his pocket, he stood peering up at the board as if he couldn't believe it. It took him a minute to accept the fact that his gate was really closed. Then he turned away and kept moving.

He headed for the café. He bought a newspaper and a small coffee. Then he left a tip on the counter and went to the window.

He drank standing up, without any apparent enjoyment. And he was still gazing blankly off into the distance, as if the scene in front of his eyes—the station, I mean, and the people coming and going, the shoe blacks and the women in heels and the GIs with their duffels—didn't exist. As if that station had been replaced by some other station, or some other, different version of this one.

WHILE HE FINISHED HIS COFFEE, I FOUND A PAY PHONE THAT KEPT him in my sight line.

What is it, Pash said when I'd reached him in the office.

Opp's flying the coop, I said.

What do you mean he's flying the coop? Pash said, after a moment.

He left the Rad Lab. We're at the station. I think he's heading into the city.

Jesus Christ, Pash said. Jesus Christ, the fucking Red bastard.

I could hear him breathing into the telephone.

Do you want me to stop him? I said.

Stop him? Pash said. What the fuck are you talking about? Why the fuck would you do that?

I didn't answer. Pash made several odd snorting noises.

No, he said. No, no. Don't intervene. Don't fucking intervene. I have to phone Washington first.

He paused, snorted again, then caught his breath.

Just don't fucking lose him, he said. Remember your fucking directives. I'll have Frank meet you out front in the De Soto.

AFTER THAT, AT A KIOSK BY THE PAY PHONE, I BOUGHT SOME CASH-ews and a *Chronicle*. While I waited for change, I opened the paper, then snuck out my camera. Over the rim of the front page, I photographed Opp a few times.

Then I glanced down again at the headlines. FORTRESSES SMASH KIEL, BREMEN, they said. 26 LOST IN BIG DAYLIGHT BATTLE.

I put a cashew in my mouth, but it was too salty to swallow. Then I focused again on Opp's face: dark eyebrows, high cheekbones, that beak of a nose.

Every so often, he brought his coffee up to his mouth.

The longer I focused, the less human his face seemed. His jaw was like a grasshopper's jaw. Then after a while it wasn't a jaw, just an inhuman apparatus.

At 5:07, he brought his watch up to his face. Then he moved out of the frame. I folded up my paper and followed.

ON THE TRAIN INTO THE CITY, HE TOOK A SEAT BY THE WINDOW LIKE any other man on his way in to work. I watched him over the paper, trying not to get caught up in the headlines. I must have, though, because I remember them still. There were a lot of headlines that day. COSTS HELD "NOT TOO HIGH FOR RESULTS," was one of the ones I remember. And U.S. FLIERS DOWN 25 ZEROS OF 50 IN SOLOMONS BATTLE.

That kind of thing. All the headlines you get during wartime, mathematical calculations of loss.

I tried not to let them distract me. I focused on the side of Opp's face, that strange apparatus. He was in possession, I thought to myself, of secrets that could potentially wipe out the planet.

That's as much as I knew. He was working on a weapon that could potentially wipe out the planet.

And there he was, a quiet man in the seat by the window.

ONCE WE'D MOVED OUT OVER THE BAY, THE WATER MADE ITSELF known. It was so bright and vast, stretching off into the haze. Opp looked out the window. Then, when the train pulled into the tunnel through Yerba Buena, he got up and went to stand by the door. Once again, he faced out the window, but now, in the tunnel, there was nothing to see. Only a light passing, every so often, from an occasional dead man's hole in the darkness.

I tried to imagine what he could be thinking. Maybe he was counting the holes. Maybe he was watching his own reflection, swimming on the glass in the window. From the side, he looked blind and determined, like a man getting ready to make a mistake, the inevitability of which he's already accepted.

Or maybe that's just what I saw. It's possible I was reading him wrong. Like I've said, I slept badly that summer. Sometimes I was up all night on the job. Other nights I was at home, and I still had trouble sleeping. Once I'd turned out the lamp, there was always that conversation with Warren to go over again.

Then I'd picture the scene: me and my little brother, out on the back stoop, the moths knocking themselves out on the streetlight.

May had gone into the bedroom to sleep. You could smell the jasmine crawling over the opposite fence. Warren was standing, leaning on the stoop railing, and I'd taken a seat on the steps.

For a while, we stayed out there without having much to say to each other. It was a strange moment between us.

Warren was shipping out the next morning. It was the end of our three days together, and now that we were alone we both felt compelled to imitate a brotherly closeness.

We sat there in silence. We were trying, I think, to come up with something to say. Something conclusive to allow us to imagine that in the course of three days, we'd gotten close. That I'd miss him, and that he would miss me. That we'd be in each other's minds even after he'd shipped out in the morning.

But it wasn't that easy. How do you miss a brother you never really knew in the first place? The last time I'd seen Warren was when he was a kid, when my mother packed up the car and asked which of us would come with her. He went, and I stayed. And then he showed up ten years later, the week before he shipped out to the Pacific, and it's true that nothing went wrong.

He stayed with us in the new house. He met May. We played cards. We had a good time. We smoked cigarettes and listened to records.

But there was still something unnatural about it. And that last night, on the back porch, neither one of us knew how to take his leave in a way that would seem normal. We sat there in the darkness, with the jasmine vines in the alley, and the streetlight flickering, and the dog a few yards down occasionally yowling, and I couldn't think of the right thing to say, so I was grateful when he started talking. But then I realized where he was going: Asking about where May grew up. Asking about where she went to high school.

I got a metal taste in my mouth. Then I stood up, stubbed out my cigarette, and headed back into the kitchen, and Warren left the next day. I drove him to the base.

The whole way there, neither one of us spoke. At the gate, with those enormous ships flying their flags behind us, we both got out of the car. We stood there awkwardly for a moment: me and my brother, who I'd never known all that well in the first place.

My last memory of him was when he was a kid, his face a moon in the car window, jutting out from the jumble of suitcases and lamps and spare pillows our mother thought to throw in there. Now he was grown and getting ready to ship out to fly planes over Japan, and the point he wanted to make never got made. That conversation just hung in the air around the back stoop, gathering the importance of conversations that never got finished.

After that, I had trouble sleeping. At work, I tried to stay focused. I remembered the major directives. *Be overaware of the details,* Pash said to us during training. *Heed atmospherics. Your gut feeling is usually right.* But after Warren shipped out, I was in a strange state. Not unhappy, exactly, just wakeful. Alert to the task of finding evidence.

Because, of course, at that point I had a good life. Even though it was wartime, I was happier than I'd ever been. I was lucky to be in the counterintelligence game, stationed stateside, living in a new house with my new wife. I liked our life together. May was so funny. So good at cards. After dinner, we sat together, and while she was racking up wins, she'd make clever jokes. And sitting there across from her, I was so happy, so I had to find whatever evidence I could find that Warren was wrong about what he'd suggested.

Then, after May and I went to bed, I often lay awake. That's when I realized how often she got up in the night.

More nights than not, she woke at some point and threw off the covers.

Silently, she'd rise from the bed. Then, gently, she'd pull the sheet back over her absence. Then she'd cross the floor and move out of the bedroom.

Once she'd closed the door, I sometimes heard water running in the hall bathroom. Other times I realized she must have gone somewhere else.

Sometimes she stayed out a long time. I lay there in bed, wondering where she'd gone off to. Did she sit at that kitchen table? Did she read a magazine in the armchair? Maybe she ventured farther. Maybe she was on the back stoop. Or maybe she was walking down the back alley, past the fences covered with jasmine, past the Millers' dog in its doghouse.

Later, when she came back into the bedroom, she was always so quiet. And where, I wondered, had she learned to slip so silently into a room? When had she practiced those noiseless footsteps?

At her touch, the latch of the door was a cat's tongue. I had to wait for an angle of moonlight from the hall window to open over the floorboards to let me know that she hadn't left me.

What a relief it was, that pale fan of light spreading over the floor. Then closing again. And May's shadow, returning to join me.

WHICH IS ALL ONLY TO SAY THAT MY HEAD WASN'T ENTIRELY STRAIGHT when I followed Opp into the city. I tried to note what I could. When the train pulled into the station, for instance, he was the first person out. I tried to follow, but I got stuck behind an old woman, and for a moment, out on the platform, I was almost worried I'd lost him.

But then there was that porkpie hat, sailing ahead. And then I'd maneuvered myself to see his whole body. He was leaning forward, walking with one hand stuffed in his pocket.

Even now, I can see it so clearly. The way he walked with that jerky stride, like a big marionette. He moved in a way that was slightly unnatural, as if someone else had the strings and was awkwardly controlling the movements.

Even so, he moved pretty quick. I had to pick up my pace not to lose him.

"THE FUCK'S HE WAITING FOR?" FRANK SAID WHEN I'D CLIMBED INTO the De Soto. His crossword was folded up on the armrest.

Opp had come to a stop in front of the station. He was standing beside a fat man who kept mopping his face with a handkerchief. I took another photograph. I focused on the space between the big man and Opp. I was looking to see if they touched each other, even just slightly. A brushed sleeve, some kind of contact. Some kind of sign revealing that the fat man was Opp's contact.

But then a few minutes later, without so much as exchanging a glance, the fat man picked up his suitcase and exited the frame. When I put the camera down, I watched him maneuver himself into the low passenger seat of a black sedan that had pulled up in front of the station.

Frank lit a cigarette and leaned back in his seat. "That fat man looked like a woman," he said.

I didn't answer.

"Unfortunately that's what happens to fat men," Frank said. "At some point they become women."

Oppenheimer was still on the curb. He was peering across the street with that same blinded look. I kept the camera trained on his face. I wanted to note the precise moment when there was a shift in his expression, so it was Frank who first noticed the girl.

"Who's the piece?" he said.

I put the camera down. Frank tilted his chin toward the opposite sidewalk. The girl had stopped in her tracks. The other pedestrians were streaming around her, and she was smiling at Opp. She'd lifted one hand to get his attention. Then she stepped off the curb.

For a moment, before she got ahold of herself, she broke into a run. She was still waving. Then she slowed herself back down to a walk, but anyway her hand was still up in the air. It seemed sort of exposed. Left out in the open.

I turned back to Opp. He'd clearly seen her. In the meantime, he'd started smiling.

Or that's the best way I can describe it: he'd seen her, he'd started smiling. But the smile wasn't entirely natural. It didn't seem to give him any real pleasure. It looked like his vision had been restored too abruptly, and, seeing her, a smile cracked open his face.

The girl walked toward him with her hand up, and he stayed where he was, one hand stuffed in his pocket, the other hand hanging free, that smile cracking his face like an eggshell.

When she reached him, she stood before him. They didn't touch. But they obviously knew each other.

"There she is," Frank said.

The girl was saying something we couldn't hear. She was gesturing with her left hand. Opp looked down at her, and he was still smiling, but he kept his hand in his pocket. I thought I saw it twitch a few times, as though he wanted to pull it out into the open.

"You think she's pretty?" Frank said.

I took a few pictures. Thick dark hair, pale skin, black dress with a looped bow at the collar. Tall, with a solid build, somewhat thick in the ankles. But her face was beautiful.

"She's got a nice figure," Frank said.

She was still standing in front of him. That smile was still wrecking Opp's face. She was saying something and laughing, but after a while, her smile wavered. Then she wasn't smiling. Then Opp tried to stop smiling, too, but it was as though his lip had gotten caught on a hook. It took him a second to get it back down.

And the whole time, she stayed where she was. She was looking up, squinting into the light. Or maybe frowning. Then with a small gesture, almost a shrug, she turned, and they walked off together, across the street and away down the sidewalk.

FRANK NOSED THE CAR FORWARD. "THAT'S REALLY A VERY FINE-figured girl," he said. "Sailing off down the street like a ship."

We followed them for a couple of blocks. Opp still hadn't looked over his shoulder. He was refusing, one hand thrust in his pocket.

"Prow riding high," Frank said. "Flags flying."

The girl had a pocketbook slung over one shoulder. She

kept her left hand pressed against it, maybe to keep it from bumping her hip. That silk bow at her neck was fluttering slightly.

"Are we supposed to think she's his handler?" Frank said.

"I don't know," I said.

"Maybe she's the bait. They send her in to get compromising photographs. By tomorrow they're blackmailing him for nuclear secrets."

I lifted the camera and focused on the space between Opp and the girl. They were walking close enough that sometimes her sleeve brushed against his. Then I let the camera drop.

"Or she's just some woman he knows."

"No way," Frank said. He stubbed out his cigarette.

Opp and the girl had stopped walking in front of a green Plymouth coupe. She stepped off the curb, glancing back at him while she did.

On her way around the nose of the car, she stayed close to the body. It was a 1935 model, the one with big rounded tire hoods that always reminded me of the front paws of a lion.

"No way," Frank said, repeating himself. "No chance in hell he came all this way, lied to a five-star general, and risked not only the entire national security apparatus but also his job just to meet up with some side piece."

Opp was waiting by the passenger seat. His hat was pulled down over his forehead. He was looking down at the sidewalk. Then I remembered I'd seen his wife once, when I'd just taken the job.

It was one of my first assignments for Pash: watching a party Opp and his wife threw, the week before they left San Francisco. I had a list of CP members and their license plate numbers, and I checked them against the cars parked in front of their house. I found a fair number of matches. Bernard Peters, for one. And a few of Opp's former graduate students. Then I just watched the guests, coming and going. When the party was finished, and everyone but Haakon Chevalier had gone home, Opp's wife moved between rooms, picking up empty glasses.

I had her name on my list. Kitty Oppenheimer. She'd been a CP member once, though her membership was now defunct.

Through the windows, I could see her perfectly clearly. All the lights were still on in the house, and the shades hadn't been drawn. She was a small woman, wearing a blue skirt and a sweater and bobby socks with her loafers. By the time she'd done a circle of the living room, she was carrying an armload of glasses.

For a while, she moved back and forth, between the kitchen and the living room. Opp and Chevalier had gone out to the back porch, and she was inside, cleaning up. Sometimes she stopped in the kitchen. Then she looked out at them through the window over the sink.

It's a strange thing, watching people you've never met. You stand outside their house on the sidewalk, and after a while, you start to imagine you know them. A woman you've never spoken with in your life is suddenly a woman you've fallen in love with. Suddenly she's a woman you're waiting for on the sidewalk, hoping she'll look out the window and see you.

That's how I felt. Of course it didn't make sense. I'd never even met Kitty in person. I had no idea what she was thinking when she collected those empty glasses, or when she carried them into the kitchen.

After that party, they left for the mesa and I never saw her again. But then I'd already spent a night watching her through her window, so I did sometimes wonder if she was adjusting. I wondered how she liked her new house. I found out somehow that they'd given her a place on Bathtub Row, where all the top scientists lived. That satisfied me, for a while. Then I found a few pictures. The houses on Bathtub Row looked pretty old, but not all that bad in the end. And I told myself even if the house wasn't great, she would have a view of those pink mountains out back, and those weird horizontal piñons.

Then I started to wonder: Up there on the mesa, in that old, rickety house, did she sometimes move around the living room, picking up empty glasses?

Did she watch her husband and his friends outside the kitchen window?

I had no idea. All I knew about Los Alamos, besides those pictures I saw, was that it had once been a boys' school. We'd gotten the owners to sell, then surrounded the campus with a barbed wire fence and built a few checkpoints. Some of the old school buildings were repurposed as dorms for the GIs and the WACs. They made the main building a lodge where the scientists could eat dinner and dance on Saturday nights. Then they built laboratories and a PX and a school for the scientists' kids.

So that's where Kitty was, in her house on Bathtub Row, surrounded by the barbed wire fence, when Opp came back to San Francisco. And that's what I was thinking about when I watched Opp looking down at the sidewalk. And maybe that's what he was thinking about, too, with his hat drawn down over his forehead, waiting on the passenger side for that girl to unlock the green Plymouth.

IT WAS GETTING DARK BY THAT POINT, BUT PEOPLE HADN'T TURNED on their headlights just yet. Before, while we were still on the train, heading out over the water, the sun had been gaudy. Now both sides of the street were in shadow.

When the girl got to the driver's-side door, she fumbled around in her purse. Walking beside him, she'd seemed at once graceful and sturdy, but now, with her head down, rooting around in her pocketbook, she'd become clumsy. Her neck was exposed. She glanced up every so often, looking for Opp on the sidewalk.

Then I noticed there was a run in the ankle of one of her stockings. It was only small, but it was there, nevertheless. When she finally got ahold of the keys, she let herself in, then reached over and pulled up the lock. Opp folded himself into the seat, then closed his door, and we had a good view through the rear windshield.

They sat for a moment together, finally alone but not touching. He still wouldn't look over his shoulder.

Then she reached out and touched the brim of his hat. Then she took it off. She held it gently in her lap, and looked down at it for a moment, and only then did he lean forward and kiss her.

I DON'T LIKE IT EITHER. I DON'T LIKE IT NOW, AND I DIDN'T LIKE IT back then: peering through the back windshield at the other side of a lie.

23

Some secrets aren't meant to come out. Some, when they do, are only misleading. Sometimes an uncovered secret is worse than having no information to start with. It's the portion of the iceberg that shows over the surface, which isn't helpful at all, at least not for measuring the shape and mass of the iceberg.

Sometimes it only serves to point out how much you don't know about the whole object. I didn't know, for example, when I watched Opp and that girl through the back windshield, why Opp waited until she touched him first before he leaned forward to kiss her.

Or what she was thinking, when she put his hat in her lap. Or what she was thinking when she sat there for a moment, looking down at the hat, and he hadn't yet kissed her.

And given those holes in the information I did have— that Opp had veered off from his preapproved plan; that he'd lied about where he was going; that he'd ended up with a girl who wasn't his wife; that he'd gotten into her car; that he'd finally leaned forward and kissed her—given those holes, what did I know about that situation?

Some uncovered secrets only point out the need to uncover more secrets, especially when it comes to a man with a position like Opp's. He ran off from the mesa, after all, having been granted the highest level of security clearance. And we were at war. Pearl Harbor had been attacked. Most of us believed that San Francisco or Los Angeles would be the next target.

Now the danger's receded, so it seems prying, watching Opp and that girl through the lens of a camera. When you're not living with an imminent threat, it's easier to think that people should be permitted their secrets. But when Opp came back, we were on guard. We'd set aside our reservations.

That month, for example, was the same month a white mob rioted for three days in the black neighborhoods of Beaumont. But I only know that because when I came home from following Opp, I sat down for a drink at the table and saw that May had left the newspaper open. She had it turned to an article about Beaumont, buried somewhere deep in the back pages.

There was a water ring from her glass, just above the photograph. The caption mentioned that five black people were killed. Whole blocks were burned to the ground, and nobody was prosecuted.

Then, for a moment, I wondered why May wanted to read about Beaumont. I'd never even heard of the place before I found that ring on the paper.

Do you see what I'm saying? We were at war. Stories like that one got buried. That same month, in Los Angeles, a mob of servicemen on leave headed to a Hispanic neighborhood and started attacking residents. Five days later, thousands of civilians were involved in the fighting, but you didn't read about that in the papers.

In San Francisco, when we followed Opp, everywhere you turned you saw banners: *Japs Move Along,* or *Japs Don't Let the Sun Set on You Here.* There were foreclosure notices on every Japanese storefront, whole streets of houses abruptly abandoned, whole neighborhoods suddenly vacant except for a few Polish families wandering around like survivors.

But no one really paid much attention. We were focused on other threats. Violence on an international scale. Opp, for instance, ran off from the mesa in possession of secrets about a weapon that could evaporate a whole city. So you understand why we believed we had to collect whatever information we could.

Even if the information wasn't complete.

Or even if it was of a personal nature. Even if it involved looking in the back window of that girl's Plymouth coupe, and taking a photograph when he kissed her.

ONCE THE GIRL PULLED AWAY, SHE HUNCHED OVER THE WHEEL AND fumbled with the ignition. Frank waited for the Plymouth to edge out into traffic, then let a few cars get between us.

"Unfortunately," Frank said, "I'm starting to think she might love him."

"Why unfortunately," I said.

"It always ends badly for the piece if she loves him."

We followed her up Fremont Street toward Market. When we'd pulled up at a red light, Frank checked his mirrors. Then he leaned back in the seat. He cradled his head in his hands.

"By page sixty-three," he said, "she's looking lovely, draped over a desk, wearing a hole in her head instead of a hat."

That's the kind of story Frank liked to make out of a case. It got on Pash's nerves. Pash was a dramatic person himself, but when other people took narrative license, it rubbed him the wrong way. He liked to insist we were in the business of uncovering facts. He got livid whenever Frank started talking like a gumshoe in a pulp. At first, he'd try to pretend he couldn't hear what Frank was saying, but his face picked up that angry, rabbity look. His eyes started to bulge, and his mouth worked under his moustache. Eventually he'd start to issue directives.

"We're not here to tell stories," he'd say. Or: "We're here to notice the events as they happen."

But Frank couldn't be stopped. We were still waiting at the red light, and he was still leaning back in his seat.

"Or maybe," he said, "she's not draped over the desk. Maybe she works for the Reds, but after she lures the scientist in, she has regrets about the whole ploy. As it turns out, she really loves him. She loves him despite the fact that he's married. So later, after she helps the Reds procure their dirty photographs, she tries to get the photographs back. She goes to great lengths. She seduces her handler, even though he's a scumbag. The scumbag lets her think he's keeping the photographs in his desk. But after she's already seduced him, she goes through his desk and realizes they're gone. He's already sent the prints back to Moscow."

"He's a Russian?" I said, keeping my eyes on the light.

"No," Frank said. "He's one of these American Reds the Russkis keep in their pocket. So now cut to the morning, and she's in her car, and she's slept with this scumbag handler. Let's say he's not just a scumbag. He's also obese. He has greasy hair and bad teeth. And now the scientist's already back on the mesa, where he lives with his wife. Let's make the wife pretty. With two sweet little kids. So then the piece is in front of her handler's house, alone in her car, and she's in love with the scientist even though she betrayed him. And now it's too late. And she's sitting alone. And it's very depressing. So instead of driving back to her apartment she drives to some lonely cliff over the ocean."

"The light turned," I said.

Frank pulled into traffic, weaving between a few cars because the girl had gotten too far ahead. "So she drives to some lonely cliff," he said, shifting into second gear, "and she parks there. And she shoots herself in the mouth with a pistol."

We were both quiet for a minute. Frank had gotten up close to the Plymouth.

"Why doesn't she just drive off the cliff?" I said.

"Why would she drive off the cliff?" Frank said. He sounded annoyed with the question.

"Why would she go to a cliff if she doesn't want to drive off it?"

"Because there's nothing to see if the piece drives off a cliff," Frank said. "There's no body left to discover."

The girl turned onto Market, and Frank held back for a minute, then turned behind her.

"No way," he said, once we were heading down Market. "Can't happen like that. It's not a good ending."

"It's not always a good ending," I said.

"People won't be satisfied," Frank said.

But then he was quiet for a few moments, as if considering the possibility. Then he shook his head again. "Plus why would she drive off a cliff? You don't drive off a cliff unless you don't want to be found."

"Maybe she doesn't want to be found."

"She's here, isn't she?"

"Driving away."

The girl was driving faster now, as if she'd found her rhythm. Frank had to pass a few cars to keep up.

"Anyway," Frank said, once he was behind her again, "it

28

doesn't matter. She can't drive off the cliff because the body has to be found. It's an unsatisfying ending, if the body's never discovered."

At the next stoplight, he looked at me. His face was bloody because of her taillights. With two fingers and a thumb, he made the shape of a pistol. Then he swallowed the tip.

"She shoots herself," he said. "Brains all over the seats."

ON BROADWAY, THEY HEADED WEST. JUST BEFORE CHINATOWN, THE girl pulled over and parked. Frank found a spot at the far end of the block. We watched them in the side mirrors.

She didn't wait for Opp to open her door. And once she'd stepped out onto the street, she brushed out the skirt of her dress with two brusque, practical gestures. Then she lifted one ankle and checked the sole of her shoe. Maybe she noticed the run in her stocking. Then she looked over her shoulder at Opp. He'd gotten out of the car and stepped off the sidewalk.

Crossing the street, they didn't hold hands, but they walked so close together it wasn't easy to see where her sleeve stopped and his arm began. By then, it was dark, and her dress was dark, too, so her pale face floated above it like some detached apparition. Where had she come from? He'd been at Los Alamos since the winter. He hadn't told us anything about a girl he wanted to see in San Francisco. She was off the radar completely.

But now, suddenly, he'd flown back and summoned her out of the ether.

I watched her closely. I noted that while her lips were soft, her gait was a bit mannish. They headed toward a door with no sign overhead. He reached it first. Then he opened it for her, and she went in before him.

"Your turn, bub," Frank said. He was already unfolding the crossword.

WHEN THE DOOR SWUNG SHUT BEHIND ME, IT SEEMED AS IF THE street outside had never really existed. The air was full of smoke. The lamps at the tables were dim. The waiters seemed to disappear every time they moved away from a table.

At the far end of the room, I saw Opp and the girl in a booth. I took a seat at the bar so I could watch them in the mirror. Then the bartender gave me a menu, and I saw the place was called the Xochimilco Café. They served Mexican food and cheap-looking cocktails. When I looked back up at the mirror to check on Opp and the girl, I realized it was almost opaque. It was as if the glass had been buttered. Opp and the girl were no more than shadows, flickering faintly at the back of the mirror. Every so often, I had to glance over my shoulder to reassure myself they were still sitting there at the table. Once I'd caught a glimpse—his hat, back on his head; the big silk bow at her neck—I turned back to the menu.

Looking down at the cocktails, I remembered the directives Pash gave us. *You note every detail,* he liked to say, striding up and down between the rows of desks where he had us sit during training. *If he orders a martini, does he order a twist? Does he order it dirty?* Often, during training, Pash got up close in our faces. There were sometimes white beads of spit on his moustache. *What color are his socks? What material are they made from? It's all important. For all you know the length of his fingernails is important. For all you know the size of his fucking ear holes is very fucking important. You don't know. All you know is you watch him. You do what he does. He drinks a martini, you want a martini. He crosses the street, you cross the street, too. You're a mirror image when there isn't a mirror. You disappear if you're doing your job right.*

Outlining directives, he could work himself into a fever. With those beads of spit on his moustache, and that angry, rabbity face, he could seem ridiculous. Frank and the other agents imitated him when he was out of the office. But I had a soft spot for him and his stories. His father was a Russian Orthodox priest. They'd moved back from California to Moscow when Pash was a kid, just in time for the Bolsheviks to start burning cathedrals.

When he was sober, he drank beers and talked about coaching football. But if he got drunk, he'd switch to vodka. Then, if you let him, he could spend hours describing his father's church: the lapis lazuli in the mosaics, the gold-leaf enamel, the dim light that filtered through the stained glass.

As a kid, he'd loved the way his father moved down the aisle, his chasuble belted with rope at the waist, a heavy cross on his chest, a trail of burning myrrh in his wake.

When the Bolsheviks took power and started rounding up priests, Pash joined the White Army. His claim to fame was serving under General Wrangel. The general, he told us, stood over six foot six inches tall. In a single tank, under heavy shell fire, he and a few soldiers single-handedly captured the fortified city of Tsaritsyn. It was a heroic time, he liked to remind us. But after the evacuation from the Crimea, when they'd washed up in Constantinople, there was too much waiting

31

around. They were all in between, uncertain about where to go next. They spent their nights in opium dens. Even Wrangel fell into malaise. He lived on his yacht, moored in the harbor, and didn't think about moving until the Reds tried to sink it.

After that, Pash moved to Germany for a year. Then he got married. He found his way to Pasadena. Wrangel was murdered by a servant in Brussels. Pash and his wife had a kid. He got a degree in physical education, and they changed their name from Pashkovsky.

Sometimes a man's life goes to pieces. Then, if he has it in him, he pulls a life together again, though it's usually not in the same shape that it once was.

In Pasadena, Pash trained for the reserves on the weekends. When he got called up the day after Pearl Harbor, they put him in charge of the San Francisco intelligence office. He ran it in remembrance of Wrangel, and also his defrocked father.

He stormed around with those beads of spit on his moustache, all action, no contemplation, until sometimes, in the late afternoon, when he'd called me into his office, he'd forget what he'd wanted to say.

He'd stare off out the window, over the bridge, past the blue whale humps of the peninsula, with his chin resting on his fingertips, pointed in the shape of a steeple. Sometimes I sat there in his office and could almost hear choral music rising off in the distance. As if the sun were made of gold leaf. As if the blue bay were lapis lazuli.

IN THE XOCHIMILCO CAFÉ, I TRIED TO FOLLOW PASH'S DIRECTIVES. I sipped my martini. I wondered why Opp had brought the girl there. Or why she'd brought him there, on the one night he was back in the city.

The martini was cheap, and the place was run-down. Both Opp and the girl seemed somewhat out of place, like they were trying to fit in somewhere they couldn't.

For a while, I listened to the sounds of glasses clinking together when the waiters cleared off the tables. On the small dance floor, a few couples were dancing. Onstage, a Mexican girl was singing in front of the piano. It was dark on the stage, and you could barely distinguish her features. Her hair was drawn back from her face. She kept her eyes closed while she sang. And when the song finished, she opened them slowly, as if waking from a deep sleep.

Behind her, the piano was swallowed in darkness. All you could really hear was her voice.

Take my lips, she sang, *I want to lose them. Take my arms, I'll never use them.*

I pulled a pen out of my pocket and jotted the lyrics down on my napkin. In the mirror, I saw the shapes of Opp and the girl flicker and rise. She followed him to the dance floor. They left their plates at the table.

Once they'd started dancing, he held her hand at his shoulder. His other hand braced the small of her back, and while he turned her around the floor, I saw her from different angles. From behind, she could have been any girl: that narrowing of her waist; the hem of her dress at the midpoint of her calves; the run in her stocking, which had worked up from her ankle. From another angle, when he'd turned her around, I saw only his back, and her fingertips clasping his hand. At a third angle, from the side, I could see the line of her profile.

Her hair was loosely pulled back on one side, fastened there with a clip. A few times, with the tip of her finger, she touched the high point of her cheekbone.

It struck me, even then, as a strange gesture. It was almost as if she were touching her cheekbone to make sure her face was still there. Then I thought, Is she crying?

I couldn't say. Either way, I don't think Opp ever noticed. His head was above hers. If she was crying, and maybe she wasn't, I don't think Opp ever realized. He never stepped back, or looked with any surprise at her face. They only kept dancing. When the song finished, the Mexican girl left the stage for a while, and Opp and the girl headed back to their table.

As soon as she sat, she reached into her pocketbook and pulled out a box of cigarettes. Almost at the same time, as if it were a choreographed aspect of a scene they'd planned in advance, Opp pulled out a lighter. Then he leaned over the table to help her.

ONCE, A FEW WEEKS AFTER WARREN SHIPPED OUT, I HEARD MAY GET out of bed. She moved over the floor and closed the door to the bedroom. Then I heard the sound of water running from the tap in the bathroom.

It went on a long time, too long for her to be washing her hands. Too long for her to be just washing her face. After a while, I started to worry, so I got up and went to the bathroom. I moved as quietly as I could. And I stopped before I got to the door, so she wouldn't see my shadow under the crack.

I didn't want her to think I was following her in her own

house. I stood in the hall and craned my neck forward. I got my ear close to the door. Then I heard her crying. Or that was my best guess. If she was crying, she was crying very quietly, trying not to make any noise. It sounded like a faint succession of coughs, made gentler by the sound of the water.

Standing alone in the hall, wondering whether or not she was crying, I remembered my brother.

I thought of him, leaning on the railing of the back stoop. I remembered the smell of the jasmine, and the moths frying themselves on the streetlights, and the way he brought up the subject of May.

At first, it all seemed so mild and pleasant. He was happy, he said, that I'd found a woman I loved. He talked about her jokes for a while, and how quick she was at cards. Then he asked where her accent was from.

"What accent?" I said.

He shrugged, and made himself busy fiddling around with his lighter. We were quiet for a while. Then he started talking again.

"Tell me again," he said, "where she's from in Wisconsin?"

He said it lightly, not looking at me directly. Staring off past the fences cluttered with vines, past the yard where the Millers' dog was lying outside its doghouse.

I answered the question. Warren nodded. "And which school did she say that she went to?"

By then, that metal taste had flooded the back of my mouth, but still, I answered the question. I hadn't yet pinpointed the problem. I only realized once I'd already given the name of the school: he'd asked the question as if I didn't know the right answer.

As if my wife might be lying to me, and I hadn't realized. As if I'd been a fool to believe her.

Then I looked at him a little more closely. What did he think he knew that I didn't?

When our mother asked us if we'd come with her, Warren went. I was older than he was. I knew what kind of life it would be. So I stayed with our father, and Warren went with our mother to Texas.

I was older than he was. I probably should have looked after him better. But I let him go. He survived it, but we had different lives. He left junior college to sign up for the army, and by the time I saw him again, he read car magazines and stood two inches taller than I did. And then he stayed with us for three nights, and maybe it was because of those years he spent in Texas, but immediately he saw what I'd made myself blind to.

Or he felt he did. Or wanted me to believe that.

I still don't know. I can only picture him as he was when he leaned against that railing, wearing a white T-shirt and blue jeans. He was tapping his cigarette box on his palm and squinting off down the alley, pretending he didn't want to offend me. When I answered his question about where May went to high school, he started to say something, but I stood up. Then I went inside. The screen door banged in its frame when I left him.

Walking back to the bedroom, I paused a few times. I almost went back to join him. It was the night before he shipped out. I thought maybe I should let him say what he'd meant to.

But then I kept going. In the bedroom, I took off my

clothes as quietly as I could. I draped them over the chair. I got under the covers. Then, in bed, I looked at the outline of May's shoulder.

I looked at the slope of her waist. I looked at the rise of her hip, facing away from me in the darkness.

What accent? I thought. And why would she lie about the school that she went to?

IN THE BLURRED MIRROR OVER THE BAR, OPP AND THE GIRL WERE both smoking. She was listening, with her head cocked to one side. He spoke, gesturing with the hand that held his cigarette. Every so often, he flicked the ash off without taking his eyes away from her face.

When the waiter came to bring him the check, they both looked up as if startled. Then they dug around for their wallets. I didn't wait to see which of them paid. I left a dollar on the bar and headed out with my face down.

"What'd you see?" Frank asked, once I'd climbed into the De Soto.

"They had dinner," I said.

"What else?"

"They danced."

"Anything else?"

I thought of her touching her cheek. I thought of the way he'd leaned forward to help her when she pulled out her cigarette.

"That's it," I said. "Dinner. And three rounds of martinis."

FROM BROADWAY, WE FOLLOWED THE PLYMOUTH AT A SAFE DIS-tance. At Montgomery Street, they turned left, then climbed the hill, and they were nearly to the top when she pulled over and parked.

I checked my watch: 10:58. They'd gotten out of the car and were heading toward a three-story building.

"No way she survives this," Frank said.

I tried to ignore him, but there was something unnerving about the way that building swallowed them whole. One minute they'd been on the sidewalk, the next minute they weren't. Once they were inside, the building remained dark for what seemed like a long time. I guess they were climbing the stairs, but at that point we didn't know. We'd lost sight of them for the moment. When the lights finally came on in the top-story apartment, even Frank breathed a sigh of relief. One by one, three windows came into play. The lights blazed on like signals.

"Out you go, bub," Frank said.

I reached into the glove compartment and took out the camera.

OUTSIDE, THE NIGHT SMELLED LIKE THE BAY. IT MUST HAVE BEEN cloudy, because there was no starlight. I crossed the street and stood in the yard opposite the building they'd entered. I found a place close to the trunk of a big, leafy tree, trying to keep myself in the shadows.

Then I lifted the camera. From below, through the lit windows, I could see the lines where the walls hit the ceiling. I could see the top cabinets in the kitchen, the still fan in the bedroom. Then I saw the girl come to the window. There was her head, and the tops of her shoulders. Then she lifted one hand.

For a moment, it almost seemed as if she were waving. As if she'd seen me, and was signaling to me from the window, just as she'd signaled to him at the station.

But she wasn't moving. She'd only lifted that hand. She was standing like a conductor does, in the moment before the music gets started, with his hand lifted and his thumb and forefinger drawn together, as if holding a bead.

Then I realized she was drawing the shades. She had the cord pinched in her hand, and in that instant I could see her pretty well. She was looking straight toward me, as if she could see me. Then, with a quick tug, she drew down the shades. Then the lights went out altogether.

I checked my watch. It was 11:05.

Then the apartment seemed to have been abandoned completely. I had to remind myself that Opp and the girl were still there, even though I couldn't see them. It was then, when I was suddenly alone, that I noticed the leaves hanging around me. They were thick and lacquered, dark green and shaped like canoes. Their undersides were lightly furred. Their spines were the color of rust.

LATER, WHEN I'D BEEN REASSIGNED, I THOUGHT OF THAT GIRL EVERY time I saw one of those trees, which are somewhat uncommon in San Francisco. But still, I'd sometimes see one. And as soon as I caught a glimpse of those leaves, I'd remember that scent: dusty and a little bit sweet. Then I'd think of that girl, driving up Montgomery Street in her green Plymouth. I'd see the way she stepped out of the driver's-side door and walked briskly up to her building.

At the entrance, it always took her a minute to find the

right key. And she was almost always alone, at least in those months after Opp went back to the mesa. All that time I tailed her, he never came back. By then, I imagine, he knew he couldn't pull off such a dumb stunt.

He knew he'd screwed up. Security on the mesa let him know pretty quick. From that point on, he understood he had to be more security minded. There were leaks on the mesa. We'd caught him in a lie. He had to prove we could trust him.

So we'd gotten him to start giving names of people who might be suspicious. He was reluctant, of course, and agonized about the whole thing, but then we'd remind him of that stupid trick, and he didn't want to lose his position. Maybe he also didn't want his wife to find out. So he gave a few names, and he didn't risk another trip back to the city.

That was all for the best. Time was ticking out on those weapons. He needed to stay there and focus.

But still. There were nights when I almost wanted him to try it again. Waiting under that tree, outside the girl's windows, I almost wished he'd drive up in a cab. Leap out, run up to her building.

But he never came. After he kissed her cheek on the sidewalk outside the airport, she walked back to the Plymouth. He headed through the glass doors into the airport. And after that he never came back.

Those months after he left, she started working later at the hospital. Maybe it was a coincidence. Maybe it wasn't. Most nights, she headed straight home after work.

That was the basic routine, though sometimes there were slight variations. Once or twice, she had a friend over to the apartment. A few times she went to a bar in the city. Sometimes, after work, she headed to the grocery store. But eventually she always ended up driving back home, climbing that hill in her Plymouth, then walking toward the front door of her building.

When she looked for the right key, she bent her neck and frowned deeply. And every night, once the door closed behind her, I waited for the lights to come on with that same uncertainty, as if she might have gotten lost on the staircase. Or as if I'd allowed her to escape on my watch.

I always breathed a sigh of relief when the lights came on in her windows. I learned to see her shadow on the living room wall. I learned to differentiate the light she turned on when she walked in and the colder light of the refrigerator spreading out through the kitchen.

Outside, standing under that tree, I wondered what she was doing. Had she poured herself a drink before bed? Had she cooked herself something simple to eat? How did she pass those final hours before she lay down for the evening?

And, when she did lie down, did she rest her head on the pillow knowing I was standing outside, looking up at her window?

Maybe she had an inkling. Maybe it unsettled her. Or maybe it made her feel less alone, as if there were someone looking out for her while she slept.

That's what I tried to believe. I didn't think she was the leak, even though Pash was convinced. By then, we had her phone tapped. We steamed open her letters. But all those months, Opp didn't contact her again. She didn't meet with any Communists, or any of his friends and former students who showed up on our list of suspects.

Most mornings, like I've said, she just reported to the hospital. All day, she met with her patients. At night she drove back up the hill. Following her in her routine, it was easy to forget that there was a war on.

Sometimes, a lamp came on around three in the morning. Then, after a while, she'd come to the window to smoke. She'd sit on the ledge. All I could see in the darkness was the light at the tip of her cigarette, flaring orange, then fading. Sometimes I was sure that she saw me. I convinced myself we were watching each other. Both of us waiting to say the first word. Both of us poised on that ledge, prepared for something we had a feeling was coming but couldn't quite comprehend yet.

When that plane passed overhead, flying so slowly it seemed impossible that it wouldn't just fall out of the night, I was sure that she saw it, too. I was sure she felt the same fear.

But in the end I had no idea. I had no clue what she was thinking when she came to the window to smoke. She and I never once exchanged words.

Once, on a Saturday, I found a book she left on a park bench. It opened up to a poem by Donne. I read it a few times, trying to make out the sense of the words, as if they were a message she'd left me.

But I can't say I understood it. It was a strange, violent poem. I left the book on the bench, adhering to Pash's directives, and as far as I know, she never went back to get it.

THE ONLY REAL INTERACTION WE HAD WAS THAT NIGHT IN NOVEMber, when she came out of the grocery store. She had three oranges in one hand, a yellow pad in the other, and a bottle of wine under her elbow.

She'd parked the Plymouth out front. At the driver's-side door, she tucked the oranges into the crook of her elbow, where she was also holding the wine. Then, with her head down, she fumbled in her pocketbook for the car keys.

I'd ducked into the store when she came out, but even through the fake banana leaves in the window display, I could see that she was struggling. I knew she hadn't slept much the previous night. That morning, on her way out to the car, I'd seen thumbprints under her eyes.

Now she was trying to accomplish too much, standing there by the door of her car, with the wine and the oranges under her elbow. She was clumsily fumbling around when, for no reason, in a weird and inexplicable act of aggression, the keys she'd been searching for leaped out of her purse.

There was a flash of silver, like a fish jumping out of the water.

Then, with a dexterity that surprised me, she reached out and caught them. But doing that, of course, she dropped the oranges and the wine. The bottle shattered. The oranges started rolling away, and without thinking, I ran out of the store and started darting around, picking them up.

Now it seems like an improbable scene. And even then, as I was starting to run out of the store, I felt a little ashamed of myself. I knew how Pash felt about intervention. I could hear him lecturing me about breaking cover.

But then I'd already started. I thought it would only draw more attention if I stopped before I'd collected the fruit.

She stood there and watched, those thumbprints under

her eyes. Red wine splattered all over her ankles. When I handed the oranges back, she just nodded slightly. Then she turned and climbed into the car.

Who knows if she'd seen me before, when I was waiting outside the store, or at the pharmacy where she picked up her pills. If she had, she didn't say so. She just took those oranges and drove off in the Plymouth.

BUT ALL THAT HAPPENED LATER, AFTER OPP HAD GONE BACK TO THE mesa. After Warren and the rest of his crew had been declared officially missing in action, their plane having gone down somewhere over the water.

By then, I'd been introduced to the fact that he'd never come back to finish what he started on the back stoop. I'd started to realize that we'd never have that conversation, or any other conversation, and that none of the things I didn't know about him or the life he led with our mother would ever become any clearer.

Then I finally asked May about where she went to school in Milwaukee.

At first, she stuck to the original story. Then she backtracked a little. She introduced a few complications. During the Depression, she said, they'd moved so often. She'd hated it, all the moving around, and now that she was an adult she liked to think they'd stayed in the one place she'd liked best.

That was Milwaukee, she said. The city where she'd been happiest. But she hadn't quite finished high school before she went back to Texas.

"With your parents?" I asked.

She looked away.

I waited, that metal taste creeping into my mouth.

"With a friend," she said.

By then she was pale. She'd set her mouth in a hard line, and it was clear that she wouldn't keep talking.

STILL, SHE DID HER BEST. SHE TRIED, AT LEAST, TO GIVE ME A NEW SET of facts to hang on to. But by then, of course, I had no reason to believe they were facts.

She was still the same woman who came to the door when I got home, the same girl who threw her arms around me and kissed me, the same girl I liked to play cards with. But after I asked those questions, something between us was different.

Those little lies she'd told at first: they'd come to stay with us like pets who require little in the way of attention. Still, every so often, they made themselves known. Slinking around the corner into a room, or jumping up on the couch and sitting between us.

They bothered me less, I think, than they bothered her. I might have accepted them. I might have moved on with our life, the same way I moved on when my mother left, when I let Warren go with her.

I could have refrained, I think, from asking more questions. But May couldn't take it. I guess she knew better than I did how uncertain the ground was that she stood on.

Then the lengths of time she stayed away from the bedroom increased, and sometimes she never came back, and finally she packed a bag and went to live with her friend Dorothy.

Or that's what she said. I never met Dorothy. And after

she left, I still lay awake. I still waited for her shadow to cross over the bedroom.

Lying there in the same house, in the same bed, I thought I'd ruined my one chance at happiness by asking too much about what lay underneath it. I stared at the door, imagining it might open, and light might spread over the floor, and when it didn't, I thought that if you want to get through this life in one piece, you should either know all the facts, or you should know nothing.

Sometimes, I blamed my brother for tempting me to know more than I needed to know to begin with. But by then, he was gone. Another one of the planes knocked down over the ocean, another name on the lengthening list of men who'd been declared missing.

And the thing is, you can't really blame someone who's missing. So then I gave up on blaming him for making me want to know more about May, and I'd get to thinking how surprised I'd been to see him when he showed up at our house.

He was taller than me, in a white T-shirt, with a duffel hoisted over his shoulder.

Lying there through the long nights, I'd think how surprising it was to see him as a man. Then I'd think I missed my brother's childhood. Then I'd think, in some ways, I'd missed my own childhood, too, or at least the childhood I might have had, growing up with my brother.

And now, I'd think, in addition to his childhood, I'd also miss his adulthood. Which meant I'd miss my own adulthood, or the adulthood I might have lived, knowing my brother.

Then it felt as if I'd been fated to miss my whole life. As if, for some time, I'd been moving through a life that wasn't really my own, and everything I'd recently lost had never really been mine to keep in the first place.

BUT, LIKE I'VE SAID, ALL THAT CAME LATER. THAT NIGHT, WHEN OPP flew the coop and spent the night with that girl, we'd only been in the war a few months. Warren still hadn't gone missing, and that girl's lamp didn't come on in the night. She didn't come back to smoke a cigarette at the window.

I just stood there for a while, under the lacquered leaves of that tree, wondering what was happening up there in the bedroom.

Whether, after she pulled down the shades, she went to him first. Or whether he went to her. Or whether neither one of them moved, and if for a while the space between them persisted.

Who, in the end, I wondered, made the first move to cross through the distance between them? Those were the questions that came up in my mind, waiting under that tree with the camera.

Those are the rabbit holes you can go down all night if you want to. Then the only way to get any sleep is to remind yourself that not all questions get answered, and all we can rely on are the observable facts. It was 10:50 P.M., for example, on June 14, when they left the Xochimilco Café. She drove a green Plymouth coupe. She lived on the top floor of her building, 1405 Montgomery Street, and at 11:30 P.M., the lights in her apartment were completely extinguished.

WHEN I HEADED BACK TO THE DE SOTO, FRANK LEFT TO GO FIND A pay phone. By the time he came back, it was drizzling. There were beads of water on the brim of his hat.

"Jean," he said. "Her name is Jean Frances Tatlock."

I thought about that for a minute. It's strange, when you've watched someone a while without knowing a name. When you finally figure it out, the name never fits.

"How old is she?" I said.

"Twenty-nine," Frank said. "Working girl. Psychiatrist. And card-carrying Commie. Pash is in the midst of a full-blown conniption."

Jean Frances Tatlock, I thought. *Twenty-nine.*

She was eight years older than May. Nine years older than Warren.

Frank craned his neck up at her windows.

"This doesn't end well," he said. "She's most definitely dead by the ending."

"Everyone's dead by the ending," I said, "if the book goes on enough pages."

"Jesus, bub," Frank said.

Jean, I said to myself again, rolling the name around in my mouth.

For a minute, once again, I let myself wonder what they were doing. Maybe she was lying with her head on his shoulder. Maybe he'd rolled away. Maybe now they weren't touching.

Then I remembered them dancing. The way he held her hand to his shoulder, and the way she brushed her cheek with her finger.

Then I thought of May in the bathroom, and that quiet coughing. And the tap running, and how noiseless she was when she came back into the bedroom. The door opened without any sound, and that angle of moonlight widened over the floor, like a fan spreading over the face of a girl who doesn't want you to see her.

It's the Jornada del Muerto desert that Oppenheimer sees when he faces out the open side of the shack. There's some debate about the source of its name: The Journey of the Dead Man, or The Journey of the Dead, or, perhaps more accurately, The Working Day of the Dead. Some historians believe it's named in honor of the Spanish settlers who fled Santa Fe in 1680, when, after over a century of subjugation, the Pueblos organized a revolt. Five years before, fifty Pueblo medicine men had been accused of sorcery by agents of the Inquisition. Three were hanged without trial; another killed himself in his cell; the others were publicly whipped then imprisoned. Then the Pueblos began to prepare. Five years later, they attacked Santa Fe, where they killed four hundred settlers and drove the rest from the city. Of the two thousand Spanish refugees who gathered in Socorro and headed south into that stretch of desert, only twelve hundred later emerged at Las Cruces.

Others believe the desert was named for a German trader, Bernardo Gruber, known for his prosperity and his elegant clothing: he owned ten mules and eighteen horses, traveled with three Apache servants, and wore a blue doublet lined with otter skin, which matched his blue pantaloons. Gruber *passed through Quarai Pueblo in 1668, where he sold some of his wares and a fight broke out one afternoon over a magic trick played with* papelitos. *Several months later, he was accused of sorcery by local agents of the Inquisition. They kept him in a cell for more than two years. His requests for a trial went nowhere. At some point he was told that his servants had disappeared. His animals had all died, or fallen into the hands of new owners. No word could be given on the length of his sentence.*

Finally, driven to that desperation that a lack of real knowledge so often produces, Gruber managed to break out through his cell window and flee into the desert on horseback. Several weeks later, the horse on which he'd fled was found dead, tied to a tree by its harness. His blue doublet was discovered nearby, along with his pantaloons, a skull, three ribs, and four bones, gnawed and scattered in the dry, woody snakeweed.

THAT'S THE DESERT OPPENHEIMER SURVEYS FROM ONE HUNDRED *feet, a desert he's known since he was seventeen. His parents sent him there from Manhattan, to recuperate from an illness.*

In New Mexico, after a somewhat solitary childhood, he learned to ride horses. He spent nights sleeping outside. Days he rode over empty plateaus, learning the landscape by heart, so that now, as he stands on the tower and turns to the open side of the shack, he faces a desert he's often imagined.

Staring out over that strange ocean of land, it's almost as if he's looking for someone: a caravan of carriages winding its way down the Fra Cristobal mountains, or a single young man riding horseback, a bobbing black point in the distance.

But nobody comes. The desert appears to be empty.

With his hat pulled low over his forehead, Oppenheimer turns and climbs back down the tower. The steel rungs press his arches until his feet hit solid land once again. He drives the jeep back into base camp, where he chats with the metallurgists packing their gear.

According to one, interviewed later, he talks about family. He discusses life at the Los Alamos camp. Then he looks up at the sky. It's blackening over the Oscura Range. "Funny," he says, "how the mountains always inspire our work." He keeps his face turned toward the range, and the clouds keep rolling over the ridges.

GRACE GOODMAN

Los Alamos, 1945

OF COURSE I DID. HOW COULD I HAVE MISSED HIM? HE WAS THE mayor of our little Shangri-la on the mesa. No matter which way you turned, you'd see him getting driven around in his jeep, wearing that porkpie hat and an old pair of blue jeans.

He was everywhere you looked. Or at least that's how it seemed. He had his spoon in every pot. He even started a women's committee, and he donated part of his record collection to the mesa radio station. After that, if you were lying awake in your dorm room, listening to Bach to calm down because every time you opened your eyes you saw mice running over the ceiling, it was Oppie you had to thank for the music.

Sometimes, he came to the square dances we organized at Fuller Lodge. Then we'd all go green with envy while he danced with some lucky girl. Or Kitty might take a break from drinking in her living room, and she and Oppie would dance, gazing into each other's eyes like they'd only ever been in love with each other.

Once, he played the part of a corpse in the theater production of *Arsenic and Old Lace*. He let them carry him in with flour all over his face, and out in the audience we almost died laughing.

But that was the kind of thing Oppie would do. He didn't hold himself too high above us. When the wives complained about working jobs on the mesa and still getting left to do all the cleaning at home, he organized a maid service. After that, there were Indian girls who walked up from San Ildefonso, wearing leather slippers and emerging out of the mist that came up with them from the river.

It was Oppie who arranged that, just like he spearheaded the effort to improve the hospital where the women gave birth. He was always trying to help, even with the trivial things. Even though he was the head of the project.

Once, you know, he even invited me to his house. Sometimes I can't believe I was there, but it's true: once I went to a party at Oppie's house on Bathtub Row, and Jack was there, too, standing in the living room, talking with Johnny von Neumann and Oppie.

They saw me when I walked in, with that bruise under my eye and my new boyfriend. All three of them were holding martinis, and standing in front of a bookcase. And usually I would have felt cowed by their importance, what with my own relatively insignificant status, but I walked into that party with a real sense of my strengths.

It was the bruise that made it possible, not the fact that I had a new boyfriend. He'd only come in recently, after all, with the latest round of explosives, and he wasn't even all that important.

No. It wasn't him. It was the bruise that gave me such substance when I walked into that party. As soon as Jack saw it, he changed. I smote him with that bruise, I really did, even though I was only a WAC, and I only got to come to that party because Oppie invited the new round of explosives. And even though Jack was standing there with von Neumann and Oppie himself, and they were all tan from their recent trip into the desert, for some secret reason having to do with the secret weapon we all knew they were building.

There they were, assembled in front of a bookcase crowded with Oppie's big books and his expensive Native American tchotchkes. Jack was standing as he always did, with one hand in his pants' pocket and the other leg jutting out slightly, like a Boy Scout who's climbed to the top of a summit. And even so, when I came in, the mere sight of me smote him.

SEEING MY EFFECT ON HIM, I DELIVERED MY MOST GLANCING, CASUAL smile. Then I scanned the room like I was looking for somebody else. I held my head so he'd see the better side of my face, and meanwhile, in a great stroke of luck, my new boyfriend chose just the right moment to help me out of my raincoat.

There I stood, unmoving, while the coat slid off my bare shoulders.

I even let my hand rest on my new boyfriend's arm like it was the banister of a grand marble staircase, and I was in an evening gown about to descend it.

It was a good moment, it really was, until my new boyfriend leaned in to see what I wanted. "What's that?" he said. "Please, Grace, you have to speak up."

He had tinnitus from all the explosions. It was something I found hard to handle, and I almost said something impatient, but then I remembered the bruise. It helped me regain my composure. I remembered how, earlier in the evening, I'd inspected it while I took out my curlers and discovered that, though its outer ring was yellow and sickly, the center was black as the night.

It was a powerful bruise, it really was. I felt it deeply. In some ways, I felt I'd gone to that party not with my new boyfriend but with that magnificent bruise, so even when my new boyfriend leaned in and annoyed me, I was able to remember it and smile up at him sweetly, then hand him my purse, and excuse myself to go to the bathroom.

I COULD FEEL HIM WATCHING ME AS I WENT. NOT MY NEW BOYFRIEND, but Jack. It was Jack whose eyes I could feel, so warm and almost wet on the back of my head that for a second I wondered if I'd started bleeding. It was all I could do not to reach my hand up to check, but instead I kept my composure all the way to the bathroom, and only once I'd closed the door did I allow myself to feel nervous and overexcited, and sit there on the lid of the toilet counting from one to ten Mississippi, hoping my heart would stop uncontrollably racing.

I HADN'T BEEN SURE HE'D BE AT THAT PARTY. THERE WERE MOMENTS, of course, when I suspected he might be. But I'd also heard rumors that he was out scouting locations.

So I'd curled my hair and worn the red lipstick he once told me he liked, but I hadn't prepared myself absolutely, and I definitely wasn't prepared for him to be standing there when I walked in through the door, as if he'd positioned himself by the entrance to greet me.

Even so, my bruise and I had impressed him. He'd watched me all the way down the hallway, and by the time I was sitting there on the toilet, I knew that it was possible that he was waiting for me in the darkness outside, and that soon, perhaps, if I gave up my hiding place, we'd be standing together alone, as we'd once been alone in other dark places.

Knowing that, it was hard to calm down. When I got up to wash my hands, my fingertips were trembling. But then I looked at the bruise in the mirror and the very sight of it calmed me. My face with that bruise: It was young and alluring. It wasn't at all the haggard old visage that sometimes showed up in my mirror in the WAC dorm.

There, again, set off by the bruise, was the good line of my nose, and there was the delicate bow of my lip. Then I smiled to myself in the mirror, as I planned to smile at Jack, because by then, of course, I knew he'd be out there. I knew he'd be waiting for me in the hallway, and that as soon as I stepped out he'd reach forward and touch me.

"PLEASE, GRACE," HE SAID, WHEN HE DID. HE HAD HIS THUMB UNDER my chin, tilting it up, so he could look down sadly upon me.

"Please what?" I said.

"Please," he said. "I can't sit back and watch this."

"Watch what?" I said. And I smiled my jauntiest debutante smile, and gave him one last look at the bruise, then threw my shoulders back and sailed into the party.

IT WAS A TRIUMPH, IT REALLY WAS, ESPECIALLY AFTER THAT OTHER occasion.

Of course, by the time I showed up to that other party, I'd been awake for over twenty-four hours. We'd all gone to June Steenberger's house because Germany had surrendered, and she had a projector in her big green McKee house, which she got because her husband was in the theoretical group.

So we all sat around, drinking colas and watching the newsreel, and June was ostentatiously pregnant. She was wedged on the couch, knitting a little pink blanket, and smiling like a dumb cow through the whole program as if Hitler's suicide and Germany's surrender and the opening of those camps were all nothing more than the background of her own personal nativity set.

At every new development they reported about General Eisenhower and the unconditional terms of surrender, she picked up her knitting again and murmured some sweet wifely comment, like "I guess we can go home now," or "What a relief it will be to have my own stove back."

There I sat on the floor, surrounded by wives with stoves to go home to, and in my state of despair I kept my eyes on the next newsreel and the horrible shadows that kept sliding over the screen, those skeletons emerging out of the camps, blinking vulnerably in the new sunlight.

And then I remembered how thin my mother got in the last weeks, when she was dying, and I slept in the big bed alongside her.

I thought of the bones in her shoulders, and meanwhile June kept knitting that blanket and talking about going home with her husband, and in order to survive how vindictive I felt, I had to take a deep breath and have pity because once, when we went to the lake, June wore a bathing suit and her thighs were pure cottage cheese.

And later, when I went off by myself to pick berries, I felt her husband watching me, with my nice legs and my tan and the little white shorts I was wearing that summer.

And usually that scene would have calmed me, but as soon as I remembered them—the berries that grew near the lake, and the thorns that grabbed at my hair when I lay down among them—the pity I felt was for myself. It was rising up to my throat, rising so high I was sure it would drown me. Because then I remembered the edge of the lake, licking the sand with its silver tongue, and that rock that jutted out into the water, parting it, causing it to subside, because of course that was the rock where Jack taught me to swim, back when the two of us were a couple.

There I was again, up on that rock, shivering wet in my little suit, trying to get the nerve to jump in.

And there was the sunlight, braided into the ripples, and Jack down below, his hand over his eyes when he grinned up and laughed, urging me to jump into the water.

And meanwhile, at June's house, the newsreel kept trumpeting on about Victory and a Great War, and June and Charlotte and Kay were conspiring about what they'd cook first when they'd gone home to Princeton, and it was miserable, but I wouldn't leave.

Out of stubbornness, I stayed a long time, celebrating the end of the war while I drowned in my own personal sorrow, and it wasn't until two or three in the morning that I finally got back to the WAC dorm.

When I opened the door, the lamp wasn't on, so it was dark when I saw my cot, and the GI chair in the corner, and the stack of big books I kept on my nightstand in case Jack happened to stop by and see them. Then I forced myself to look back at the GI chair, and confronted the nest of young rats that had somehow ended up there.

They were wriggling and squirming, blindly nestling in toward their mother, and I had to blink at them for a while before I realized they were actually socks. I'd knotted them up after doing my laundry, but there hadn't been time to put them away before I headed to June's house.

So there they were, a nest of baby rats, and by the time I'd figured it out, my heart was racing, so then I got into my cot to calm down.

But of course the harder I tried to lie still, the harder my heart insisted on beating, so there I lay in a panic until at some point the next day Charlotte and Freddy stopped by the dorm and invited me along to that other party.

THAT, AS IT TURNED OUT, WAS A VERY BIG PARTY.

At that point, of course, most people thought we'd go home. Most people thought we were up on that mesa to build our secret weapon before Germany could do the same thing.

We didn't know, for example, that a memo had already been sent to the general in charge of firebombing Japan, telling him to spare Hiroshima so that we could be the ones to destroy it. We weren't even supposed to know it was a weapon we were working on.

But I knew. Jack told me, when we were together. He

didn't give me too many details, but I knew, and so did most of the other women, and we all thought we were racing the Germans.

So in May, when Germany surrendered and Hitler killed himself with that secret girlfriend he married just before handing over the cyanide tablet, most of us went along to that party thinking it might be the last party, and even from outside the lab, Charlotte and Freddy and I could hear people singing. Mike Michnovicz was playing the accordion, and it was clear that we'd gotten there late, because in the hall someone was throwing up in a trash can, and inside the lab it was already too crowded.

Someone had rolled in two GI cans from the barracks and filled them to the brim with Shangri-la punch. Then they'd built a tower of crushed grapefruit juice cans and empty lab alcohol bottles, and they'd chilled the punch with steaming blocks of dry ice. A little clutch of GIs had draped themselves around Mike, who was playing some kind of mournful Sinatra, and I stood there with Charlotte and Freddy and tried to arrange my face to look pleasant.

Then someone gave me a beaker of punch. Later, I lost track of Charlotte. For a while, I listened to some excited little GI telling me about how before he came up to the mesa, he'd been in Utah developing a new incendiary that couldn't even be doused out by water. He told me they'd built a min-iature replica of Tokyo, down to the books on the shelves and the mats on the floor, and how when they dropped those bombs on the actual city the thing went up like it was built out of matchsticks.

He said they didn't even camouflage the bellies of the

planes anymore, because they flew beyond the range of Japanese defenses.

He said not only Tokyo but Nagoya, Yokohama, Osaka, Kobe, and Kawasaki were basically gone at this point, and then I excused myself and went somewhere else, and a scientist with thick glasses regaled me with a story about how he'd got his hair cut at the barber chair by the cyclotron.

It was a story I'd heard ten thousand times. But I nodded and smiled as if I cared very much, and someone else who was listening in said if only the whole world ran as smoothly as our little Shangri-la on the mesa, where haircuts are free, no one is poor, and everyone has such excellent health care.

And meanwhile, I scanned the room and realized Jack wasn't coming.

He'd never show up, I thought to myself. It wasn't a party for people like him. It was just a bunch of GIs and WACs and unimportant scientists, and for a while I felt safe and lost and a little bit dead, but then I saw Oppie's hat over the crowd.

Then I knew Jack was coming. Knowing that, I came to life and felt nervous. Then I went to the GI cans to refill my beaker, and that's where I was standing when I saw him walking in behind Oppie.

He was wearing a work shirt with his blue jeans, which is what most of the scientists wore, unless of course they'd come from Europe, in which case they wore formal clothes, as if they'd come out west from a funeral.

But Jack was from Princeton, and he'd gotten that tan, and he looked like a hero out of a Western when he crossed that party to shake hands with a group of admiring GIs.

Then, suddenly, I was so flooded with such confusing and unreasonable terror that I drank all my punch and passed back my beaker.

And even then, after that extra beaker of punch, that weird unreasonable terror was still tingling in the roots of my stomach. I had to take a deep breath and remember that this was only another lab party, and that was just Jack. But of course my heart had been beating too fast since I saw those baby rats in the armchair, and now, drinking my punch, watching Jack stride through the crowd, everyone else in the room lost their features.

Slowly, the walls started to melt. Then the lab equipment began to float off, and the only thing I could see was Jack's face, his tormented and unhappy expression, while he nodded earnestly, talking in the corner with a pretty young blond girl.

I could see her as well. She was wearing one of those dumb peasant blouses and a long braid over her shoulder, like she thought she'd taken the train straight from Vassar into the pages of *Little House on the Prairie*. There she was, with her shoulders bare, smiling at Jack and touching her braid, and even though they were standing on the other side of the room, and the walls were slowly melting around me, I could see his face exquisitely clearly.

I realized how haunted he looked, with his dark eyes and the shadow of a beard on his face, listening to that dumb little girl so intently.

And then I remembered the Dostoyevsky novel he'd assigned me to read, back when the two of us were together. I remembered how on the front page there was an ink drawing of a haunted student-murderer with eyes just like Jack had in that moment. I stood there by the cans of Shangri-la punch and gazed into Jack's regretful student-murderer eyes, and for a moment, I allowed myself to forget that he might be unhappy because of the weapon we were up on that mesa to build.

I forgot that completely. Instead, leaning on the centrifuge, I thought: It hit him hard, also.

I thought he, too, must have stayed up all night. And maybe he reached for the copy of *Crime and Punishment* that he'd lent me, which I'd left on his nightstand, with my dog-ears and the passages I so carefully noted.

And maybe it was the aching accordion music, but I managed to stir up a great deal of pity for him, and how much he must have missed me, or how much he must have missed that careful and obedient girl I was in the days when I read beside him. By then the room was swimming in a not entirely unpleasant way, and Charlotte and Freddy had gone off forever, and time slid nicely by until Jack came over and found me.

Then we were together, leaning on the centrifuge, laughing at my clever jokes, alone with each other again, along with a burly new man from explosives.

I DID, IN MY DEFENSE, ASK MYSELF IF I'D HAD TOO MUCH TO DRINK. But it was always so hard, up there on the mesa, to predict how the altitude might affect you.

Once, when I was his young, eager student, Jack explained to me how massive bodies warp time and space, so that time moves more quickly for a person on top of a mountain than it does for someone who lives down below it. And from that point on, I allowed myself to believe that our sea-level lives no longer existed, or that if they did exist still, they did so in a time that was no longer our own, a time we'd left behind when we rode the shuttle up to the mesa, where it was hard, because of the altitude, to predict the effect of all that alcohol.

But I did ask myself if I'd had too much, and I seemed to still have my composure. I hadn't made any mistakes, standing with Jack and that new man from explosives. I even made a few funny jokes, and kept my face turned to the good side, and overall managed such a compelling performance that the explosives man asked if he could take me to dinner.

I agreed, feeling Jack's eyes on the side of my face. And when the explosives man went off to fill my beaker with water, Jack and I were alone.

There we were, standing in that wavering room. He fixed me with his troubled eyes.

"Please," he said. "Don't go to dinner with him."

"Why shouldn't I?" I said.

"He beat his wife," Jack said. "She got a divorce."

"But then at least he's divorced," I said.

And for a moment, I felt very fine. But then, of course, I saw that Jack wasn't laughing.

He wasn't laughing at all. He was looking at me, instead, with such unbearable sorrow that I immediately realized how badly I'd miscalculated the joke.

Then, of course, I repented my error. But before I could think what to say to undo it, the explosives man had come back with my beaker, and Jack had excused himself and gone off in search of a less accusatorial part of the party.

LEFT ALONE ONCE AGAIN, I BERATED MYSELF FOR FORGETTING HOW crucial it had become for me not to participate in the narrative of guilt and renewal he'd been crafting ever since the event.

In the beginning, of course, when the event had been scheduled, he'd accepted the duty to endure my untidy bereavement. Several times, for instance, he allowed me to come over to his house to sit beside him and weep, blowing my nose and wrinkling my forehead and rehashing the ancient arrangement, though of course we both knew he still had a wife, and his wife was still an irreproachable person.

For hours, in those days, he remained there beside me. He accompanied me in that stage of my sadness, he really did, and even after the awful event, when I'd taken a bus from Albuquerque to Santa Fe and the shuttle back up to the mesa, he came over and slept in my cot.

All night, though I was bleeding so disgustingly it got all over the sheets, he slept with his arm over my shoulder. And even when I finally felt tired, I forced myself to keep my eyes open. I didn't want to miss a moment of him still lying behind me.

Even later, when the shooting pains in my stomach began and I was afraid I was dying, I was reassured by his presence. I even began to feel somewhat hopeful, because though what I'd just done was wrong, Jack was lying with his arm over my shoulder, as though he cherished my life so completely he'd lay down his own to protect me. Horribly, I know, because what I'd just done was a crime, I began to imagine that now that I'd done what I had, maybe we could get back together, if not forever, then for the time being, or for all of time as it moved on the mesa.

Only later, when he'd gone back to his house to get ready for work and I was sitting by myself on the toilet, waiting for the much-promised clot to slide out, did I remember the priestly way he'd kissed my forehead before heading out. And then, of course, I knew it was over. Then I realized he'd only come back to finish what was left of his allotted repentance, because repentance, unlike need, can be finished.

While need goes on forever, repentance has limits, and at some point in the future, if he hadn't reached it already, Jack would complete the necessary atonement to counterbalance the sin he'd committed, and then he'd be allowed to forget me.

How clueless I'd been, I thought, sitting there on the toilet. In those previous weeks, each time I'd left his house after airing all my grievances, I'd imagined we were coming to a new understanding. I'd headed back to the WAC dorms, through the crusts of old snow, past the stunted junipers and the Quonset huts with their laundry strung up on clotheslines, and I'd imagined I was a character crucial to the course of the story.

Not a wife, no, but a crucial character still, like the goodly Christian prostitute who accompanies the unhappy student murderer to the distant Siberian steppe, where together they repent his murder forever.

But repentance, I realized, while sitting there on the toilet, never goes on forever. And with each act of kindness I required from Jack, he was heading toward forgiving himself.

From that point on, I didn't go back to his house. I cast no painful aspersions upon him. For most of March and April, while the war in Europe was winding down, I forced myself to keep my own grief.

I stayed in the office past closing, and at night I went to the PX, where I ate unhealthy food and drank warm Coca-Cola. All through those terrible weeks, I played bad songs on the jukebox and forbore any expressions of sorrow, leaving Jack alone with whatever remained of his guilt, and in doing so I forced him to hoard it. I made his debt to me start earning interest, and it was only because of that debt that he crossed the room to find me at that party.

And I felt how badly he wanted to touch me, and it all went as I'd hoped, until I made that stupid joke, and squandered in one awful moment the entire balance due of repentance that had been so extraordinarily painful to build up in the first place.

THAT'S WHAT I WAS THINKING ABOUT, WHILE I LEANED ON THE CENtrifuge and didn't listen to the man from explosives, who at some point had returned with my beaker.

And then Mike Michnovicz abruptly ceased on the accordion, and the whole lab was swallowed in a silence so horrible and clattering that someone immediately put on a record, and I watched Jack talking with a group of GIs, and then I watched myself get up from the centrifuge and walk over to put my hand on his shoulder.

Then we were dancing together. He was smiling down at my pretty, young face, which I'd tilted upward to gaze into his eyes, except it wasn't me. It was some other girl I'd momentarily mistaken for myself, and from my banished position, invisible and insistent, I watched them dance like a ghost who can't accept that she's dead and keeps stubbornly hanging around with the living.

And then I finally saw my mistake. I almost started laughing, leaning on the centrifuge, wondering how I'd initially missed it. I was not, I realized then, a well-intentioned prostitute, but the horrible ghost of a murdered old woman.

Then I reexamined the events of the past months. I remembered that once, during the previous weeks, when I was forcing Jack to fall into debt, I did commit one small indiscretion and go back to his house and cry, and say that now that we'd descended so far into squalor, why shouldn't we keep on descending.

There must be a bottom, I said, and now that we've come so close we should reach it.

And then, of course, we ended up in his bedroom together, getting undressed in his bed, and only then, lying there with my skirt up, did I begin to suspect that this might be a mistake I was making.

I began to fear that the bottom was still very far off, much farther than I could have expected. And it was still so soon after the event, and the nurse had warned me several times not to do this.

And then suddenly I was very afraid, and I knew that afterward I'd lie awake alone in my dorm room, looking up at the ceiling and waiting for the crazed mice to start running.

Then, for a minute, I did what I could to turn back the train. I told Jack we shouldn't go on. I said I'd changed my mind. I said it could only make my suffering worse, but then I saw how disappointed he looked, how pained and fundamentally saddened.

And of course I was still working under the mistaken impression that I was the Christian prostitute, so I gave up my selfish resistance. I told myself that the train had long since left the station, and we were already on our way to the steppe. Then, finally, I got myself to relax. But afterward, when he'd pulled himself out and a distance had opened between us, and we were lying there close but farther and farther apart, him rising up to the surface, me sinking deeper into the darkness, I did in fact start to suffer.

It was almost past bearing, to think of returning to that nurse's back office. Then I wondered where else I could go. Certainly not to the Shangri-la clinic, where though everyone did have such excellent health care, no one was providing that particular service.

And where, I thought, could I go? Where in the world would they help me?

Beside me, still rising, Jack lit a cigarette and contemplatively smoked it.

It's a crazy world, he said, that we live in. Many millions already dead, and many millions still dying.

In one strike, he said, our weapon could incinerate a whole city. They won't even have time to take shelter.

Just think, he said: The buzz of one plane overhead, a single silver belly in the blue sky, and suddenly the whole world will be burning.

Then he shook his head. He said all we can do is tend our own garden. And then he happened to mention that to that very end, he'd volunteered for a carnival thing the following weekend, a fair organized by the wives to raise funds for needy Los Alamos mothers.

Needy Los Alamos mothers!

My laugh, hearing that: it sounded like a rusty old gate swinging open.

It sounded like the caw of a usurer with her throat cut.

Hearing it, Jack stopped talking abruptly and looked at me with revulsion: to hear that rusty laugh, escaping the maw of a murdered old woman.

FROM WHERE I LEANED ON THE CENTRIFUGE, A MURDERED OLD USU-rer resting her bones, I watched Jack and that pretty girl dancing.

Then the song stopped, and the girl went off in one direction, and Jack went off in another. For a moment I wanted to find him, and tell him I was still living, but then I remembered that ghosts always act as if they're still living, so I downed my beaker and looked up at the wife beater, who was still jabbering on, and though I'd long since lost the thread, I watched his face move and wondered whether this was indeed the face of a man who, in some former life, might have enjoyed humiliating his wife by causing her to feel completely defenseless.

For a moment, examining him, I felt something like caution. But I told myself I'd already been murdered, and dead women don't need to be fearful, so then I asked the wife beater if he'd walk me back home. Then, for a while, we looked around for my coat, and only when I'd been safely swaddled did we head out together into the darkness.

IT WAS WITH AN ODD FEELING OF CALM, AS IF FLOATING JUST OVER my head, that I watched myself walking home with the wife beater from explosives. Looking down, I noticed that my shoulders were thinner than they'd been last summer, when I played on the rocks by the water, wriggling my little brown body. But I'd cried too much since then, and lost weight all through the winter, and now I had the shoulders of a very old woman.

Then I saw that, though in keeping with his reputation he was somewhat burly, the wife beater in fact had very small hands. His wrists were almost touchingly slender, and somewhere off in the distance, he was telling me about his nine-year-old daughter: a girl, he said, who liked science and horses.

Listening to him droning on, I thought about June knitting that blanket. Then I remembered that blond girl with her braid and her exposed shoulders, and I thought: So many daughters.

So many daughters, I thought. And so many parents, though of course my own were now dead, my father, surprisingly, having gone first, and my mother having gone after.

Floating high overhead, I was barely listening while the wife beater talked, thinking instead about how, after my father's death, I'd come home after that one year at Hunter, one glorious year I'd enjoyed very much. But after my father's death I was needed at home to take care of my mother, who was still sick with the disease she got before they left Russia.

You never escape in this life, my mother once said, at least not once you start running. And that's what I was thinking about while the wife beater talked. I was remembering what a careful and obedient girl I'd always been, because my mother was always so sick, and how for that one year at Hunter, I was set free.

For one whole year I was in love with my freedom, until I came home and my father had died, and I had only three months left with my mother.

In those final months, I washed her face. I brushed her hair back from her temples. I lay with her in the big bed, and I watched her while she slept, and sometimes, gripped by the fever dreams she was having, she whispered in Russian, and sometimes she whispered in Yiddish, and though I didn't understand either language completely, I kept my eyes open and watched her lips moving.

And now here I was, a hundred million miles away, at a different altitude altogether, deep in the secret heart of the country she'd fled to, walking home with a man I didn't know, past the Quonset huts and the clotheslines where people's dresses and pants and shirts were hanging still, until a breeze came by and they seemed to be dancing.

And then, of course, I thought about Jack.

I thought about the substance of his body. I thought about how he never quite fully dried himself off after a shower. How, like an excitable little boy, he toweled himself off in a hurry, then rushed out with his neck still dripping wet and joined me in his bed, where we sat cross-legged and naked.

Through his bedroom window, you could hear owls. You could hear the rustling of the aspens, their leaves full of children.

You could smell the lake, glittering somewhere, and the fresh mud of the roads. That bedroom was like a tree house out of a book, and we were like kids, telling spooky stories at night, and giving each other the shivers, our skin so alert that the mere brush of a finger was like a stone slipping through the skin of the lake, sending rings widening over the water.

That's what I was thinking about, walking home with the wife beater from explosives: that second childhood in Jack's bedroom, which felt like my first, my own actual childhood having been spent speaking in whispers, never running, and trying so hard to live up to my end of the deals I made every night—the desires I said I'd forsake, the pleasures I'd live without—if only the world would leave me my mother.

And therefore what a wicked and keenly felt freedom it was, to be a child again in Jack's arms, the world having already taken my mother.

That's what I was considering, when the wife beater and I reached the WAC dorm, and he reached toward me and snaked his hand into mine, and from above I watched myself slow down and turn toward him, making it easier for him to lean forward and kiss me.

But then he simply gazed down at me fondly, and asked again if he could take me to dinner. And looking up at his hopeful face, I was flooded with such awful weariness of the whole thing—the girlish youth, the murdered old age—that I simply laughed, and asked if he wouldn't prefer coming up to my dorm room.

"I think," he said, stammering somewhat, "that I'd like to get to know you first."

You'll never know me, I thought.

Then I heard the call of an owl.

And then I remembered lying with my legs spread on that table in the nurse's back office, and I wondered how interested the wife beater would be in getting to know me if that's what I told him. Or if I told him I loved Jack so much that it killed me.

You don't get to choose what you know, I thought, looking at the wife beater. And then the owl hooted again, and I felt I might get swept off into the darkness, so in a moment of desperation I grabbed the wife beater's wrist and pulled him forward and forced him to kiss me.

LATER, ONCE HE'D UNDRESSED ME, I WAS INTERESTED TO DISCOVER that, far from revealing the brutality he was rumored to possess, the wife beater was earnest and loving.

It was a bit painful, to be honest, to be fixed so intently with that earnest and loving expression. It was like a light shone in your face. After a minute or two of that expression, I had to close my eyes and turn toward the pillow.

Then, getting made love to in the dark, I felt a bubble of sadness expanding inside my stomach, and I wondered if there was any more empty feeling than having a stranger moving inside you.

Lying there in the darkness, I felt like an abandoned house, wandered into by a man.

I felt like a secret closet he'd found. Or maybe more like a young girl, hiding at the back of the closet, knowing that he'd never come find me.

Yes: that's what it was. Getting made love to by the wife beater was like one of those games of hide-and-seek when you know your hiding place is too perfect. Then night falls, and the calls of the people who know you grow faint, and you understand that you'll always be hiding.

That's what it felt like, it really did, and it was such a sad, empty feeling, and also so oddly like the game of getting made love to by Jack, which was a game I'd once endowed with such transformative meaning, that I felt at once as if my sorrow would eat me. Then I looked up at the wife beater and said, "You can hit me."

He froze.

"Go ahead," I said. "Hit me in the face if you want to."

But this only seemed to confuse the wife beater further.

"I mean it," I said. "I want you to hit me."

Hovering over me in the darkness, he looked afraid. He blinked at me a few times. Then he began to earnestly make love to me once again, but by then I couldn't lie there anymore, looking up at his fatherly, lovemaking face, allowing him to play the part of somebody tender, to atone, perhaps, for some other crime against some other woman. Then I pushed him.

"Get out of me," I said, and headed off to the bathroom.

I STAYED ON THE TOILET FOR A LONG TIME. I WAS WAITING FOR THE wife beater to get it. I hoped eventually I'd hear the sounds of him leaving. But I didn't hear any sounds. Then I got up from the toilet and washed my hands for a long time, until finally I felt I couldn't hold out against the pressure of his stationary expectance.

When I went back into the bedroom, I was annoyed to discover that the wife beater was lying as if completely unperturbed by my long absence, the only difference in his position being that he'd tucked himself under the covers.

Smiling, he lifted my side of my sheet.

"You don't have to stay over," I said.

Jack, for instance, never stayed more than one or two hours, and was careful to always sneak home before morning.

But the wife beater had nowhere to go. There was no one left for him to deceive, his wife having already left him.

"I want to stay over," he said.

Then I lay down beside the wife beater. I kept my face turned to the ceiling to avoid his earnest and loving expression, but even so, I felt his eyes on my face.

"Do you want to talk?" he said after a while.

"Not really," I said.

"What's that?" he said. "I'm sorry, I have this tinnitus."

"NOT REALLY," I said.

Then I turned my back to him, and soon he'd fallen asleep in the position of someone reading your book over your shoulder. He lay that way all night, breathing heavily in my ear until morning.

AS I LAY AWAKE BESIDE THE SLEEPING WIFE BEATER, I THOUGHT ABOUT Jack. I remembered the troubled way he'd looked at me when I made that dumb joke, as though he'd stumbled into the ghost of an old woman he'd killed.

So he killed me, I thought. And yet, I'd always felt that he loved me.

All those months when we were together—sitting cross-legged in bed, or hiking up to the ruins, or swimming in the lake and adventuring in the brambles—I'd never felt that he wished harm upon me.

Maybe, then, I said to myself, adjusting the impression I'd formed while leaning on the centrifuge, I wasn't actually the murdered old woman. Maybe I was only that half-wit half sister who gets accidentally axed after witnessing the intentional murder.

That, I realized, was a more logical story. When Jack came up to the mesa, he hadn't intended to murder some orphan. He'd wanted to be involved with a moral kind of intentional murder, the deaths of enemies in declared war, and the only flaw in his execution was that he'd been interrupted by a bumbling half sister.

It was therefore understandable, I thought, that Jack hated to see me, lurking at the centrifuge, accusing him of having committed an unforgivable murder. Then I realized that if I wanted to get him to love me again, the only possible way was to demonstrate that I wasn't dead yet, and that he hadn't committed a crime he couldn't ever atone for.

IN THE MORNING, WHILE TYING HIS SHOES, THE WIFE BEATER ASKED if I was free that evening for dinner. After work, he said, he planned to attend a meeting for scientists who were concerned, now that Germany had surrendered, that we were still forging ahead with the project. Afterward he planned to eat dinner at Fuller Lodge, and he wondered if I'd be so kind as to join him.

I said I hadn't heard about the meeting.

"It's for the scientists," he said.

"Which scientists?" I said.

He looked at me, his thick eyebrows furrowed. "Probably a lot of them," he said.

"But who, exactly?" I said.

"Everyone's concerned about going on with the weapon," he said. "Senior scientists, especially. They think Oppie should shut down the project, now that the war in Europe is over."

So then I told him I'd meet him there at the chapel, and that afterward we could head to dinner together, and all day, when I was putting calls through at the office, I choreographed my entrance into that meeting. I'd wear the yellow dress, I decided, and curl my hair, and try to look extremely unmurdered. I hoped to stand in the doorway illuminated by sunshine.

Around noon, however, I went outside to eat lunch and was disappointed to see a rainstorm heading toward us. It was one of those storms you sometimes saw on the mesa, coming from such a distance that it moved as an isolated disturbance in a sky that was otherwise sunny. Then I realized I'd forgotten my raincoat, and I didn't want to show up looking sodden, so I decided to run home after work. But by the time I'd extricated myself from the office, the storm had gotten so close that I couldn't see where it started and stopped. Now it was only the weather, the skies all around having darkened, the wind having picked up, and by the time I'd headed back out to the chapel, I was really racing the rain.

I could feel it catching up to me. Off in the distance, a couple of buffaloes had somehow gotten through the barbed wire, and they stood there in the wind, watching me with their glassy black eyes, balancing on their delicate ankles like enormous, shaggy bumblebees.

It struck me as strange and alarming, the way the wind was ruffling their fur, though otherwise they stood perfectly still, and I almost stopped to watch them for a moment. But then I kept running, trying to beat that storm to the chapel, and good thing I did, because it caught up just as I crossed the threshold.

Outside, the rain started lashing the earth, and the aspens were genuflecting like women in mourning, crying wildly and tearing their hair, and inside there was a somber, serious meeting in progress. It was a sea of scientists, all of them men. The only woman scientist on the mesa was Diz Graves, and she was pregnant, and I don't think she was there at that meeting, because when I ran through the foyer I pulled up short before a sea of men in their work shirts, and a scientist I didn't know was standing up at the lectern.

I stood just outside the doorway, hesitating to intrude on a meeting that wasn't intended for me. But even so, I stayed where I was in the foyer and listened while the scientist at the lectern said that, up until now, we'd been racing the Germans.

But now Germany had surrendered, he said, and Japan didn't have a nuclear project.

Japan was, he said, for the most part already defeated, by sea and by land and by air. Our naval blockade had ruined their economy, and our bombing campaigns were systematically destroying their cities. At least 85,000 civilians, this scientist stressed, had been killed in the firestorm in Tokyo. Nearly 9,000 tons of jellied petroleum incendiaries had been dropped on Nagoya, Osaka, and Kobe.

We're already burning them alive, this scientist said. We don't need this weapon to do it.

Then he stopped talking abruptly, staring out at that sea of men as though he'd suddenly realized that there wasn't a face he knew in the whole bunch. I felt for him, I really did, and I almost wanted to wave at him so he knew that I saw him, but then a few scientists stood up and applauded, and he looked reassured, and descended the stairs from the lectern.

Then I turned and looked outside. The sun had begun to peek through one rift in the clouds, and though it was still raining hard, the rain was now illuminated by sunlight, silver slanting diagonally down through the aspens. And inside the chapel, a new scientist had climbed up to the lectern and said that if we did continue, we should be obligated to share any developments in the project with Russia.

This weapon, he said, shouldn't be used as a negotiation point. We shouldn't play diplomatic games with this weapon.

And furthermore, he reminded us, the Russians had lost tens of millions of men fighting Hitler, while we debated joining the war. For now, he said, they're still our allies. But if we don't share our secrets with them, we'll be making them our enemies. They'll have no choice but to defend themselves against the threat of the secret weapon we're making.

Then he sat down, and Bill Friedman stood up and said that he agreed, and that anyway, as every physicist should understand at this point, the whole concept of operating according to national boundaries was foolish.

He said such boundaries were hypothetical in a day and age in which whole nations could be destroyed by one weapon.

And what about radiation, he said. And what about fallout. Do they operate according to national boundaries?

By then the sun had gone out again, and the rain stormed down through the leaves, causing them to fall as if it were autumn, to swirl down to earth or to cling to the wet black trunks of the trees like notices on telephone poles.

There's no conscionable reason to actually drop one of these weapons on a Japanese city, Bill said. Then he banged his fist on the lectern. If we are going to continue work on this weapon, he said, we need some kind of guarantee that it won't be dropped.

Test it, sure, he said. But what possible use could there be in destroying another Japanese city.

Then the chapel filled with applause, and Bill returned to his seat, and contemplating those words—*radiation* and *fallout,* words I'd never heard of and couldn't imagine—I felt awfully uneasy. And then I caught sight of Jack. He was sitting in the second row beside Oppie.

There was Jack's head. I felt it in my stomach: the weight of that head, which I'd known on my shoulder, when we sat beside the lake and looked out on the water.

And because I was looking at him, watching the back of his head, I saw Oppie rise and move toward the lectern. It was difficult for me to tear my eyes away from Jack's head, but still, every so often, I did look up at Oppie. I remember how he looked, standing up there at the lectern: his hat, his heavy eyebrows, how thin his neck was.

By then, the rain was pounding so hard it was difficult to hear what he was saying, and I had to lean forward to make it out when he said he understood the scientists' concern.

He said he would do everything in his power to communicate to the generals the necessity of sharing information with Russia. And he swore, in addition, that he would do everything in his power to advocate only testing the weapon.

But, he said, even if, in the worst-case scenario, it were used once, dropped on one Japanese target, he truly believed that it would function as a preventative measure.

A horrible loss of life, he said. And yet. What if that single demonstration of the weapon's unspeakable effectiveness finally caused the governments of the world to comprehend that war is too dangerous to be waged?

Imagine, he said, how many lives could be saved by such a prohibitively dangerous weapon.

That's what our work could amount to, he said. A violence to end all other forms of violence. A weapon to end the use of all weapons.

Meanwhile, in the chapel, the mood had started to shift. Now people were nodding. All the good scientists of Shangri-la who had gathered there in the chapel were beginning to feel a little more hopeful, and a little more proud of the work they were doing, so by the time Oppie had finished talking about how, in any case, all of us were scientists, and a scientist's primary duty was to know, to know and understand the world as he saw it, you knew those men would stay on the mesa.

Then Oppie sat down beside Jack. And meanwhile that storm headed off down the mesa, and the sun began to shine through again, and the aspens stood up and shivered.

Then it was quiet, and no one else went up to speak, and finally the scientists began to filter out of the chapel. Outside, it was one of those lemony evenings after a rain's washed the sky clean, and I was standing there in the sunlight, wearing my yellow dress, smiling at those men as they passed.

And then Jack had also gone by, barely glancing up to acknowledge my presence, and when he was gone I stood slain in his wake.

For comfort, I had to repeat: *A violence to end all other forms of violence. A weapon to end the use of all weapons.*

And for some reason, those words gave me hope. They made me feel somehow hopeful and strong, like a person who could bear any blow. Like a person prepared to get all the way to the bottom, which maybe explains why, when Oppie walked past after Jack, I had the nerve to touch his sleeve and say, "Thank you."

He glanced down, and though I wasn't meant to be there at all, he didn't look exactly surprised. His head was tilted off to one side, and I'm not sure I've ever seen such an unhappy expression.

Later I learned from some disgruntled scientists that even before that meeting was held in the chapel, the target committee had already convened in Oppie's office to determine which Japanese cities would be the first targets. So Oppie must have known they'd be dropped and not merely tested, despite what he'd said up there at the lectern. But I didn't know that back then. At that point, when he saw me in the doorway, it only seemed as if, despite all that grinning, and the dancing in the lodge, and the waving from the jeep, he was actually a terribly unhappy person.

He looked down at me in the doorway as if I were a ghost

he'd seen many times. As if he knew just who I was, or who I'd been, and why precisely I'd come back to disturb him.

FROM THAT NIGHT ON, THE WIFE BEATER AND I OFTEN ATE AT FULLER Lodge after work.

The food there was better than the food at the PX, and though the wife beater was less senior than Jack, it did make me feel somewhat important, or at least somewhat involved, to be sitting there with him and his friends from explosives.

Because they'd only just come to the mesa, you could see how much they were enjoying the camp-y feel of the place, wearing their checked shirts and their blue jeans, like the most recent guests to show up at the dude ranch. There they sat at our long wooden table, merrily scraping their Fiesta-ware plates, describing a mountain lion they'd heard the previous night, or the inefficiency of the Indian girls who came up in the mornings. And meanwhile I laughed, and advised them on the best place to go swimming, and the whole time, I hoped that Jack would come in and see us.

But he never came. And by then it was June, and after that it was July, and though the war in the Pacific had dragged on for months, we all knew it would end soon.

I felt my time running out.

I felt it slipping away, while the wife beater and I ate at the lodge, and I informed all the wives about where on the mesa to buy the best spinach, or how to get letters out past the censors.

Sometimes, to pass the time after dinner, we'd go to somebody's house and drink cola and gossip about the most important scientists. One night, for example, one of the explosives' wives told me that Oppie was under the thumb of the army.

I looked at her closely. She wore horn-rimmed glasses and had a soft face. Then I leaned forward and whispered: "Do you know about the weapon?"

And she went instantly pale, and started fiddling with the glass throat of her cola, which meant that she didn't know any details, so either her husband wasn't important enough to have high-level security clearance, or he did, and he still hadn't told her.

Then I forgave her for having a husband, and let her go on with her story, and she told me she'd heard that Oppie had committed some sort of gross indiscretion. They'd followed him when he went to San Francisco to visit a woman, she said. And he didn't want that to come out. So they had him up against a wall. They were using it as psychological leverage, she said, so he'd cooperate on other fronts.

Like what, I said.

Like informing on spies, she said. And persuading the scientists to finish the weapon.

LATER, WHEN I WALKED BACK TO MY DORM ROOM WITH MY NEW BOY-friend, I felt inexplicably mean.

I thought about Jack, and how he and Oppie were close. Then I wondered how much Jack knew about that trip back to San Francisco.

I wondered whether Jack knew and didn't tell me, or if he didn't know, despite acting like he understood all the secrets that were kept on that mesa.

Then I thought about Oppie in that chapel, saying we were scientists, and a scientist's duty was to know, and to understand how the world worked, and later, when the wife beater was making love to me in my cot, I couldn't stand it anymore and suddenly bit him.

He pulled back abruptly and stared at me from above.

Then I moved to bite him again, but he pushed me back down on the mattress.

"Don't," he said, in a strict and somewhat frightening voice.

I almost grinned. But then, regretting his tone, the wife beater kissed me on the forehead, and smiled somewhat goofily, as if he was embarrassed, and afterward, when I'd come back from cleaning myself out in the bathroom, I found him sitting propped up on the pillows.

"We need to talk," he said.

"OK," I said.

"I don't want to hurt you," he said. "I care about you. I respect you."

"Sure," I said.

Then I kissed him, and turned out the lamp, and while I was trying to fall asleep for the night, I thought I was so tired of people keeping their weapons secret until the very moment they decided to kill you.

THAT MORNING, WHILE THE WIFE BEATER SHOWERED, I STOOD AT THE sink, brushing my teeth and watching him through the clear Plexiglas door.

He kept his eyes closed under the water, so he couldn't see me while I inched closer, until I was standing just outside the door, examining him while he soaped off his chest, and it was then that I realized that I didn't care to know what he was thinking.

I looked at his body—his chest, the dark hair that grew there, and on his forearms, and even on his delicate wrists—and it was so opaque, an impenetrable collection of physical features, a form full of inaccessible thoughts, and I realized that it didn't perturb me.

And how many nights, I thought, watching the wife beater lift one arm and soap his armpit, had I lain awake, wondering what Jack might be thinking?

When he'd slept with me that last time, for instance, and when I'd resisted, pleading with him to stop, had he imagined it was a kindness to finish? Had he felt there was some final sweetness in the way he stroked my back until I relaxed, the way he held me close until the moment he'd finished?

Or had it been something else? Had he felt, after those weeks when I kept myself apart, the desire to punish me for my independence? Or, alternatively, listening to me while I explained about the mice on the ceiling, had he felt an urge to sever our connection completely, and was that last time, when he slept with me in his bed despite all the fears I'd so clearly expressed, a final and definitive strike: the only possible break from the unpleasant system we couldn't otherwise seem to escape from?

I didn't know. I couldn't figure it out, no matter how many nights I stayed awake, trying not only to know what Jack was thinking, but to feel it inside my own skin, to enact the whole scene again, this time playing both parts, feeling the desire in both of the bodies.

And now here I was, peering through the glass door at my new boyfriend's face, and I didn't care to know what he was thinking. I had not even the faintest passing curiosity about the thoughts beyond his closed eyelids. And that's what I was wondering at when suddenly the wife beater swung the door open.

Surprised by a sharp edge, I staggered back, only to be surprised again by another sharp pain behind me. And because I'd been attacked on both sides, I had nowhere to run, and could only buckle at the knees like a goat, or a woman begging for mercy, and I think I may have blacked out for a moment, because when I came to again, the wife beater was helping me back up to my feet, and I caught a glimpse of myself in the mirror.

There was a cut crossing my cheekbone. And when I lifted my hand to my head, I felt warm blood matting my hair.

Then, slowly, I started laughing.

"Are you OK?" the wife beater was saying. "Do you think you need stitches?"

But I couldn't stop laughing.

The wife beater gaped. "What's so funny?" he said.

"Nothing," I managed. "Nothing is funny," but tears were still spilling out of my eyes, and I still found it hard to contain my weird laughter.

IT WAS THE FOLLOWING FRIDAY, I THINK, THAT THE BRUISE AND MY new boyfriend and I all went to Oppie's house on Bathtub Row.

And though the last time I'd seen Jack was when I made that joke in poor taste, this time I was perfect.

"Watch what?" I said, smiling lightly when Jack touched

my cheek in the hallway. And then I sailed off, and his eyes followed behind me.

It was the bruise, I'm sure of it, that made it so he couldn't resist me.

Because, of course, can a woman you've already killed get a bruise? Can you worry for a dead woman's physical safety?

No. You only worry for a woman still living. So I moved around that party with the vitality conferred on me by my bruise, and I didn't find myself awed in the least by those thick copies of Dostoyevsky and Proust, not even by the Bhagavad Gita in Sanskrit.

Indeed, standing there, perusing the bookshelf, I wondered whether Jack only liked Dostoyevsky because he knew that Oppie did also. That made me smile. I felt so blithe, moving around that well-furnished room. I even smiled at those Native American tchotchkes. Child of an immigrant, I thought to myself, trying to make himself feel like a Native.

Because of course though Oppie was the mayor of Shangri-la, his father, like my own parents, had come over from Europe, and they might have been rich, but I, too, knew what it was like, to sit at the table with your immigrant parents, listening to them while they struggled with English.

I thought of Oppie as a little boy at that table, and then I saw his collection of rocks, and the hawk's feather he'd placed in a glass, and I thought: Such incomplete children they are, these powerful men.

And then I remembered that nurse's back office, and I ran my fingertip up the soft edge of that feather.

What do these children know, I thought, about killing? What do they know of the intimate details of dying?

Then, for the first time, I looked up with new interest, and saw the women who had come to that party.

I saw Kitty first. She was sitting alone in an armchair. Her legs were pulled up underneath her, and she was wearing a pleated skirt and frilly bobby socks, and she was smoking a cigarette that she tapped off periodically on the ashtray she'd balanced on the fist of the armchair.

And even though she'd always ignored me, and mostly didn't show up to meetings of the women's committee, I loved the way she sat in that chair, her shoes kicked off, one arm folded over her chest, surveying her guests as though deciding which one she ought to say something unkind to. And what had she given up, I thought, to find herself here? And who had she become to support her powerful husband?

So I loved her, and I loved Charlotte, and I even loved June Steenberger, unbearably pregnant by now, her forehead covered with sweat and trying not to fall over. She was standing there in the corner, with her hands supporting her own lower back, holding her whole body up while her dumb husband drank another martini. And I loved them all, all those women who'd hoped we'd go home once Germany had surrendered. I loved them because of my bruise, which made me generous and forgiving, so that I walked through that party holding my glass of gin like a flag, keeping my face turned to the good side, and showing those women that I, too, knew what it was to persist in the face of a violence you couldn't quite comprehend yet.

And whenever the wife beater came over to stand too close and ask what I needed, I put my hand on his arm. I even laughed at his jokes, because even as he delivered the punch line, I knew exactly where Jack stood in the party, and as a result of that knowledge, everything in the room—the hawk's feather, Kitty's glass ashtray, June's gleaming forehead—had been sharpened to the edge of a knife, and there was a thin ringing in one of my ears, as if I were the slate on which the knife had been whetted.

All night that ringing continued, and I could feel Jack's eyes on the back of my head, and I kept laughing and drinking as the night slipped over its edge. Then Oppie passed around more of his famous martinis, and someone set a Peggy Lee record spinning, and Oppie danced an elaborate, old-fashioned waltz with a girl in a blue dress, and Kitty watched expressionless from her armchair, and later we'd all drunk so much we forgot to turn over the record.

Then there was noise enough between the clinking of glasses and our wild laughter, and in the midst of all that clattering, I. I. Rabi pulled his comb out of his pocket and played it like a harmonica.

By then, June had gone home, leaving her husband, and the girl in the blue dress had gone to sleep on the couch, nestled under a Navajo blanket.

A FEW TIMES, THROUGHOUT THE COURSE OF THE EVENING, THE WIFE beater asked if I'd like to go home. He asked in that way people do when they themselves want to go home, but I pretended I didn't get it, and told him I was having a fine time, and of course Jack stayed as well, though he never talked to me or my new boyfriend.

Everywhere I went in that room, I could feel him watching me, or watching my new boyfriend. And my new boyfriend watched me as well, and I moved around that living room aware at every moment of where they were standing and who they were watching.

We were in each other's sights, we really were. Everywhere I went in that hot, crowded room, the awareness of the game we were playing caused the hairs on my arms to stand up and prick, and by then, of course, I was very alive. By then the murder in question hadn't yet happened. That murder was still in the future, and the only thing we had to decide was which one of us would commit it.

By then, the other couples had long since gone home, and even the sleeping girl had somehow dragged herself off, and the wife beater kept coming over and suggesting that I might be tired, so finally I decided to face him.

"Go home yourself," I said, "if you're so eager to leave."

"But how will you get home?" he said.

"I'll be fine," I said.

He blinked. "You won't walk home alone?"

"Of course not," I said. And then he was gone, and Jack and I were alone, and I thought, We all have such strange ideas about danger.

IT WAS JACK, OF COURSE, WHO WALKED ME HOME IN THE END AND we didn't remember my raincoat. And of course instead of walking me back to the dorm, we walked back to his house, moving under those awful stars, past those shivering clothes on their lines, and it was only then that I felt something had shifted.

It was a sudden and terrible loss. The whole night, inside that party, I'd been exquisitely thrilled. But as soon as Jack and I were outside together, moving through that darkness that smelled like the lake, I began to feel myself emptying out. I looked out at the jagged, black line of the mountains, dark as black ink spilled on black paper, and in that moment, for some awful reason, I remembered those baby rats.

Then I was really afraid. I couldn't even look up at Jack, who was walking alongside me in silence.

Maybe, I realized, now that the wife beater was no longer a threat, I'd lost what I'd gained in his presence.

Maybe now, once again, I was the ghost of a long-since-murdered woman.

Realizing this, while we walked home along the dried ruts left by the wheels of the jeeps that passed over that road in the springtime, I tried to feel living. I tried to feel as alive as I'd felt in the party. But outside, in the dark, a fear had snuck in, a blade prying the edges of a stuck box.

And when we finally got back to Jack's house and he went to the bathroom, I wandered through those once-familiar rooms as you'd move through a museum. There was the couch where he once lay with his head on my lap. There was the bowl where he kept his grapefruits. There was the shower from which he'd come dripping wet to sit with me and laugh in his bedroom.

I moved through those rooms as silently as I could, and I'd no more have touched a single thing I found there than I'd have reached across the red velvet ropes to touch a painting in a gallery. Instead, when I'd come to that bedroom I remembered so well, I stood there with my bare arms, shivering slightly, holding myself to try to keep warm, until I felt Jack enter the bedroom behind me.

Ever so gently, he removed my pocketbook from my shoulder. Then he unzipped my dress, then moved to drape it over a chair, and I stood where I was and watched while I followed him to the other side of the bedroom.

There they stood: Jack and myself. And she looked so young, as young as I was when Jack and I met. As young as I was when we played by the lake, when he smiled up at me on the rock and called me to jump into the water.

He touched me so gently, as gently as you might touch a young girl, an innocent girl you've recently rescued, and it was as it had been when I'd just arrived on the mesa.

There I was, so recently orphaned, so recently plucked from WAC training and told I was going to Europe, then sent by cover of night on a train heading deeper into the country, across fields of corn and through mountain tunnels, then taken from the mouth of the train and placed on a bus that rattled over the cracked red earth of the valley, passing San Ildefonso and the brown Rio Grande, and finally jagging in switchbacks up the side of the mesa.

I stood there in the bedroom, watching that girl I was when I'd just passed the checkpoints, and I almost wanted to cry.

I saw, finally, how stupid she was. How unknowing of what was to come. How she felt that the worst was finally behind her, with her nice legs and her little white shorts and her foolish laughter when she returned from the lake to this house that was never her own, but where she still bumbled around and felt happy.

Standing there in the bedroom, watching my former self and Jack kissing, I felt so sorry for her in Jack's arms, and so

97

deeply ashamed of her dumbness, that I couldn't help it and did start crying a little.

Then Jack lifted his fingertips to the bruise. Then he kissed it so gently.

"Oh, Grace," he said. "My little Grace."

Then he picked me up and carried me to the bed. "Sweet Grace," he said, and I was so cold, lying there with no dress, lying there with no coat to protect me.

Nakedly, I got under the blankets. Then I felt Jack's body beside me. And then it was the two of us there, lying underneath the same sheets that I'd pulled up to my chin when I slept there as a young girl. In the same bed, I lay naked again, and this time when Jack kissed my throat, I thought about that murderer's axe.

I thought about the cold, sharp edge of that weapon, and a warmth began to spread through my body.

Now, I thought, here it is.

This, finally: this is what the dead long to come back for. This fear, this spreading warmth, this exquisite new youth that knows it will die, and how, and when, and exactly how much it will hurt when it happens.

THAT NEXT WEEK, THE WIFE BEATER WAS GONE.

So were a bunch of the most important scientists, like Jack, for instance, and von Neumann and Oppie. And of course they weren't allowed to say where they were going, and the rest of us were supposed to not guess. And I did my best, I really did.

I went through all the motions, putting calls through to intelligence, trying to piece together the scraps of informa-

98

tion I overheard, eating at the PX, reminding myself to still put on my lipstick, and toward the end of the week Charlotte came by my room and said that June's husband told her tonight was the night they were testing the weapon.

Even then, I didn't say, what goddamned weapon. I didn't say, why tonight of all nights.

I only tagged along with Charlotte to the base of Sawyer's Hill, where a bunch of other women were waiting. And none of us knew what to expect, not even June, who was standing there nervously touching her stomach. And meanwhile the whole night smelled like the lake, and then of course I remembered learning to swim, and the feel of the water, and the way it parted so softly to let me slip under.

Inside my body, while we waited there at the base of the hill, I was sinking so softly into the lake, deep down into that darkness where nothing could touch me, where the storm had already passed and the gales had already blown themselves out and all I had left to do was let myself go all the way to the bottom.

I stood there so calm and so patient, letting my eyes adjust to the darkness, and eventually I could differentiate between the dense, matted black of the mountains and the more watery black of the sky. A few times it drizzled, and then we were cold, and whenever it came around, I took the thermos June passed, letting the warmth from the whiskey run through me.

We waited there a long time. Four o'clock passed, then four fifteen, then four forty-five, and at five o'clock I almost gave up and went in, but just as I was reaching to hand back the thermos, the sky went perfectly white.

Then the earth under our feet lurched toward the mountains, and the mountains tilted a foot to the right, and the trees leaped off the sides of the mountains.

I grabbed for somebody's arm, and I saw that the women around me had turned into X-rays, and that my own arm was an X-ray as well, our bodies having become in an instant nothing more than revelations of the bone cages we'd lived our whole lives in.

Somewhere in the silence, Charlotte was whimpering weirdly. A few moments later, a low rumbling rose up from the floor of the valley, and I thought the great flood was finally coming, and for a moment it seemed as if we should be running.

But then I remembered that vision: all of us bone. And I thought, What nonsense. We're in no danger, we've already died, and what use could there be in running toward safety.

WHEN IT WAS FINISHED AND THE TREES HAD RETURNED TO THE mountains, we stayed there for a while. By then the sky had burned out to orange, then purple, then inky black, and the rumbling had died back to silence, and we stood there in the cold like a statuary of salt figurines, holding each other close, craning our necks over our shoulders, as if there were anything left to see anymore, or as if seeing it clearly made any difference to the destruction of the city we'd already run from.

AT THE PARTY THEY THREW AFTERWARD, PEOPLE'S SPIRITS WERE HIGH. The scientists who hadn't wanted the test to be done stayed at home, but the others came out for a victory dance.

In that big lot in front of the lodge, Richard Feynman was playing the bongos on the roof of a jeep, and Mike Michnovicz had his accordion out, and he was trying, I think, to make it sound happy while the WACs came streaming out from the WAC dorms.

For a while, caught up in the celebration, I looked for Jack. Then I looked for my new boyfriend. But I didn't find either one, so I kept drinking and at some point in the evening, Oppie turned up, wearing his hat.

Then a cheer rose in the laboratory where I'd ended up, and Oppie grinned, and by then I must have been asking people where Jack had gone, because finally someone pulled me aside and said he'd been given leave to go back to Princeton.

Why, I asked.

Because his wife's having a baby.

Then I stood there for a while. Later someone came by and handed me a full beaker.

I THINK IT WAS A SATURDAY, SEVERAL WEEKS LATER, WHEN OPPIE called an assembly to let us know the bombs had been dropped. He took the stage, as he'd taken the stage in the chapel, but this time it was the auditorium and the weather was sunny.

He told us our bombs had been a success. They'd gone down on two Japanese targets: Hiroshima, and then Nagasaki. He said in both cases they'd exploded as they were meant to, and we'd finished the job we'd come up to accomplish.

Then he pumped his fists over his shoulders, and for a moment I remembered his getting carried onstage, covered in flour, playing the part of a corpse in the mesa theater production.

But there he was, still pumping his fists, though I wasn't really sure he looked happy.

THE PARTY THAT NIGHT WAS UNUSUALLY QUIET. IT WAS THROWN IN the GI dorm, and most of the scientists didn't even show up.

Freddy stayed in, for example, and so did the wife beater and most of his friends. And I almost stayed in my room, but then I got restless and lonely, so I put on a dress and went to the party.

For the most part it was only GIs and a few other WACs. They'd mixed up some punch, and later someone opened champagne, and everybody got pretty loaded, trying to forget what we'd seen that night, when the mountains shifted two feet to the left, and the trees jumped off the mountains. Everyone in that party had really committed themselves to drinking. The lab didn't smell right, and people were sweating, and a woman wandered by with the sleeve of her dress torn, and while I lined up to refill my beaker I was thinking this was really a gross and disreputable party, so it was a surprise to me when I saw Oppie.

He was standing there in the corner. He didn't shake his fists over his shoulders. He didn't smile. He just stood quietly, smoking a cigarette, and by then the rest of us were so drunk I'm not sure anyone else noticed his presence.

But I did. There he was in the corner, wearing his work shirt and his boots, and I remembered his hawk feather, stuck so jauntily in that jar, and suddenly, for a moment, my heart ached to see him.

He looked so young. He looked as if he might cry. For a moment, I felt really bad for him. I thought he'd done something he knew he couldn't ever forgive, and therefore couldn't begin to atone for.

But then the moment passed. I'd cared too much already. I'd stayed up too late, wearing out my powers of caring, so then I gave up, and right away I knew I'd be sick.

I only just got outside before I had to kneel and shove my head into a juniper bush, and only when I'd finished and wiped off my mouth did I realize Oppie was kneeling beside me.

Then I felt another wave rising, so I shoved my head back in the bush, and the whole time, Oppie stayed there beside me, the two of us kneeling on the cracked earth as if we'd come there to pray for forgiveness.

"I'm sorry," I kept saying, "I'm really sorry."

And he didn't answer. He just stayed there beside me until I'd stopped throwing up, and then he helped me off my knees. I brushed off my dress. And by then, I think, I'd gotten sort of used to his presence. By then he didn't seem like the great Oppie, the mayor of our Shangri-la, he just seemed like another lost soul, wandering around a camp we should have abandoned.

HE WALKED WITH ME THE WHOLE WAY BACK TO THE WAC DORM. AT some point I noticed that there weren't any clothes on the clotheslines.

Then I thought somewhere else in the world, the survivors of those two bomb strikes—if there were any survivors—were even now wandering through a city that no longer existed.

Later, I read more specific accounts. I was sitting in the hair salon, and I read an article in a magazine that mentioned a girl whose leg had been broken when the bomb exploded nearby, and how all night while the black rain poured down around her, she waited under a sheet of tin with another woman whose left breast had been sheared off her body.

I read about a man who, running from the conflagration of the houses on his street, kicked the severed head of a man and shouted, "Excuse me, excuse me!"

And then I read about another woman who wandered for days through the ruins of the neighborhood where she used to live, holding the charred corpse of her baby, looking for the husband she'd lost in the chaos.

But I read that magazine later. That night, when I was walking back to the WAC dorm with Oppie, all I could really imagine were the mountains shifting two feet to the left, so I asked Oppie why he'd called it the Trinity Test.

He told me it was in honor of a good friend.

"Was he Catholic?" I said.

He told me it was from a poem she loved.

Then we walked for a while in silence. Later I asked him what became of his friend.

She died, he said. Her name was Jean.

I said I was sorry. Then I told him my mother died also. Then we walked on for a while in silence, and only later, when we'd gotten close to the WAC dorm, did I ask him how his friend died.

She killed herself, he said. She drowned in the bathtub.

I said I was sorry. Then I asked about the poem she'd loved, and he said it was a poem by Donne. Then he recited the whole thing by heart. And then, very politely, he left me at the front door of the WAC dorm.

THERE I STOOD IN THE NIGHT, WATCHING OPPIE RECEDE. HE WALKED somewhat jerkily, as though he were strung up on a line. He kept one hand in his pocket, the other hand hanging free, and while I watched him moving away, blending in with the dark trees and the dark mountains, I repeated what I remembered back to myself.

Batter my heart, three person'd God, I whispered into the night.

And while I headed up the stairs, I thought, *For you as yet but knock, breathe, shine, and seek to mend.*

And when I opened the door, hoping there wouldn't be any rats in my chair, I thought, *Break, blow, burn, and make me new.*

And later, brushing my teeth, looking at my aging face in the mirror, the bruise having faded, leaving me alone with myself once again, I whispered, *For I shall never be free.* When I lay down to sleep, I waited for the mice to begin running over the ceiling, but by some unknowable grace they were still, so I just lay there in the darkness that seemed to have poured out of a faucet, a darkness rising slowly around me, and repeated, *For I shall never be free.*

By then I was getting it wrong, but I didn't care. I only wondered what Oppie's friend Jean had been like. I wondered whether he loved her, and whether or not Kitty knew.

Then, finally, I wondered if Jean would have wanted a bomb to be named in her honor, whether she might have considered that outcome when she lay down in the bathtub and opened the taps, but before I had time to come to any conclusions, I began to drift off to sleep, and just before the whole world went dark, I thought again: *A violence to end all other forms of violence.*

And: *A weapon to end the use of all weapons.*

~

Oppenheimer spends the last hours of daylight in the confines of base camp, where site personnel are completing their preparations. The medical group issues coveralls, caps, gas masks, cotton gloves, and booties to be worn over shoes. The chief of the fallout team issues commands to his monitors by radio transmitter. They've chosen code names from The Wizard of Oz; *orders are directed to Dorothy, the Cowardly Lion, and the Tin Man. Now the meteorologists have launched their weather balloons, and as the sun sets, they drift northeast in bright clusters.*

At the control hub at South Shelter, ten thousand yards from the shot tower, technicians check the detonator signals for the last time. Some are out in the desert, scattering debris. At the last minute, someone decided that an effort should be made to test the bomb's impact on city structures. Pieces of sheet metal and lumber, intended to represent houses, have been placed at varying distances from the tower.

At some point, someone was given a box of white mice and ordered to tie them to the signal wires running between the bomb and base camp. Now a technician runs out to check on the mice and finds they've all died of thirst before they had a chance to survive the explosion.

At dusk, circuit testing is called to a halt. The activity at base camp starts to slow, and the only disruption that occurs is a young scientist who suddenly grows hysterical and has to be removed under heavy sedation.

ONCE HE'S GONE, THE CAMP GROWS QUIET AGAIN. AFTER NIGHTFALL, the darkness is massive. The clouds have thickened over the desert, its elements undifferentiated by starlight.

In the mess hall, to pass time, some of the scientists place bets on whether the bomb will ignite the atmosphere. If so, they wonder, will the fire consume only the state, or will it consume the whole planet.

Others, trusting the theoretical group's calculations, bet on the force of the explosion. Some of the scientists go to sleep. Oppenheimer does not. He remains in the mess hall, rolling cigarettes, drinking black coffee, and reading—according to several witnesses—poems by Baudelaire. At some point, rain starts pelting the tin roof of base camp.

ANDRIES VAN DEN BERG

Paris, 1949

IT WAS ONLY A FEW YEARS AFTER THE END OF THE WAR—MAYBE 1948, or 1949—when he and Kitty came to our little garret in Paris for dinner, and as soon as he walked in the door, I knew that nothing had changed.

Maybe there were a few superficial differences. His hair was cut shorter, that much is true. And let's not forget that he'd become famous. In one year, can you believe it, he was on the cover of *Time* magazine twice. The Father of the Atom Bomb! Or maybe it was the cover of *Life*. One or the other, he'd been on it twice, and I bought copies of both. I kept them on the coffee table, until Jacqueline put them away in the bookshelf.

Once, I picked up a magazine at a newsstand and on the cover there was only a lab stool and his porkpie hat. That's how famous he was. He'd entered the metonymic realm!

Of course, between you and me, I can tell you that hat wasn't exactly an original choice. He only started wearing it after Bernard Peters joined up with our group. Opje might have been his advisor, but we all looked up to Peters. He'd been sent to Dachau for Communist activity. Then he escaped and made his way to Berkeley, wearing a brown felt porkpie hat.

A few months later, Opje was wearing one also. But what does it matter? By the time Opje came to visit in Paris, that was his hat on the cover. You saw it at every magazine stand you passed. It even showed up in the newsreels. You'd go to the cinema and there he was, sitting with Eleanor Roosevelt and a bunch of bigwigs in bow ties, and every time I saw him presented like that—quoting Donne and the Bhagavad Gita, his hair cropped so close his head looked like a skull—it made me laugh.

Could that really be Opje? I had to rub my eyes!

There he was on the screen, looking so somber, the same guy who once kept his hair in that unruly cloud. Once he took me riding over a mountain pass near Santa Fe, and he wouldn't turn back when it started to hail. He must have had some kind of death wish! Those hailstones were like marbles, but Opje wouldn't take shelter. We rode over that pass covering our heads with our arms like we were under enemy fire, and when we finally got back to the house it took a whole bottle of whiskey to warm us.

That was 1938, or maybe 1939, the summer Barb and I visited Opje in New Mexico. There was no electricity in his cabin, and no running water. We drank our whiskey out of tin cups. We ate Vienna sausages straight from the can. It was lucky I brought my pocket knife with the inlaid turquoise handle, because as soon as we got there, Opje realized he didn't have an opener.

What would we have done? We might not have eaten all week! But even so, Opje would have had a fine time. He never ate much. He had a few bites, and then he sat back and while the rest of us were finishing, he recited poetry, or talked to us about permanent free fall, and when he had to piss he did it outside under the stars, and when he came back in he was smiling.

That was the Opje I knew in Berkeley, not the Opje up there on the screen. But time does funny things. Or that's what I said to myself, when I was waiting for him and Kitty on the balcony outside our little apartment. Inside, Jacqueline arranged the tulips she'd managed to find, and I tried to imagine what Opje would look like.

It was spring when they came, but it was still cold. I sat there on the balcony looking out over the spirally rooftops and the low, miserable clouds, and at one point Jacqueline came out and asked me to sponge off the tables. But I was so caught up in wondering whether Opje had changed that I completely forgot what she'd asked me. Instead, inspecting those rooftops, I thought that, to a certain extent, I would have to "face facts." He probably wasn't the same Opje I'd known back in Berkeley, when I was working on my monograph on Native American myth. How could he be? A lot of time had intervened. There had been a war. Some people said that Opje had won it.

Now he was a great American hero. He was in Paris for an international conference on diplomacy in the atomic age. He'd given his country a power that set it above every other country on earth. By then, every week, Radio Moscow made some new announcement about how close their atom bomb was to completion, but no one really believed them, and in Paris, waiting for Opje to show up, I tried to prepare myself for the fact that he might have been changed.

I told myself he probably wouldn't walk in the door looking just like he had when he was another assistant professor at Berkeley, with that big cloud of curly hair and that belt he wore with the Navajo buckle.

While Jacqueline finished the soup, I stayed out there on the balcony, looking out over the bare trees and the gray city, feeling more and more cross about the things time does to the people we care for, and then, finally, a cab pulled up, and Opje stepped out.

Sure enough, even from above I could see he looked different. He wasn't wearing his hat. His hair was shorter, and it had gone gray. His overcoat must have cost him a fortune.

Then Kitty stepped out behind him, and I'll tell you what. She was wearing a mink coat, and her hair was done in an awful new style, cut just under her chin, and sort of rounded and sprayed in the shape of a helmet.

I was so disappointed! I imagined them climbing the stairs, passing the shared bathroom we used on the stairwell, and there was a knot in my stomach when I went to the door. But then I opened it up, and there they were, and I saw that underneath her new helmet, Kitty was still almost as pretty as she was in the old days, back when she and Opje first met and she came with him to a dinner party we threw at Barb's house.

Now she was wearing a pair of diamond earrings the size of small grapes, but when she went up on her tiptoes to kiss me, and Opje grinned, and held out a salad in a big wooden bowl, and a bottle of Château Cheval Blanc, I knew right away that they were the same people.

I took the wine and Opje held on to the salad, and they moved through that little Paris apartment—the only thing we could afford, between my lecturer's pay and Jacqueline's graduate stipend—and acted as impressed as they would have acted walking into that house on the coast that Barb inherited from her parents.

That apartment was no bigger than the laundry room in Barb's house, but Opje seemed genuinely delighted. He loved the exposed beams and the view over the rooftops. He walked around acting so excited and happy to be there, and it was clear right from the start that though our lives had taken two different forks, he didn't hold himself above me.

He was still the same guy he was when he lived in that house on Shasta Road, with the hammock slung up on the back porch. And he was just about to put the salad bowl down when Jacqueline swooped past, murmuring apologies, and sponged off the tables. Then she smiled shyly and let him put the salad bowl down, and I saw Opje notice how pretty she was.

I'll tell you what: that made me feel good. I realized then how lucky I was, to live with Jacqueline in that little apartment. She was so pretty and sweet, and such an excellent cook, and the spread we laid out for Opje and Kitty was simple but it was as good as anything they'd have been served at any pretentious French restaurant.

We started with the onion soup and a loaf of excellent bread, and I'd spent more than I should have on a few bottles of good Languedoc. Then we opened the Château Cheval

Blanc. And by the time we'd finished that bottle, I'd remembered Opje's famous martinis.

Those martinis! He used to keep glasses chilled in the freezer. Even in that little house, where he sometimes slept on the back porch and ate nothing but peanut butter out of the jar, he always kept a box of the best gin in his pantry.

I told that little story while we finished our salad, and we all had a good laugh, and then we decided the only proper thing we could do to celebrate the old days back in Berkeley was to make a few of Opje's famous martinis. Then Opje and I went to the kitchen, leaving Jacqueline and Kitty to get to know one another, and for a moment, just before we closed the door, I remembered that Barb once said Kitty could be a difficult person.

But then I thought maybe that was just Barb. She was always oversensitive, and Jacqueline was so sweet she could have charmed Stalin, so I wasn't concerned in the least when Opje and I went to the kitchen, and while I rummaged around for some olive juice and vermouth, we caught up on the old days in California.

We talked about the monograph I was writing back then, my collection of Native American myths. Then Opje asked me about the new project, and I told him this one was an ethnography in photographs, a study of Europe after the war. And we both knew without saying that it was a new direction for me. My specialty was Native American myth, and I found the new subject depressing. But of course I'd been denied a visa to return to the States, and then Opje acted so interested in the new subject, and so impressed by the new direction I'd taken, that by the time we'd found the olives, it didn't matter one bit.

There was Opje, leaning on the counter, asking me all sorts of excellent questions, and I'll tell you what, it made me so happy just to be standing there in the kitchen with Opje, talking about our work like we used to.

Then I asked him if he'd had time, since the war, to go back to studying permanent free fall. He couldn't believe it! But how could I have forgotten permanent free fall? All those conversations, late into the night, sitting on his back porch and looking up at the stars while Opje explained that somewhere out there in the darkness there were spots of matter so massive and dense they simply vanished.

They collapsed into themselves and disappeared, and so did every little thing that passed by them.

Even sound. Even light! Or that's what he told me, sitting on that back porch in Berkeley. Every little thing that passed too near those spots bent in and around them and started to spiral until they'd disappeared, vanished as though they'd never existed.

Later they called those spots a name. They called them black holes, I think, but it was Opje who predicted them, all the way back at that house on Shasta Road. Standing there in the kitchen while Opje poured the gin into the glasses, we laughed about those nights for a while, and then Opje told me he hadn't had much time to get back to physics.

He looked a little sad about that, so I changed the subject. I asked him about California. I'd heard he'd moved back there after the war. Of course by the time he came to Paris, they'd moved to Princeton. But for a year or two, after the war, when he'd left the Manhattan Project, he was in California again. So I asked him if he'd seen any of the old gang that used to gather on Shasta Road.

He couldn't believe it! But how could I have forgotten the name of that street? I remembered everything about that little house, like how he kept the windows open all year, so the smell of eucalyptus swept through the kitchen.

In the winter, he built great big crackling fires. Then we sat around in the redwood-paneled living room, with Navajo blankets draped over our knees, and even though we were only a few miles away from San Francisco, we felt like frontiersmen.

We were so far away. The war in Europe was happening on a different planet completely, in a different universe. We gathered around Opje's fire and drank his red wine, and even those black holes seemed to be closer than Europe. Still, sometimes, after reading the news, we came up with schemes to send ambulances to the rebels in Spain. We raised money for refugees from Germany. On the home front, we got involved in the dockworkers' strike and organizing a teachers' union at Berkeley.

We had so much energy in those days! We didn't just talk. We put that union together. Everyone chipped in, people of all possible backgrounds, and there was no internal strife whatsoever.

That's what Opje and I had to remember, standing there in the kitchen of that little apartment. It put a smile back on my face, I'll tell you what. There I was, smiling like a fool, still on the hunt for the vermouth, and meanwhile I asked

Opje all about the old gang: Haakon Chevalier, and that Sanskrit professor, and Bernard Peters, and his wife, Hannah.

I even asked Opje about his graduate students. Those admiring kids! They smoked Chesterfield cigarettes because that's what Opje smoked. They flicked the ash off with their pinkie fingers, because that's how Opje did it. When they talked they sort of quietly mumbled, *nim nim nim nim,* because that's how Opje delivered his lectures, and they also came up to that house on Shasta Road. They sat with us by the fire, and when we were hungry Opje cooked eggs à la Opje.

Did we ever laugh about that, all those years later in Paris! I said I remembered how he scrambled those eggs with peppers he pulled from a strand, and Opje told me he learned to make them during one of the summers he spent as a kid, camping in New Mexico: pitching his tent alone, listening all night to the screams of the mountain lions that slept in the trees.

It was a woman, he said, in a nearby hacienda, who taught him to make eggs à la Opje. And for a second, when he told me that, he looked just like he did back in Berkeley: that wistful expression, those sensitive eyes.

Then I reminded him how those boys ate their eggs: Like they hadn't eaten in months. Like it was their last meal on the planet! Standing in that kitchen in our Paris apartment, where I finally found an old bottle of vermouth, we had a good laugh about that. Then I asked Opje if he saw any of those kids when he moved back to California, and he told me he hadn't.

Then he changed the subject, and later I asked if he remembered when he tried to get Bernard Peters a job in the

Physics Department, but the chair told him one Jew in the department was plenty.

Then I found him a jar to use as a shaker, and while he mixed the martinis, I asked if those boys had teaching jobs now, or if, like me, they'd had trouble finding work because of our politics during those years. And then I began to feel a touch maudlin.

I sometimes did, when I remembered those difficult days after the war, when things had gone south with Barb and I was sending letter after letter to the State Department, asking for the grounds on which my employment kept getting revoked.

But then Opje finished mixing the drinks, and we carried them out, and just looking at Jacqueline cheered me right up. She'd gotten up from her chair to change the record I'd chosen, and she was looking so sweet, wearing men's trousers and chewing on a wisp of her hair.

What a beautiful girl, I thought, and then she turned and looked at me with a somewhat odd expression, almost confused, as though for a moment she didn't know me. And in that moment she looked so vulnerable and alone—like the girl she must have been before the Occupation, when her parents sent her away from Paris to live with her grandmother in Metz—that I wanted to go over and kiss her.

But then she came back to the table, and the four of us drank our martinis, and I did notice that Jacqueline was a little quieter than she usually was, but then she rose and went into the kitchen, and when she came back, carrying the cheese plate before her, I suddenly remembered Barb's face.

I remembered it as clearly as if she were standing right

there. And I'll tell you what: it almost brought tears to my eyes!

I really felt, for a moment, as if we were all back in Berkeley, the four of us, having a dinner party together. So then I went into the bedroom and got out the big turquoise ring and the agate-inlaid hunting knife that I got from a Hopi man when Barb and I were in Utah, and then we finished the cheese.

Then Opje made a second round of martinis, and it was all so much like the old days that suddenly I remembered that afternoon back in Berkeley, when we all drove down to the picket line on the docks, and how afterward we went back to Barb's house, that sprawling mansion perched on a cliff.

I asked Opje if he and Kitty remembered that house, and if they remembered driving back there after the strike, and how we all ate that Chinese supper Barb made, with the salty mandarin oranges. Poor Barb! She was such a bad cook. But even so, we always had a good time bringing friends back to that house. Even all those years later in Paris, I still remembered how much fun we had that night after the strike.

We stayed up late drinking martinis, thrilled by the progress we'd made at the docks, and by the time we'd finished that Chinese supper we were so exuberant we ran out into the darkness and threw off our clothes and swam naked in the big tiled pool.

That pool! I'll never forget it. It was heated, and there were lamps on the sides, and the light swung through the water in nets. Outside, that pool was surrounded by shaped cypress trees standing sentry, and those enormous stone sphinxes that stared duskily at us while we swam, resting their chins on their crumbling forepaws.

I told that story while Jacqueline changed the record again, and everyone just split their sides laughing. We were having such a fine time together, remembering those nights back in Berkeley, while the candles Jacqueline had bought burned down to the wicks, and her white tulip arrangement, lit from below, began to look as if it, also, was melting. And then, out of the blue, I remembered that I still had three of the good bottles of port I'd salvaged from my marriage to Barb. I went into the kitchen and pulled them out of the back of the cabinet, and as soon as I uncorked the first one, I could smell California.

There it was, at the back of my palate: the warm earth, and the dusty spice of eucalyptus, and the ocean blowing in from the coast.

It stopped me in my tracks. For a moment, in the kitchen, I stood there with tears in my eyes.

Then I brought the bottle out to the table and we all drank it down to the dregs, talking about the old days on Shasta Road. We didn't even realize how much time had passed! We stayed up so late that at some point, Jacqueline went to the couch and yawned like a kitten. Then she wrapped herself in a blanket, and later, she started reading a book.

And later, Kitty went to the balcony to smoke another cigarette, but Opje and I were still laughing about the struggles we had with that teachers' union, so I went to the kitchen and opened another bottle of port.

Then I realized it was the last bottle I had from that case I'd salvaged from the wine cellar at Barb's house. Then I hesitated for a moment, but what better time to finish that bottle than with my good old friend Opje? So then I pulled out the cork, and back at the table, Opje and I started talking about the time Barb and I visited him and Kitty at that cabin in New Mexico.

Then I remembered how Barb and I had made love all night in that bare little bedroom, with its four-poster bed and the wood beams, and it filled me with love, remembering that.

And then I thought again about that night when we all went swimming, after we'd come back from the dockworkers' strike.

And Opje said, we were good in those days. And I said yes, that's what it is. We were all so good in those days.

Then we toasted to that, and poured ourselves another glass, and I kept saying, "Do you remember this?" and "Do you remember that?" and then Kitty came in from the balcony and said it was time to go home. They had an early flight back to the States, so Opje helped her back into her mink, and he put on his overcoat, and we clapped each other on the back one more time, and for a moment I almost imagined I was saying goodbye to him at that pass in the mountains, as if he were going on in the hail and I were turning back to go home.

One of us heading west, the other going back east.

And I almost cried, to think of everything that had happened since Opje and I rode over that pass, and how much more time might go by before we met again at those mountains.

WHEN I WENT BACK INSIDE, JACQUELINE HAD GONE TO SLEEP.
She'd left all the dishes out on the table, which annoyed

me for a moment, but then I went to the balcony and finished the port, and then even though it was cold, and the rooftops were steely and wet, I was in California again. I could even smell eucalyptus, and the desk lamps that were switched on in people's apartments were like little oranges, looming in the dusky groves, and I felt such fondness for Opje as he was in those days in Berkeley, and also for those boys he taught, and for Bernard Peters and even for Barb, who was so pretty back then, with her blond hair and her brown shoulders.

Sitting there on the balcony, I was swept away by my fondness for Barb, with her disorganized American laugh and that sprawling house she inherited from her parents and didn't know how to look after, with the tiled swimming pool and the shaped cypress trees, and the way we all rushed out together, caught up in that moment of unbridled youth, and stripped off our clothes and swam naked.

I felt so fond of everyone in those days that I decided, right then and there, to write a letter to Barb to ask her if she remembered that night. So then I went inside and got a pencil and paper, and came back out and sat down at that table, the one Jacqueline had decorated with a blue porcelain cat, and I wrote to Barb and told her about our excellent night, drinking Opje's martinis and catching up on the old days.

I told her Opje and Kitty seemed happy together, and I said it made me remember how happy we all were in Berkeley: driving back up from the strike, eating that Chinese supper, and throwing off our clothes to go swimming.

Then, carried away by my fond feelings, I told her I remembered how generous she always was, how loved she made me feel, especially in the beginning. I told her how beautiful

I always found her, particularly on that night, her wet hair streaming behind her, her shoulders bare, her eyes shining toward me in the darkness.

I went on and on. I told her, joking, that I remembered how bad her cooking was, and how she never really knew the meaning of money. But I told her that now, after all, none of that mattered. None of the unpleasant things mattered, I wrote. I'd forgotten them all.

I couldn't even remember, I said, what we fought about in those days, and all that remained still in my mind was how beautiful she was in the water, and how much I loved her, and what a gift it was to me to have known her.

Then, feeling warm and happy and satisfied with the generous spirit that had caught me in its arms since Opje walked in the door, I cleaned up the dishes. And I realized that Opje and Kitty had forgotten to take their big salad bowl with them. And I'll tell you what, even that was just exactly like Opje!

He was always forgetful. His mind was hung up on bigger concerns, like solar decay and permanent free fall. So that salad bowl made me smile, and I smiled again whenever I saw it sitting there on our shelf, even though for a few days after that party, Jacqueline was in a bad mood, one of her inexplicable sour ambitious phases, when she worked on her dissertation all day and snapped at me if I interrupted.

But even so. I was in a high state all week, and well into the next one, when unfortunately I received one of Barb's tiresome, embittered responses, saying she didn't remember that night the same way that I did.

She told me she remembered that I'd pressured her to

get naked, and that she'd been excruciatingly self-conscious, even under the water.

And even so, she said, despite her repeated objections, I'd insisted on turning the lights on.

Later, she said, in the following months, she'd been mortified whenever she ran into our friends, not because of how we'd all gotten naked, but because they'd heard me ignore her when she asked me to not turn on the lights.

For months, she said, she was embarrassed, though now when she looked back on that night, she wished that instead of feeling embarrassed, as though it were her fault I'd ignored her, she'd felt what she should have: anger, and pain, to be so disregarded by the one person she'd decided to trust.

But we're always blind, she said, in the moment when we need to see.

Then she told me that, for the record, by the time Opje and Kitty were married, he didn't live on Shasta Road anymore. It was Jean, she said, who was with Opje when he lived on Shasta Road. Jean went with us to the dockworkers' strike. Then Jean and Opje broke up, and a few months later Opje got together with Kitty, and a few months after that, Kitty was pregnant. Then they got married and moved into that ranch house.

And Jean, Barb said, had to watch him move on that quickly, as though her memory didn't haunt him at all.

It must have been very painful, Barb said. Such a complete eradication of what they were together.

Then Barb asked, incidentally, if I ever wondered whether I'd wound up on the blacklist because of my connection to

Opje. And she reminded me that all his former students—those *nim nim* boys I was so fond of—had ended up drafted, or blacklisted, or imprisoned for taking the Fifth. Barb said some people in Berkeley thought he'd given the names of his former Communist friends, perhaps to keep his position on the bomb project.

A real trail of ruin he's left in his wake, Barb said.

And now he's running around like that little Dutch boy, giving talks on world peace, trying to put his finger in the hole in the dike, but it's only a matter of time before the Soviets test one of those bombs.

Then she said that, speaking of water, it was Jean, not Kitty, who was with us that night we went swimming, and she asked whether I knew that Jean had drowned herself in her bathtub.

Then she said that while I'd certainly described a very fun dinner party in Paris, she couldn't believe Robert Oppenheimer was happy, not with all that blood on his hands.

Tens of thousands of dead in Japan, she said, and more dying still as a result of the radiation sickness our government made such a point of denying.

He may have seemed happy, Barb said, but she'd seen Kitty in the salon, and Kitty told her things had been bad since they left the mesa, that Robert had been very troubled, and that she was the one who bore the brunt of the burden.

(So they go to the same salon, I thought, and wondered if Barb also wore her hair short now, and rounded and sprayed into the shape of a helmet. Then I imagined a whole bunch of American women with their hair sprayed in the shape of a helmet, and I thought, What's happening in California! Is there some army forming, some battalion of embittered American women, all wearing their hair like a weapon?)

Then Barb said, in conclusion, that while she appreciated the sentiment in my letter, for her, the unpleasant things still existed.

If you want to forget them, she said, so be it. I can't force you to remember what you don't want to. Regardless, I wish you well, and I hope life with the most recent graduate student is everything impossible you've always allowed yourself to believe in.

At one A.M. *it's still raining. The test is scheduled for three o'clock, and several scientists approach Oppenheimer in the mess to express their concern about exploding the device in this weather.*

They favor postponement. In weather like this, if the bomb does explode, the rain will absorb the radioactivity. The wind could unpredictably shift. Who knows how far the dangerous material could spread.

Oppenheimer listens, then consults Hubbard, the chief meteorologist on the project. Hubbard consults his instruments. He assures Oppenheimer that the storm will pass before sunrise, then recommends delaying the test to sometime between four and five o'clock in the morning.

Drawn by the commotion, General Groves joins the group. He dislikes Hubbard and mistrusts his predictions. "I'll hang you if you're wrong," he says to the meteorologist.

Groves is suspicious of information based on balloons. But he's also opposed to postponement. The bombs, he feels, must be delivered on schedule. Imagining the scientists might persuade Oppenheimer to put off the test, he now orders Oppenheimer to accompany him to the command hub at South Shelter, ten thousand yards from the test site. They drive through the rain, then enter the shelter, where they join a group of several generals, technicians, and scientists, including Oppenheimer's brother, Frank, whom Oppenheimer has put in charge of the shelter.

At 2:30 A.M. it's still raining. Oppenheimer and Groves go outside. They pace the grounds, their eyes turned toward the sky, which is occasionally rent by flashes of lightning. In those moments of light, the mountains come staggering out of the darkness.

"If we postpone," Oppenheimer says, according to Groves, "I'll never get my people up to pitch again."

So he wants to finish. At least according to Groves. He wants to get it over with, to head off this uncertainty about whether the device will really go off.

The rain is still pouring down on the tower, the detonator wires, the bodies of the dead mice, but Oppenheimer and Groves decide the test should proceed. They go back inside. They reschedule the test for five thirty.

SALLY CONNELLY

Princeton, 1954

I'LL GET TO ROBERT, I PROMISE.

I'll tell you everything he told me that afternoon—about Jean and the friends he lost and what he imagined the army would do with the bombs he delivered—when he came into my office at the institute and said he wanted me to know the whole story.

But first I need to go back several steps.

Once upon a time, when I was twenty, before I worked for Robert at the institute, I was married to a person named Stan. Stan was a nice, decent person from New Jersey. I married him in 1952, two years before Robert's security hearings, seven years after he left the position at Los Alamos. That was when we were still at war in Korea, and Robert was still advocating against testing the H-bomb, and I'm going to get to him in a moment, but I need to get this all out while I can.

When I met Stan, I was still a junior at Rosemont. I didn't care much about science. Ever since I was a girl, I'd been caught up in secret ambitions to write a Great American Novel.

But that was something I never admitted out loud. It would have been an absurd thing to say, like announcing I hoped to become king of England. Who had ever heard of a girl writing a Great American Novel, let alone a debutante from the Main Line.

Anyway, my parents disapproved of their daughters' pursuing the arts. A dignified, marriageable degree in art history was one thing, but actually pursuing an artistic life was for WASPs who could afford to flaunt their neuroses.

We, on the other hand, as representatives of our religion, had to show at all times how cheerful and mentally stable we were. How in control of our sensuous aspects.

My parents wanted us to play sports. We competed, but never too aggressively. It was essential to never reveal anything resembling a temper. My father rowed like Grace Kelly's father. My mother played tennis, on the court my father built in the backyard, because the clubs on the Main Line weren't open to Catholics.

Still, my secret dream was to write novels, though on the outside I took tennis lessons and worked hard to pretend that my great ambition in life was to accomplish an exemplary husband.

Unfortunately, however, in those days, I was twenty pounds overweight.

Sometimes, at night, in my dorm room at Rosemont, I ate bowls of cereal.

I stuffed my face full of soggy spoonfuls of Wheat Chex, which I'd bought during the day in the attempt to be healthful. By nighttime, however, when I'd finished my simpleton's art history homework, I'd get caught up writing draft upon draft of some terrible novel, some sprawling, disjointed blob about American Characters in the Nuclear Era.

For hours and hours, I'd escape into the lives of the characters I'd invented. I'd duck into the personalities of people who weren't like myself in any way, and while I wrote, giddy with freedom, I'd forget all appropriate concern for my figure. Then, in the morning, bleary eyed and appalled by how many bowls I'd consumed, I'd squeeze myself into a dress and go to class to be pretty.

MAYBE A STRONGER-WILLED GIRL WOULD HAVE GIVEN UP THE PURsuit of a husband to follow her dreams of writing in earnest.

But then I had to consider the enormous effort my parents had made: the company my father had built out of nothing, the faultless veneer my mother had polished, the insults they'd so gracefully borne, and all in the belief that their daughters would flourish.

Every time I considered rebellion, the awareness of their sacrifice deflated my will.

At the end of the day, any rebellious energy I had left was spent on eating too much cereal, pointlessly and absurdly resisting my mother's wish that we girls should stay slender.

I DON'T KNOW WHY I RESISTED SO FIERCELY. IT'S CLEAR TO ME NOW that my mother's desire rose out of nothing but love. She herself had escaped a long line of women whose bodies were fed to their children. She hoped we'd rise above that. For us she wanted the dignity of life without a womanly body.

In other words, her intentions were pure. But for some reason, at night, I felt compelled to resist them. I stuffed my face with cereal. Then, in the mornings, with my undignified body spilling out of my dress, I went to class so unhappy.

I could barely keep it together to sit still and look pretty. I only just managed to make the right kinds of friends, in order to meet the right kind of husband.

LEFT TO MY OWN DEVICES, I'D NEVER HAVE FOUND HIM. I WAS TOO tired and unhappy after all those long nights. I was lucky my roommate Kathy had the energy to step in and assist me. The only reason I ever met Stan—and Robert, as a result—was because Kathy dragged me along with her to Princeton to go on a double date with her and her new boyfriend.

We drove up together in the Studebaker her parents had bought as a present for her coming-out party: not the Charity Ball, but the private cotillion our parents threw, just so we Catholic girls wouldn't miss out. Kathy and I wore white dresses beaded with seed pearls. We danced with boys from exemplary families, and I tried not to gaze over their shoulders at the engraved silver trays of *petits fours* and *friandises*.

WHAT A MESS I ALWAYS WAS. I WAS LUCKY I HAD KATHY TO LOOK OUT for my interests. She ruled them with an iron fist.

Sometimes, remembering how determined and unscrupulous Kathy was about building alliances on my behalf, I start to get angry. Then I feel so bad for her I could weep.

Building marital alliances was her only pursuit. In some other existence, she could have arranged to make me the seventh wife of Henry VIII, thereby reversing the ecclesiastical schism. But in the early fifties at Rosemont, all she had was me and her Studebaker and the eligible friends of her boyfriends.

While we drove up to Princeton, the leaves lining the highway were changing. Kathy was driving with both hands gripping the wheel, sitting up very straight, wearing a cute pillbox hat and the white kidskin gloves she'd bought for herself at Strawbridge and Clothier.

The radio was turned to a channel on which several panelists were discussing the war in Korea, and how Truman had ordered atomic devices to be assembled at Kadena Air Base in Okinawa.

Apparently B-29 bombers were flying practice runs from Okinawa to North Korea, dropping dummy atom bombs. The panelists on the radio were debating the effectiveness of using nuclear weapons against North Korea, despite the fact that every important building in the country had already been destroyed by our bombers, and despite the fact that the Soviets had nuclear weapons as well, and had already tested two additional bombs since their original 1949 test.

And meanwhile I sat in the passenger seat with my hands crossed on my lap, looking at the changing leaves outside the window and wrestling with that hollow gnawing sensation I often mistook for real hunger.

When we crossed into New Jersey, I began to root around in the pockets of my camel-hair coat, where I was delighted to discover a Fireball I must have been saving. I tried to be subtle when I unwrapped it, but the cellophane was crinkly, and I could feel how tense Kathy was getting.

Nevertheless, however, I allowed myself to believe it might be possible to enjoy it.

Once I'd popped it into my mouth, however, the project became increasingly stressful. I had to suck it without making a sound, which involved shifting it from side to side while preventing it from knocking my molars.

By then, my eyes were watering. Kathy was forcing herself to keep her eyes on the road, but her expression was increasingly flinty. A few times, I glanced over and caught that telltale flare in her nostrils.

"Don't you want to save your appetite?" she finally said.

Then I couldn't enjoy it, so I spit the candy back into its wrapper. I noted that it was white and lightly veined with pink threads, so that it looked like the underside of an eyeball.

Not knowing what to do with it, I held on to it for a while, until I thought Kathy wasn't paying attention. Then I slipped it back into my pocket.

"That's disgusting," Kathy said, five minutes later.

By then, the car was so full of her disapproval that for a moment I wondered if she'd make me get out and walk. In the end, however, she didn't, and finally we came to Princeton and parked. Then I followed her into the restaurant.

We took a seat at the table and I removed my camel-hair coat, revealing my mohair sweater and the tasteful pearls my mother had bought me, which unfortunately did nothing to hide my dolphiny figure.

Still, I wasn't too nervous. I was expecting Kathy's boyfriend to show up with an unattractive but socially advantageous companion. That was the kind of alliance Kathy tended to forge me.

But when Kathy's boyfriend walked in the door, it was

with a person so tall and handsomely swarthy I felt immediately sick to my stomach.

Then they sat down—the handsome roommate on my side of the booth—and began to explain how they'd become friends in the air force. They'd both been deployed to Korea for several months before completing their service and returning to Princeton, and while they talked about their experiences flying planes, they both seemed somewhat larger than life and extraordinarily handsome.

Then I began to suspect that a person as handsome as that particular roommate would be disappointed to have been set up with such a fat girl, a dolphin in a pearl necklace.

Nevertheless, however, the dinner progressed, and the roommate seemed inexplicably happy.

That only aggravated my panic. It was almost as if he couldn't see how fat I really was.

It was as if he'd missed it completely, so the awful revelation was always just coming.

Then I began to wonder if Kathy had given up on arranging a socially advantageous connection, and whether that roommate was in fact somewhat low on the totem pole of people I should have been dating. Perhaps, I realized, that was his motive for missing the fact that I wasn't slender.

It was as if he'd been told in advance that I'd make a good match: that my parents had a house on Cape May and a tennis court in the backyard. As if, given those details, he'd decided before showing up that no matter what I happened to look like, no matter which flaws he discovered in my character, he'd inevitably manage to like me.

I wondered about that while I sat beside him at the table,

keeping my flippers pinned to my sides. And the more he seemed to miss the true facts of my physical form, the more hollow and hungry I felt, and when the waiter brought out the bread, I grabbed myself a whole fistful.

I felt Kathy watching. Her nostrils were beginning to flare. So then I returned the bread to my side plate.

Meanwhile, her boyfriend started talking about how the whole point of bombing campaigns was to shatter enemy morale. He said we'd been so successful in our campaign in Korea that every last trace of North Korean civilization had been reduced to heaps of smoldering rubble. North Korean leadership, he said, had instructed its remaining population to start tunneling underground in order to solve the shortage of housing.

And there I sat like a good dolphin, overflowing in my seat beside that handsome roommate, who still hadn't managed to notice my fatness. He seemed to be sitting beside me in a state of perfect contentment, and after a while, it was simply too much to bear. Then my hunger took over. I heaved my fins up from my sides and cut an enormous bloody bite of my steak.

There I was, a dolphin cutting her steak. I knew it was a ridiculous sight, but I didn't care. By then the rebellious streak had kicked in, and even though Kathy was poking me under the table, I just kept eating.

The straighter Kathy sat up, the more I slouched like a slob. The more daintily she nibbled her cod, the more bloody steak I stuffed into my snout.

Then I ordered a bourbon. I didn't even like bourbon. I just ordered it with the same glee I usually felt when I'd given a character an interesting trait.

Still, however, the roommate managed not to notice. When my bourbon arrived, he was still smiling, and treating me very politely, as if he wasn't at all disappointed with the manner in which I'd started behaving.

Then I almost laughed, because I realized that nothing was real. This was a purely literary adventure. Kathy and I were only two differing protagonists, one thin and one fat, one good and one bad, perfect opposites of each other.

I SHOULD MENTION, AT THIS POINT, THAT I HAD A TWIN SISTER.

This has to do with Robert, I promise.

Before we get to that story he told me, I need to establish that my poor mother had suffered the indignity of bearing twin daughters.

Despite her refinement, and the fact that she spoke perfect French and was skilled in the art of flower arrangement, she conceived twins, and it was when that news was delivered that my father's mother, who suspected my mother of putting on airs, laughed and brought her down a few pegs by saying, "My dear, only sheep carry twins."

It sometimes can't be countenanced, these bodies we go around with, like chattel.

Despite her perfect French, my mother was inflicted with the indignity of carrying twins, so you can understand why she was later so concerned that her little girls should be slender.

And it wasn't her fault that I was always so hungry, or that beside my sister, in photographs of our ballet class, I always looked so stout in my tutu. And it certainly wasn't my mother's fault that I hated ballet and took to secretly writing,

137

and that rather than writing attenuated little ladylike son-nets, I wanted to cram it all into a novel.

It was nobody's fault but my own that I was so fat and insistent, which meant that my sister had to get thinner and thinner in order to compensate for my fatness, so that by the time I got to Rosemont, where I ate too much and wrote novels, my sister was at home wasting away, having given up college and everything else to dedicate herself to the art of her thinness.

I'M GETTING TO ROBERT, DON'T WORRY.

My sister pursued the precise art of her thinness with the cool, detached serenity of the most gifted artists.

All day, while she moved through her routines, her eyes seemed to be fixed on a point just beyond the visible world. In the morning, she made her bed very neatly. At night, she spent a long time calmly moisturizing her hands.

She had many routines of that kind, which she pursued while I was at Rosemont.

She spent hours in the library, where she conducted the majority of her research. Otherwise, she spent a lot of time in the car with my mother. By then, she looked simultaneously like a very young girl and a very old woman. Placidly examining her well-preserved hands, she waited while my mother ran errands. Otherwise, she rested in our childhood bedroom, and during those years I thought I despised her.

WHAT I WANT TO MAKE CLEAR—AND THIS, I PROMISE, IS RELATED TO Robert—is that our roles seemed to have been predestined.

We had no control of the system.

It was an archetypical issue, bigger than just me and my sister.

It was an issue represented on cave walls. My sister was Persephone married to Hades. I was Persephone over the summer.

All summer, I ate the fat fruit, and to atone for my greed, my sister chastised herself through the winter. She remained in the penitent dark, while I ran around in the wheat, enjoying that golden splendiferous season when swans rape pretty girls on the hillsides.

We were stuck, in other words, in the hands of a myth.

It took us up in its sway well before we were conscious that it was at work. On Sundays, for instance, when we went to church, my sister's exemplary socks stayed pulled up to her knees, and mine always sagged down to my ankles.

When my sister kneeled down to pray, she kept her eyes closed like a saint. But mine kept popping open, some voice inside my head commanding me to disobey, to open my eyes and watch the more obedient people.

With their eyes closed, they prayed for those fallen members of our congregation, slain overseas, and watching them pray, I always felt hungry.

Sometimes, on the way out of church, a member of the floral committee would stop my mother to talk, then look down at me and my sister in our matching camel-hair coats. "What beautiful girls," she'd say, or "Such pretty children."

And my sister took the compliment well, gazing off into the distance as if she hadn't heard it, like Mary in a Renaissance painting, inexplicably mournful already, though Jesus is still only a fat little baby.

My sister took those compliments well, and beside her, sweating in my camel-hair coat, I felt nothing but the demands of my hunger.

ONCE, WHEN I WAS MAYBE ELEVEN, A FEW WEEKS AFTER THE WAR ended with the bombings of Hiroshima and Nagasaki, my parents threw a victory party.

Their friends all came over, and we celebrated with firecrackers on the hill behind the tennis court.

A few weeks after that, I came down to have breakfast before heading to school and happened upon a newspaper my father had left on the table.

By then, I guess, stories had begun to come out about the extent of the damage caused by the A-bombs: the steadily growing numbers of dead, the diseases and starvation and homelessness and birth defects.

And there must have been a feature article about the damage that day, because the photograph on the front page showed a row of bodies in a Japanese hospital room, all of them emaciated, prone on thin mats, many of their limbs badly burned. It was over a month after the bombings, and there they were still, lying in pools of blood and pus, and I only glanced at it for a moment before I felt too ill to look anymore.

Nevertheless, however, before I'd looked away, I'd already seen a man with no face.

His face was a smudge of black charcoal.

Seeing it knocked the air from my body.

Some people celebrate, I thought. Some people set off firecrackers on the hill behind the tennis court, and they wear camel-hair coats and knee socks and go to school and eat breakfast.

And some people starve, wasting away in crowded hospitals full of people who no longer have faces.

It made me feel sick. But God help me, it also made me so hungry.

I felt the claw of my hunger, and I wanted to eat. I wanted to be a well-fed survivor.

So then I finished the bowl of cereal that I'd poured, and I went back for seconds, and when the box had been emptied I went to the refrigerator, where I devoured both string beans my mother had saved.

Then I opened the freezer and pulled out the cookies my mother kept hidden. And I knew I didn't have very much time, so I didn't bother to thaw them out or even put them in the oven, I just started using my teeth to tear off rock-hard hunks of those cookies.

It's amazing my teeth didn't break off. If they had, I guess, I'd have eaten them also. As it was, I kept eating those frozen cookies until my sister came down to the kitchen. Then I tried to shove the bag back into the freezer, but my mother was already there in the doorway.

She stood there in her yellow wool suit with mother-of-pearl buttons, and her white gloves that only just came past her wrist bones, and she was shaking with fury.

At that point, I couldn't spit out the last bite. But I also couldn't swallow it. The bite was far too big, and solidly frozen, so I could only stand there by the freezer, holding an egg-sized rock in my gullet.

"What are you eating?" my mother said.

I couldn't answer.

By then my mother was shaking with rage. She was so small and so angry. I had attacked her; I'd stolen her secret hoard. I'd violated what space she'd preserved on this planet, and her whole face was a furious bird's beak.

"What are you eating?" she said again, and still I didn't answer. It was as if I had one of her eggs in my mouth. Then she took a few steps closer and faced me.

"You liar," she said. "You little snake."

Both of us, I think, were frightened by the scale of the thing. It was so much bigger than we were. It was a conflict on a scale we couldn't manage.

Some people eat, and some don't. That was the main problem. In Ireland, for instance, during the famine, as we were often told when we were children, mothers were expected to starve while their children ate. They were expected to give of their bodies, to rise above the necessity of their hunger, and there I was, in the nice house my mother provided, wearing the nice clothes that she bought me, unabashedly and selfishly eating, and before either one of us had quite comprehended the problem, my mother had already taken my jaw in her hand and pried open my mouth so I'd spit out the cookie.

Then we stood side by side, looking down at that mess, the regurgitated food in her palm.

And only then did my mother become human again, not some vengeful mythical angel.

Then she was nothing more than a small woman, or perhaps a large bird, hunched and inconsolable beside her snake of a daughter.

AFTER THAT, MY MOTHER WENT OUT FOR A DRIVE.

I stayed in the kitchen with my twin sister. And it was then that I realized that while my mother and I had been enacting our own personal drama, my sister had gone to the table. She was staring at the newspaper, and her whole body was trembling.

She hadn't touched the cereal she'd poured for herself. That morning she went to school without eating.

My sister could submit herself to a cause. She had the willpower I lacked, and a crueler sense of aesthetics.

AFTER THAT MORNING, SHE ATE LESS AND LESS.

She also started the project she continued from that day forward, collecting photographs from Hiroshima and Nagasaki.

She arranged them in the book our mother bought her, along with factoids about the lingering effects of the blasts. She had a clear eye for how such images should be arranged, an understanding of design that I lacked. Once, for instance, in our junior year at St. Stephen's, in the unit of home economics when we were learning how to decorate our bomb shelters in a style befitting our aspirations, we were sitting under our desks, and I was embroidering a needlepoint. I only half-listened while the teacher droned on about beautifying a room with no windows, about adding a feminine touch to an underground bunker. Mostly, however, I focused on anticipating the needlepoint my sister was making, in the hopes that maybe I could outdo her.

Her work was always more perfect than mine. She had predictably impeccable taste. By contrast, my style was exuberant and confused. I couldn't ever resist the inclination to add. So when the teacher stopped talking and we'd come out from under our desks and shared the samplers we'd sewn in our shelters, mine was sloppy and fat, a bloody mess of embroidery threads.

Then my sister revealed the sampler she'd made. All of us stared. The teacher turned pale. Because, of course, her sampler was perfect. It was entirely empty. A pure white circle of cloth, bound in a wood frame.

Which, needless to say, was much better than mine, untouched as it was, and still spotless.

ALL OF WHICH IS TO SAY THAT IN THE RESTAURANT KATHY HAD CHOsen in Princeton, while she flared her nostrils and my sister starved, I sawed my dolphin fins in the air and cut through the bloody steak I'd been given.

Meanwhile, Kathy's respectable boyfriend was saying that friends of his from the force had come home with stories of being compelled—for lack of meaningful targets, since even the smallest villages had already been completely destroyed—to drop their bombs into rivers, or on footbridges, or into little copses of trees.

And meanwhile the roommate had finished his beer. And he smiled at me every so often, and seemed to be having an excellent evening, unaware that our story had taken such a violent turn, me having cut all ties with Kathy, finishing my second bourbon, heading out into the darkness with or without him.

From that point on I ignored all Kathy's efforts to intervene on my behalf. By the time she insisted that it was time to head back to the room we'd reserved in the boarding-house for nice girls visiting Princeton, I was already somewhat drunkenly making my way back to that roommate's dorm room, my laughter fat and obscene in the darkness, his hands creeping over my dolphiny body. Then I was under him on the bed, with my fat fins flopping each which way, and then I realized my stockings had torn, and for a moment I felt trapped and frightened.

Then I slipped out of my body. From somewhere above, I watched my reckless body in bed. My hair was a mess. My clothes were a mess. Even my breasts were a gross, exposed mess, and there was the roommate's hand inserting itself into my mouth, and I was sucking it like that kind of girl, the kind of girl my mother never imagined her girls would become, and by then, watching myself, even high up on the ceiling, I could have cried, though of course, as I knew well, it wasn't that roommate's fault in the slightest.

He was only playing the part I gave him to play, just as I was playing the part I'd given myself, the role I had to play to appropriately balance the others.

And then, of course, pinned there in that roommate's bedroom, I thought of my sister.

I thought of her lying at home in our childhood bed-room, looking through the pages of her hideous book.

I thought to myself that she had been steadily retreating from life since the day she decided to eat less. And ever since the same day, I'd been forced to charge into life with an abandon that just wasn't healthy. I'd lived as if there were a thread between me and my sister, as if I'd gone to retrieve her from the underworld, and tied one end of the rope around her dwindling waist, and the other end around my own, and now I was running uphill, charging into the land of the living.

And it hadn't been exactly easy for me. Maybe living in the reckless fat way that I lived was easier than starving myself like my sister. But still, it hadn't been easy, exerting all the effort to live for us both, and now here I was, trapped in this bed, and I looked over my shoulder and realized she wasn't with me.

She wasn't at the end of the line. There I was, alone in my distress, utterly alone in that bed with my pearl necklace still on and my gross breasts slopped all over my body, and I was suddenly angry.

Then I started sweating. I wanted to sit up, but I couldn't. His weight was pressing down on my body, weighing me down, with his hand shoved in my mouth like I was some fat naked catfish, violently pulled out of hiding, and I thought: Enough. Enough. I've had enough of this lonely role that I'm playing.

Then I gagged out the hand and heaved myself up from the bed. I covered my chest with my arm and told him I was going out to the sofa.

He asked me if I was OK. Then he apologized if he'd done anything wrong. Then offered to let me sleep on the bed.

Nevertheless, however, I was insistent, so once I'd rooted around for my sweater, and buttoned my skirt over my stockings, I went out to the sofa, and in the morning, when I woke up, Stan was banging around making coffee.

He was wearing a plaid shirt buttoned up to his neck. He looked fresh faced and happy, the image of a wholesome American boyfriend.

"Good morning," he said, and he smiled, and handed me a cup of freshly made coffee.

WE SEEMED, SOMEWHAT UNBELIEVABLY, TO HAVE EXPERIENCED TWO disparate evenings. I'd been prepared to feel ashamed of myself for having acted like one kind of girl and then suddenly flipping into another, but Stan beamed down upon me as though we were both starting out fresh as new people.

Later, I learned that Stan had a remarkable ability to forget that which was at all inconvenient. In that moment, however, I wondered if he was amnesiac, or crazy. Somewhat unnerved, I took the cup of coffee he'd made. He stood smiling above me, as though he'd come out of his bedroom and been surprised and not one bit displeased to find me sprawled on the couch, washed up overnight like an overweight mermaid.

When I joined him at the table that was set up in the kitchen, he told me he'd been accepted to Princeton's doctoral program in politics. Then he supplied the details of his graduate stipend, and the conditions of family life in faculty housing, as though he were answering questions I'd asked him. He was behaving as though I'd sat down in the kitchen to interview him for the position of husband, and to be honest, sitting there, quietly drinking my coffee on the morning after I realized my sister had abandoned me for her fast, I began to wonder whether I might in fact be interested in having Stan fill that position.

Politely, keeping my ankles crossed, I listened while he covered the salient points: his service in the air force, his course of study, his family background, the suburb they'd moved to.

Then he asked me a few questions: what I majored in, if I wanted children, where my family summered, my father's profession.

He seemed pleased with the answers, or pleased enough to forget the previous evening, and as I continued sipping my coffee, assisted by Stan's remarkable ability to forget things, I began to feel like a respectable person.

I began to imagine the house we might share, the garage, the bedspreads, the little frilled pillows.

Then I began to enjoy telling Stan about how much I wanted children, about how well I got along with my mother, about how I'd always dreamed of a daughter.

OBVIOUSLY I WAS MAKING EVERYTHING UP.

I didn't think I'd marry Stan. I didn't love him, and I believed my mother wouldn't approve of the match. I had already begun to suspect that though Stan did go to Princeton, his family probably wasn't quite up to snuff: otherwise why would he have been at that table, interviewing for the position of husband.

So I was making everything up. It was all just a new story I'd decided to tell, one that was less frightening to me than the last one.

By the end of that cup of coffee, I'd described to him our house in the suburbs, our fictional daughter, our fictional son, the sports he played, and the lunch box she carried.

I was telling such a good story that Stan seemed truly touched. He was becoming fond of those children. When the hour was up, and it was time for him to go to the library and study, he asked for my address so he could write me a letter.

A letter! Not even a phone call. As if I were so pure and old-fashioned I could only be reached via post.

FOR A WHILE, AFTER THAT, STAN WROTE ME LETTERS, AND I RESPONDED in kind.

At first, it was just a minor part I was playing. The girl who wrote him letters back was only one voice in the novel. In the meantime, even as she spun her quaint yarns, I kept up my other lives, still sometimes eating too much, still writing fat novels in secret, and still sometimes performing regrettable roles on the double dates I went on with Kathy.

Nevertheless, however, I enjoyed my correspondence with Stan. I enjoyed it so much that every time he suggested a trip up to see me, I elegantly parried his efforts.

For many months, we just kept writing. In sweet, economized prose, I wrote to him of our summer house, the yard he cut on the weekends, the beach where we played with our children.

And maybe that pattern could have gone on forever, but that spring my father called to tell me my sister had died overnight.

Her heart stopped, my father said. I had to come home for the funeral.

AFTER THAT, I WENT AROUND, GOING THROUGH THE MOTIONS OF life, no longer holding the thread that attached me to my sister.

Six or seven months later, I married Stan, and for a while I guess we were happy.

NOW I NEED TO TAKE A BREAK. I NEED TO CLOSE MY EYES FOR A WHILE.
Actually, wait. Don't go. If I stop now I'll never start up again, and I want to get this all down.

It is what it is, a whole horrible mess. Believe me, I hate it, too. But now that we've started let's just keep going. I want to tell you what happened after I married Stan, which is how I ever met Robert to start with.

AS SOON AS STAN AND I WERE ENGAGED, I DROPPED OUT OF ROSE-mont. Then I lived with my parents at home. Stan felt it was proper, and I agreed, so for a few months I lived in my childhood bedroom while my mother and I made plans for the wedding.

By then, things had changed in my family. My parents were lost. They didn't comment on Stan's last name, or ask me about the clubs his parents belonged to. My mother failed to wonder about Stan's swarthy complexion. She simply accepted that a wedding was coming. Then we went to Saks and found a nice dress, with lace sleeves, and a long line of cloth-covered buttons. At the florist, we chose the white calla lily arrangements. I sat in the store with my hands in my lap and agreed with all of my mother's decisions.

BY THEN, I HAD BECOME A MORE OBEDIENT DAUGHTER. THERE WAS no longer any need to rebel. My sister was gone, and my father had faded into the background, so it was me and my mother in that story together.

Sometimes, she drove me downtown to the art museum. We stood in the rooms devoted to Renaissance paintings, surrounded by virgins and Roman soldiers and saints, serpents and lambs, satyrs and sylphs, and dark-eyed Christian martyrs whose breasts were about to be sliced off their torsos.

For dinner, my mother cooked meals I'd liked as a child— lamb chops and canned *petit pois*—and in gratitude, I didn't eat much.

Afterward, we sat together and cut place cards out of thick ivory paper.

Sometimes, when we'd finished our work, we'd go up to my childhood bedroom and sort through my sister's belongings. She'd left so little behind. There were a few of her dresses still hanging up in the closet, but her desk was perfectly clean, and her drawers were perfectly empty. The only artifact I could find was that book she labored over so long: the photographs she'd collected of those bombed cities.

When I pulled it out of her drawer, I felt as if I were peering into something forbidden and lurid, something kept hidden in the back rooms of disreputable bookstores, a book that girls in the suburbs weren't meant to discover.

While my mother hovered behind me, I peeked at one or two of the earliest pictures—streams of people in black and white, processing like orderly ghosts through an utterly demolished city, their arms held out from their sides, their forearms hanging down, trying to avoid friction between their burned limbs.

Later, there were pictures of patients in the hospitals, the petechiae that showed up to warn them they'd die of radiation poisoning, the thick scars that disfigured their faces, the anxiety in the eyes of those patients who lined up in the waiting room still exhibiting no signs and only waiting for the secret poisoning to make itself known, without knowing when or how it would do so.

Under the photographs there were captions in her neat print. Under the photographs of those ghosts, she'd written, "Some were vomiting as they walked." And under the photographs of petechiae, "These were a reliable sign that the patient would die." Under a photograph of the rubble, a month or so after the bombs dropped, she'd written: "By September, the ruins were covered in green—goosefoot, purslane, daylilies, clothbur, sesame, bluets, panic grass, and feverfew—the underground organs of plants having been stimulated by the bomb, so that all fall they grew verdant and fat over the ashes and the bones of the unclaimed dead in the city."

Then I closed the book. I put it back in the drawer. The only other artifact I found from my sister's life was that sampler she hadn't embroidered, which was shoved at the back of one of my own desk drawers.

I must have stolen it.

There it was again: that blank circle of cloth, framed by bent wood.

I placed it on her empty bookshelf, and later, I took it with me to Princeton.

SOMETIMES, DURING THOSE MONTHS, IF I COULDN'T SLEEP BECAUSE I was sad, or because I was nervous about the upcoming wedding, my mother sat on the side of my bed and stroked my hair until I felt sleepy.

I liked them so much, those last months with my mother.

I hoped they'd never end. As the weekend of the wedding approached, I became increasingly nervous, and the night before the ceremony, I couldn't sleep.

Then I went to my parents' room and woke my mother up, and we lay in my childhood bed until morning.

BEFORE LUNCHTIME, STAN'S PARENTS ARRIVED, ACTING OVERDRESSED and self-conscious.

My mother ignored them. Which goes to show how much things were changing. My mother had always been strict about manners, but on the morning of the ceremony, when Stan's parents arrived, she ignored them completely and focused on helping me fasten my hair with the mother-of-pearl comb that she lent me.

Around noon, Kathy arrived. In the absence of my sister, I'd appointed her as my maid of honor. She and her exemplary boyfriend had broken up, and she sulked around unhappily while I got dressed, and wasn't polite to my mother, and only rose from the divan to assist me when I asked if she'd help me button my dress up.

Then she tried to help badly, and made it seem as if she couldn't do it.

Witnessing this, my mother rose from her seat. She gave Kathy a look that sent her shrinking out of the bedroom, and then she easily buttoned that dress. It wasn't even a struggle at all.

I'd lost weight since my sister died, and by then I was 117 pounds.

Standing behind me, buttoning all those cloth-covered

buttons, my mother looked small and severe. She was wearing her dark purple wool suit with matching pillbox hat, and she looked like a stern little girl, holding a big doll very tightly.

There we stood together, in front of the mirror: me and the woman who had once pried open my jaw.

Clearly, we had both changed. We had both been very affected.

In an odd tone of voice, she told me I looked beautiful. I asked her if she knew how much I loved her.

WHEN THE SERVICE STARTED, MY FATHER WALKED ME DOWN THE aisle. He stumbled once, but we kept going.

Then he gave me away to my new husband.

At the altar, he released me and returned to his seat, and my mother didn't look at him. She was staring directly at me. I stared back at her from the altar. Neither one of us smiled through the whole service. We never took our eyes off each other, and beside me, missing it all, poor Stan wore a gray suit and looked happy.

POOR STAN. WHEN I THINK OF HIM NOW, STANDING SO FULL OF HOPE in his suit, I almost think that I could start crying.

After the wedding, at the reception, under the tent my parents put up on the tennis court on our back lawn, everyone except me and my mother ate shrimp cocktail and chicken salad on crackers.

That night, Stan and I slept in a hotel. He made love to me as you'd make love to a bride, and afterward, though he hadn't, he worried he'd hurt me.

Once he'd fallen asleep, I lay awake.

I missed my mother. I missed my childhood bedroom. I counted the hours until we could return to have breakfast.

Then, in the kitchen, where I'd once found that newspaper and ate those frozen cookies, Stan the happy newlywed wolfed down his breakfast.

Cheerfully, he ate every last bite of the running yellow yolk, the bacon flanged with wet fat, as though he'd never had a sister who died.

As if he'd never opened a dead sister's book to see written in her neat print, "All fall they grew verdant and fat over the ashes and the bones of the unclaimed dead in the city," he scraped his plate clean, and when he'd finished, Stan and I drove to Princeton in the station wagon my parents had bought us.

Then I was a wife. The Korean War was still being fought, and by then the air force had dropped more incendiaries on Korea than they'd dropped in the whole Pacific Theater in the entire Second World War, and also I woke up as a wife.

I walked around as a wife, and in the afternoons I called my mother and talked to her as a daughter.

I CALLED MY MOTHER AT LEAST ONCE EVERY DAY. SOMETIMES WE talked for hours on end.

In the beginning of my marriage, when I wasn't working at the institute yet, I had a lot of time to myself, more than I'd ever had when I took art history classes and went along with Kathy's romantic arrangements.

So I'd call my mother, or go out for walks, and sometimes, idly, while listening to Stan's records, or flipping through a magazine, I'd wonder if now that I had so much time, I'd finally write that Great American Novel that I'd once dreamed of writing at Rosemont.

Sometimes, I tried, but the scale of the whole thing seemed stupidly ambitious and gross. Then I tried writing stories, until one day I figured out it was easier to write poems. I could spend a long time carefully revising those poems, expending a great deal of energy futilely attempting to fix all their flaws, until one day I figured out that the best way to perfect them was to systematically delete all the words.

Then I realized it would be easier not to start them at all.

After that, I mostly just wandered around our apartment, wondering what it would be like to be a movie star, or where I'd like to travel in Europe.

Sometimes, I tried on the dresses I kept in our closet, and enjoyed cinching the belts tighter and tighter, because by the time Stan's classes started in August, I was 112 pounds, and I'd begun to feel very light.

Sometimes, I didn't get dressed until noon. I didn't make any friends. At night, I made dinner and watched Stan while he ate it.

AS THE SEMESTER PROGRESSED, I BEGAN TO TAKE MORE AND MORE pleasure in cooking dinner and watching while Stan demolished every last bite.

He had no need, I observed, to notice whether or not other people were eating. At dinner, Stan looked to nobody else for permission as to whether he should put food in his mouth.

He ate with pure, simple pleasure, with no apparent feelings of guilt about eating with so much abandon in front of a girl whose sister had recently died.

He seemed to have forgotten, in fact, that my sister had died of not eating.

He seemed to have forgotten I'd ever had a sister to start with. He never mentioned it once. He simply felt hungry at dinner, and that he therefore deserved a full meal, and a wife to listen to him while he ate it.

Then the pounds began to really fall off. By the end of September, my skirts hung loose on my hips.

Then I was 108 pounds, and my weight was going down some each morning.

IF STAN NOTICED THE CHANGE THAT WAS OCCURRING IN MY PHYSI-cal person, it didn't perturb him.

He accepted my transformation. He never stopped eating, for instance, to ask when my hip bones had begun to jut out, or why I bought that scale, or how I'd come to love cooking.

None of it really surprised him. He'd always expected, I think, that the world would reward him for his decency and his patriotism and his hard work.

So it was in accordance with his expectations that the world provided a thinner wife who began to love cooking. Every day the world rewarded him more, until one day, finally, Stan suffered a setback.

It was in the middle of his first semester that Stan came home with a bewildered expression.

He hadn't received his graduate stipend. He'd thought it had been some correctable error. But when he went to the financial aid office, he was told he'd been mistaken to think he was getting a stipend.

The officer assigned to Stan's case pulled out his file, examined it closely, then made some comment about immigrants and their children bleeding the university dry.

When Stan responded in protest, the officer showed him several pages of detailed statistics that had been collected on the criminal nature of Sicilians, and the lesser intelligence of the Irish, and Stan left the office without receiving his stipend.

When he came home and reported all this, he seemed ready to cry.

I felt for him when he told me. Poor Stan. He'd been so hopeful. He'd imagined it was all working out in his favor. It hurt me to see that his hopes had been so thoughtlessly dashed, to watch him come to the edge of the optimism and the sweetness he'd so amazingly managed to maintain all these years, so therefore I jumped in to help him.

I told him I'd go to work, to pay for the rest of his graduate studies.

Then Stan began to cheer up. By the time I brought out his butterscotch pudding, the setback had managed to reverse itself nicely.

There Stan sat, spooning his pudding into his mouth, completely unaware that I wasn't helping out of the spirit of wifely devotion.

He had no idea that I was helping him not out of love but in the name of a cruel and simple aesthetic.

By then I was disappearing so quickly. I was whittling myself away in the spirit that had infected my sister as well, the cruelty of simply snipping the thread, and it wasn't Stan's fault that he missed it.

There he was, doing everything right, accomplishing the things he was meant to accomplish, and no one ever told him that in addition to accomplishing things, he also had to stop and notice the changes that were occurring inside other people.

So he accepted when I offered to work, and then he finished his pudding, and then he took me to bed and I let him, though by then I'd stopped feeling much when he was moving inside me.

THE NEXT DAY, I STARTED LOOKING FOR JOBS. I HADN'T FINISHED MY marriageable bachelor's degree, but I could type well, and I dressed neatly and had my mother's complexion, so a few days after I started looking, I found a secretarial job, filling in for a girl who'd gotten pregnant.

The job was in the office of the director of the Institute for Advanced Study, which is how I met Robert, and how he came to tell me his story.

That was October of 1952. It was still a year and a half before his security hearings, and he was the chairman. I typed his letters, and filed his papers, and generally oversaw his busy schedule, which obviously left me no time for my writing.

AS SOON AS I STARTED, I FOUND THAT I ENJOYED THE POSITION. I liked mindlessly typing, and answering the telephone. I liked to be too busy to think.

In those days, in addition to his work at Princeton, Robert was serving on the General Advisory Committee of the

Atomic Energy Commission, so he was shuttling back and forth between Washington and New Jersey, giving opinions on thermonuclear testing and the deployment of tactical nuclear weapons, such as those that had been assembled in Okinawa.

Between his advisory role, and his public speeches, and the appearances he made on an increasing number of congressional investigatory committees, he and I were almost manically busy.

He liked to dictate messages while he was walking between various meetings. He always walked very fast, leaning forward, moving on the balls of his feet. Sometimes he was in such a rush that he forgot to put on his coat before leaving the office. Often he forgot to eat. Then suddenly he'd remember, take two bites of a sandwich, then put it down and forget where he'd left it.

Otherwise, he smoked cigarettes. He never stopped smoking, and he never stopped moving, and I followed everywhere in his wake, taking notes for various memos and letters.

At that point, of course, he was still influential. I'd known of him before I worked in the office. When I was at St. Stephen's, he was on the cover of *Life*. And even when I was at Princeton—nearly a decade after they dropped those bombs—he was still famous, but by then the tide had started to turn.

Truman's people saw him as weak. In the months after Hiroshima and Nagasaki, he'd met with Truman and said he felt he had blood on his hands. Truman wouldn't meet with him after that.

Then Robert started to campaign against the development

of the H-bomb. And then Russia started testing atom bombs, and everyone was terrified, and schoolgirls were learning to hide under their desks, and by the time I went to work in Robert's office at the institute, Eisenhower was running a successful campaign on issues of security in the nuclear age.

By then, McCarthy was on the rise in the Senate, and Robert didn't present as hard a line about the Soviets as he probably should have. He still occasionally advocated transparency about nuclear secrets, to eliminate the need for an arms race. And at the same time, stories had started to surface about his former connections to the Communist Party.

The Justice Department, for example, had a person who was claiming he'd witnessed Robert at a housewarming event thrown by members of the CP in San Francisco, while Robert was working at Los Alamos. Robert insisted that the guy was a crank, but nevertheless he was nervous. He had gone back to San Francisco, he told me. He'd gone to visit a friend. But he didn't think he'd gone to that party.

Then it came out that Joe Weinberg, one of Robert's graduate students, had been caught on a wiretap, talking about the A-bomb with the head of the San Francisco CP. So that worried Robert also, because he feared he'd be called to testify against Weinberg.

And at the same time, he was agitated about the state of the arms race. He was desperately trying to persuade Truman not to test the first H-bomb.

But Truman wouldn't see him, so Robert wrote letters.

One day, he'd write to Truman to try to persuade him that testing an H-bomb would cause environmental damage that could never be fixed. Then he'd write a letter to General

Groves and say the use of an H-bomb could only ever be called genocidal. Then he'd wait a few days, and he wouldn't hear back, so he'd launch a new tactic, and try to seem hard-line by urging somebody high up in the army to deploy more tactical nuclear weapons.

That was his strategy to get them to hold off on testing an H-bomb. He felt that the air force was the most bloodthirsty branch of the military: they wanted hydrogen bombs in their back pocket, but Robert didn't trust them not to blow the whole planet to pieces. So then, working against them, he'd cozy up to the army, advocating tactical nuclear weapons in order to seem sufficiently hard-line and security conscious.

But then the following day, worked up into a lather by something hateful McCarthy said on TV, Robert would write some morally high-flying letter about freedom and transparency, and he'd vow to never testify against his former friends.

The following week, having received a disappointing response to his letter about not testing the H-bomb, and realizing that Eisenhower would probably beat Stevenson in the upcoming election, Robert would spin off a personal memo, considering the morality of testifying against somebody minor in exchange for confidence on the topic of H-bombs.

He didn't like the idea of testifying, but he knew he'd go to prison if he pled the Fifth. He didn't feel he could do much from prison.

Those were the gambles he weighed during those frantic months, when we paced around Princeton, smoking cigarettes, occasionally stopping for a few bites of a sandwich, and then, in November, Truman tested Ivy Mike, the first H-bomb, vaporizing the entire island of Elugelab, and blowing radioactive coral out of the water that fell on ships over thirty miles away from ground zero.

Three days later, Eisenhower beat Stevenson by a landslide.

Robert didn't know what to do.

The day after Ivy Mike was exploded, he'd dictated a letter of protest, resigning from the Science Advisory Committee.

But the following day he asked me not to send it. He said he'd revised that idea. He was intent on retaining influence, in case Eisenhower won the election.

Then Eisenhower did win, and Robert had me tear up the letter. Then he dictated a report for the State Department's disarmament panel, saying nuclear weapons on the scale of the H-bomb threatened all of civilization as we currently knew it.

Every day, there was a new letter. Sometimes the letters were at odds with one another.

He was, in other words, caught up in a panic. I recognized it at once. There was far too much bloody thread on the sampler.

AFTER EISENHOWER WAS ELECTED, LEWIS STRAUSS WAS THE FRONT-runner for chairman of the Atomic Energy Commission, and it was then that things began to get really heated.

Strauss hated Robert. There had been some insult at a birthday party, something as dumb and minor as that. Strauss, in addition, believed in absolute secrecy about anything having to do with nuclear weapons.

Robert believed it would all come out at some point, so why not open the box in the first place.

Several times, in various testimonies before various committees, Robert belittled Strauss's position on nuclear secrets. Then, suddenly, magazines that had praised Robert since the end of the war began to print pieces with a different tone altogether.

Now they mentioned allegations of Robert's connections to the Communists. They made personal insinuations. A former girlfriend was mentioned. She'd been a member of the CP. He'd gone to visit her in San Francisco, and later her suicide was reported, in the bathtub of a third-story apartment.

BY FEBRUARY OF 1953, WHEN I'D BEEN WORKING AT THE INSTITUTE for four or five months, McCarthy was at the height of his powers, and Robert was persuaded that they were coming for him.

No matter what concessions he made, no matter which friends he agreed to testify against, no matter how forthrightly he supported deployment of tactical nuclear weapons, he felt he was doomed.

One day he'd decide to write an article for the Sunday *Post,* getting ahead of the thing. He'd say he was determined to reveal all the details of his associations in Berkeley, including the former girlfriend they'd mentioned.

But the next day he'd decide that there were some secrets he had a right to keep quiet.

And the next day he'd announce that he wanted to go back to teaching, and we'd dictate a memo about that.

But then he'd call me back into the office after I'd gone home to make dinner and dictate an entirely contradictory note, detailing twenty-one points for preventing nuclear warfare.

AT THE END OF THE MONTH, HE DELIVERED A SPEECH BEFORE A closed meeting of the members of the Council on Foreign Relations, urging an end to the secrecy that shrouded the arms race.

Secrecy, he said, could lead only to rumor, speculation, and ignorance.

"We do not operate well," he said—and I know this because I helped him write it—"when the facts are known, in secrecy and fear, only to a few men."

"Follies," he said, "can occur only when even the men who know the facts can find no one to talk to about them, when the facts are too secret for discussion, and thus for thought."

It was a direct attack on Strauss, and Strauss knew it. By May, when our walks around campus were warm enough that I had to start peeling off layers, sweating under my coat while I tried to keep up with Robert, Strauss had initiated a full-blown smear campaign against Robert.

He placed broadsides in *Time, Life,* and *Fortune,* attacking Robert directly. There were more questions about Robert's friends and connections, more insinuations about his family background and about his potentially traitorous opposition to the hydrogen bomb.

In July, an armistice agreement in Korea was signed. A no-fly zone was established, though a peace treaty never got brokered.

In August, Strauss formally assumed chairmanship of the

Atomic Energy Commission. Then the Russians tested the Sloika, and Robert's position against testing more H-bombs started seeming weaker and weaker.

SOMETIMES, WALKING BEHIND ROBERT WHILE HE STRODE AROUND campus, the leaves on the trees having grown bigger and bigger until now finally they were enormous and tired, hanging there like big dusty green mittens, I wondered if he'd ever realized it was a new person walking behind him, not his usual secretary, taking notes while he dictated letters.

He was so caught up in Washington business that he didn't seem able to see me, and for a while, in the early days of my new position, I wasn't sure whether it was Robert or Stan who was more unaware of my existence.

It was as if I were disappearing, dwindling away, my whole life becoming as fine and bright and pointed as the thin line of light the sun makes when it's almost slipped beyond the horizon.

It was such a pleasure. At night, I'd sit across from my husband, who ate his meatloaf and didn't see me. And the next morning, I'd report for my duties at the institute, and there was Robert, looking right past me, asking me to follow him to the station while he dictated an important new memo.

Then I was down to ninety-nine pounds, and really, I was getting so happy.

SOMETIMES MY MIND RACED, I WAS SO HAPPY. THEN, IF I COULDN'T sleep, I went to the kitchen to call home to my mother.

She, too, was often awake. For hours, we talked to each

other in whispers. I twirled the phone cord around my pointer finger. I twirled the cord around my neck.

She called me her baby girl. I asked about the club. I asked about the tennis court. I told her how much I missed her.

Then I hung up, and climbed back into bed with my husband.

SOMETIMES, EVEN THEN, I COULDN'T SLEEP. SOMETIMES I COULDN'T bear to be alone in the darkness.

Then I'd wake Stan up and put his cock in my mouth, because I felt I had to do something to justify waking him from his peaceful slumber.

So I'd put his cock in my mouth, and often it made me less hungry.

By then, that kind of thing was the only intimacy between us. I was down to ninety-five pounds, and something had changed so it hurt to have sex. It was like sandpaper when he was inside me. So then I just put his cock in my mouth, and after a while I started to like it, like sucking a little stone when you're hungry.

LISTEN, I'M SORRY IF THIS STORY DISGUSTS YOU.

It disgusts me as well, but I know I won't say it again, and I want to finish, now that I've started.

That summer and the following fall, when I was working for Robert, I kept losing weight. Sometimes I fainted. But if this worried Stan, he didn't say so. It's possible he believed that all women fainted.

At the end of the day, despite all the fainting, Stan seemed basically pleased and content to have a thin wife who cooked him dinner and worked to support his graduate studies.

I liked it, too. There was something very fine about fainting. I particularly liked coming to, after that long moment of darkness.

Then I'd look up and see Stan kneeling above me. There he was, saying my name, and at first his lips were moving in silence, and then I heard what he was saying, and I realized that in Stan's mind, I was still gone.

For him, I was still lost in that darkness.

So for a few minutes, all on my own, I could watch him from somewhere else.

I could watch him full of the perfectly luxurious knowledge that he couldn't have me. I was entirely my own for a moment.

But after a while, I'd start to feel bad about leaving him there in the lurch. Then we'd go through the whole post-faint routine. Where am I, I'd ask. Who are you. What happened.

Needless to say, I already knew. But still, I let him tell me. I allowed him to give me my position again. And then I let him carry me into the bedroom, and tuck me in, and put me to sleep, and throughout that year, I often had a bruise on the back of my head, and also I was basically happy.

By then I was ninety-two pounds. I'd surrendered myself absolutely, and I walked around with such a calm, blissful look on my face that everyone thought I was in love with my husband.

IN ADDITION TO WEIGHT LOSS, ANOTHER POSITIVE DEVELOPMENT OF that year was that I managed to strengthen my focus.

During my years of eating too much, I'd been inefficient. I was exhausted and weighed down by the effort.

Once I gave that up, I became clear-eyed and quick. Robert was like that as well. I should mention that he was losing weight also.

During those months, when he was attempting to redeem the crimes he felt he'd committed, by regaining his influence on the committee, his eyes also burned like a saint's eyes. He also seemed to grow lighter. He'd always been thin, but now he walked around in a portion of his former substance.

By then he knew his phones were tapped, and he suspected they'd planted moles in the office. It was hard for him to keep still. In his office, or while we waited outside an auditorium, or as we walked to the train station, I noticed that sometimes, in his agitation, his hands started to tremble.

There were times when he couldn't even light his own cigarettes.

Then, avoiding the phones, he communicated largely through letters. He'd go to Washington all the time, to testify before different committees, and when he came back, his eyes burned brighter than ever.

He felt responsible, he said, for the bad state of affairs.

He'd made those bombs in the first place.

He hadn't seen how bad it would become, and now, having arrived at the knowledge too late, he felt that the only way to redeem what he'd done was to maintain what waning influence he had left. Nevertheless, however, he felt his pursuers approaching.

In those days, he made every new person he met read that Henry James story, "The Beast in the Jungle," presumably to make them know how he felt. That is to say, that he was a beast in the jungle, pursued by some as-yet-unknowable hunter.

Needless to say, he was misreading that story, which, as I learned at Rosemont, and as Henry James makes very clear in the numbingly didactic ending, is really about a man who misses the one love of his life because he's so preoccupied with an imaginary pursuer. If you read that story with your eyes open at all, you'd know right away that it's about a man who's made blind by his fear, but by then Robert wasn't reading things clearly.

He was agitated to the point of excessive quickness in everything he attempted. His positions shifted each day. One day, for instance, he'd be on one of his tears about setting himself free, turning his back on Washington, returning full time to his teaching.

The next day, however, he'd be back at work plotting strategies to regain the influence that he'd lost, because he didn't really want to be free.

He wanted to be forgiven the sins he'd committed.

ONE DAY, A CREW CAME TO FILM HIM FOR A DOCUMENTARY THEY were making, and in preparation he asked me to run back to his house and pick up his copy of the Bhagavad Gita.

So I went running off to Olden Manor, the director of the institute's house, which was lodged among all the finest houses in Princeton, stately brick manors with white columns and long plantation porches.

They reminded me of the houses in the neighborhood I grew up in, and of houses in movies about the old South, haunted by the ghosts of the slaves who were once whipped there. All those ghosts: women with scars on their bodies, men with no faces. They called to me in whispers among the stately old sycamore trees that lined the well-maintained sidewalks.

I went as quickly as I could, following the directions Robert gave me, and when I finally did find Olden Manor, I saw a dead mallard at the end of the driveway.

It was lying there at the side of the road, its green head gleaming, its neck doubled back in a U, and its one open black eye staring straight at me.

WHEN SHE CAME TO THE DOOR, KITTY WASN'T HAPPY TO SEE ME. SHE was wearing blue jeans and she seemed unsteady. She glared at me in the doorway while I explained why I'd come. Then she went inside to find the Bhagavad Gita.

While she was gone, I thought about those insinuations that had been made, about the girlfriend in San Francisco and the trip Robert was meant to have taken. But before I had time to come to any conclusions, Kitty came back with the Bhagavad Gita. It was a small, battered pink book with a creased spine, held together with Scotch tape. Somehow it made me sad just to see it.

But I took it, nevertheless, then ran back out past the dead mallard and all the plantation houses and found Robert with the film crew. I gave him the book, and he started flipping through the worn pages, looking for some line he'd forgotten.

And then, a few minutes later, when they sat him before the lights and the boom and asked him what he was thinking when the Trinity Test first went off, he looked straight at the camera with that dark, beseeching expression and said:

"I was thinking of that line from the Bhagavad Gita: 'Now I am become death, the destroyer of worlds.'"

Watching him deliver that line, it struck me that he probably wasn't thinking that when the bomb really went off, or he wouldn't have needed to send me home for the book, so that he could look the line up.

But that wasn't the point. The point was that for Robert, there was no language short of myth to describe his bad situation.

That was something I understood.

By then, I realized, he felt he could summon no words of his own to explain what he was thinking and how he was feeling.

All he could do by way of language was send me running back through the plantations to pick up his Bhagavad Gita.

So you see, we were both in the same bind. We were both living in myth. We were fighting archetypical battles. We'd taken up roles that had been handed down to us from above: good and bad, sinner and saint. Both of us had blood on our hands. We went around Princeton carrying tablets. We were delivering speeches we hauled down from the top of the mountain, trying to redeem the damage we'd caused, heading for the underworld, looking for 129,000 lost people, or a single lost girl, hoping either to bring her back up or to stay down there in the underworld with her.

BY THEN IT WAS AUTUMN, I WAS DOWN TO EIGHTY-NINE POUNDS, and my pity for Robert was growing.

At night, lying awake, I thought about his suffering. I searched my brain for ways I could relieve it.

At some point in the fall, I began bringing him presents.

One day, for instance, I brought him one of Stan's records. It was a recording of *The Goldberg Variations*, because I knew Robert liked Bach. Another day, I brought him a book of Renaissance sonnets that I'd read at Rosemont.

When he took it, he let it open at random, and when he looked down at the page, it seemed for a moment as if he might start crying.

Then he looked up, and he saw me.

From then on, I think, he really saw me. I'd called him Dr. Oppenheimer up to that point, but then he asked me if I'd call him Robert, and from then on, I felt as if he really saw me.

Moving around campus, as that fall became winter, we were two figures in a Renaissance painting. Everyone else was driving their cars and eating their hamburgers, listening to Patti Page and Perry Como, and Robert and I wandered around in our robes and our oils, surrounded by serpents and sylphs, and pomegranates and chariots and dogs with multiple heads, all of them roiling blackly around us, invisible to everyone else we passed on that campus.

By then, McCarthy had come to the peak of his power. Washington was caught in the worst grips of the Red Scare. That fall and that winter, hundreds of civil servants were fired on the flimsiest possible pretexts. Everyone, even the president, cowered in fear. And even so, McCarthy still delivered that speech charging Eisenhower's administration with appeasing the liberals. And Eisenhower was so scared of losing the votes of McCarthy's allies in the Senate that he didn't respond, so really it was McCarthy he was appeasing, and Robert's file—as he well knew—was worse than those of most of the bureaucrats who'd been fired or even imprisoned.

By then, he was really alone. His Washington friends wouldn't touch him, and his Berkeley friends had long since turned against him. They started turning when his testimony against Bernard Peters was leaked to the papers. Then they'd turned even further when he didn't stand up in Joe Weinberg's defense, or plead the Fifth, as David Bohm did, which was why Bohm was blacklisted and imprisoned.

But Robert chose to testify. He admitted that Weinberg had been close with several members of the CP.

And then, of course, in addition, he'd advocated the deployment of those tactical nuclear weapons at the borders of Communist states, so whichever friends he had left from Berkeley had all turned against him. He was alone that winter in Princeton, except for Kitty, maybe, and me, and maybe that's why he started to see me.

THAT WINTER, WE WERE NEVER INSIDE. WE SPENT MOST OF THE DAY walking around campus. He smoked cigarette after cigarette, and sometimes he asked me for my opinions.

When I gave them, he'd reflect upon them quietly, then answer in a serious voice.

By then, he'd grown somewhat gaunt. His porkpie hat was becoming comedic, like a hat on a dancing skeleton.

I, too, had grown thinner. That winter my hair had begun to fall out.

So we were together, at least in that sense. We were sliding down the same hill, our cheekbones leaping out of our skin, our eyes lit up by invisible fires, licking the rims of invisible ruins.

In December, just before Christmas, I walked with him to the station.

He and Kitty were heading down to Washington to meet with their lawyer. When we arrived, Kitty was waiting. She was wearing a cream-colored wool coat, black pumps, and a black dress with a cinched belt. Her hair was freshly coiffed, and on her face, while she watched us approach, there was an expression of fury.

Then I remembered that mallard, and I was sure that she'd killed it.

I knew in my heart that she'd snapped its neck with her bare hands and left it to die at the end of the driveway.

WHEN THE TRAIN PULLED IN, ROBERT HELPED HER UP THE STEPS. AT the top, she turned one last time to give me a furious look. I wondered, for the first time, if she thought there was something between me and her husband.

And there was something between us. But it was never romantic. Or it was romantic, in the sense of an old story about pages and knights, warriors battling against the dark forces.

But there was nothing sexual.

By then there was nothing sexual about me at all. Maybe there had been, back in those days when I ate sodden cereal and wrote novels at night and watched the leaves changing on the side of the highway.

But by the fall of 1953, those days were over.

I was eighty-eight pounds and my forearms were knotted with veins. My limbs were like a very large insect's, and sex wasn't an issue. It was too painful. My body simply couldn't accept it.

IT WAS ON THAT TRIP TO WASHINGTON THAT STRAUSS MET WITH Robert and informed him that a new review of his background and policy recommendations had resulted in his security clearance getting temporarily revoked.

Strauss delivered a letter that had been prepared by the AEC. It detailed the charges against Robert.

I can't remember how many there were, but the list went on for pages. There were political accusations, and personal accusations as well: everything from his advocacy against testing the H-bomb to a night he spent in San Francisco with that former girlfriend, when he was married, and privy to the highest-level nuclear secrets.

Having delivered the charges, Strauss told him that he could resign right away, or that he could choose to contest, but that if he chose to contest, there would be a hearing, and personal information might come to light.

I KNOW ALL THIS BECAUSE ROBERT'S FRIEND TOLD ME, THAT LAWYER whose name I've forgotten, a tall man in a suit with a bow tie.

He summoned me to Olden Manor two days before Christmas, when Robert and Kitty had just returned from that trip to DC.

Stan and I were meant to leave in the morning to go stay with his parents for Christmas. I was meant to have the day off.

But that lawyer called in the morning, and asked if I could come up to the house, so I put on my camel-hair coat.

I looked at myself in the mirror by the door. That coat was getting old. It was even tattered, which in the old days would never have been allowed by my parents.

But things were different now. The coat had grown tattered, and it was too late to fix it before running off through the streets lined with sycamores, past those plantation houses, and up the driveway where that mallard had been lying with its wrung neck.

When I rang the bell, nobody came. Then I pushed the door open. Then I stepped into the chaos. There were women coming and going from the kitchen, and men walking purposefully between rooms, everyone ignoring my presence until finally that lawyer stepped into the foyer and saw me.

He shook my hand and thanked me for coming. Robert, apparently, was resting upstairs. The lawyer led me into the living room and sat me down on the white brocade sofa.

In the dining room, three men I didn't know were bent over a tall stack of papers. And in the living room, by the kitchen door, two women were conferring quietly in the corner, smoking oddly long cigarettes, standing so still with their long, elegant necks that I thought to myself that they were like two potted plants.

Kitty, however, kept coming and going, storming around with her fury. She was still wearing the same black dress with a cinched belt at the waist.

Then the lawyer sat down beside me and told me that Robert had been given only two days to respond to the charges against him. He was, the lawyer told me, in a very bad state.

The previous night, when he came back from his meeting with Strauss, he'd been very agitated, so he'd taken one of Kitty's pills. Then he'd collapsed in the bathroom. The next morning, he'd woken, and written a letter back to the commission, letting them know that he contested the charges.

He refused, he said, to resign. He didn't care what information came out. He had always been loyal to his native country.

And so, the lawyer told me, the hearings had been scheduled for April. Robert wanted to write another letter responding individually to each of the charges, some of which were patently false, and others of which might have been true but still had no bearing on his loyalty to his country.

While the lawyer explained that he'd tried to discourage Robert from contesting the charges, and gave me a summary of the contents of that letter, I watched Kitty storming around, bringing empty glasses back into the kitchen.

Meanwhile, the lawyer in the bow tie was saying that the hearing would be a circus. He said it would be a real inquisition.

He said that painful things would come out, personal things that Robert had meant to keep hidden. Then he fell silent for a few moments, and watched Kitty coming and going.

When he started talking again, his voice was a little bit quiet and wistful.

Personal things, he said again, while we sat together on that white brocade sofa, might be leaked to the public.

In this day and age of paranoia and snooping, he said, you couldn't expect privacy to be respected at all.

Then he told me again that he'd advised Robert to resign without contest, but Robert had refused.

He believed, he said, in the truth. He wanted it all to come out.

That's what that lawyer told me. Then he was called by one of those men standing at the dining room table. He excused himself, and for a while I sat there, alone in Kitty's living room, on a white brocade sofa that reminded me of my mother's.

Twice, I saw Robert's daughter with her dark hair and her blue eyes wandering by like a sylph: into the kitchen, then out of the kitchen, and back up the wide, carpeted staircase.

Once I saw Robert's son venture halfway down the stairs. Then he turned and went back up.

And still Kitty was storming around, and I started to wonder when in this process Robert had told her about the night he went back to San Francisco to visit that former girl-friend.

Was it before she gave him one of her pills? Was it after she'd roused him from the floor of the bathroom, when she was sitting beside him on the cold tile?

Or had he told her about it years back, maybe even when they lived on the mesa, when he first began to suspect he'd been followed?

Or, stranger yet, was she still in the dark? I watched her, storming around with that ferocious expression, and after a few minutes that lawyer's pretty blond wife brought me a drink.

Then I was alone again for a while, and out of boredom I

reached into the pocket of my camel-hair coat and pulled out a hardened white eyeball.

I almost laughed. Then I looked at it for a minute, that remnant of the old days when I drove in Kathy's Studebaker and the leaves changed on the trees lining the highway.

Then I unwrapped the cellophane and let that eyeball drop onto the floor. It bounced twice, then rolled off under the sofa, and I knew I'd never find it again, in my coat pocket or anywhere else.

WHEN THE LAWYER CAME BACK, HE APOLOGIZED FOR HIS RUDENESS. He told me he'd called me to the house to ask if I'd stay in Princeton over the break.

He reiterated that Robert wanted to answer each of the charges in detail, and suggested he might need help with dictation.

Then I went home, and when Stan got back from work, I told him I was staying in Princeton over the break.

He'd just walked in the door, and he was still smiling.

Poor Stan. Full of hope and a sense of his good fortune, he was moving toward me to kiss me, but when I said that, he pulled up short.

For a moment, he looked confused.

"But you can't," he said. "We're going to my parents'."

"He needs me," I said.

"He's only your boss," Stan said.

"You're only my husband," I said.

And then, for the first time, I realized: all those months, I thought I was a wife.

I thought my new goodness and my new, more organized

180

aesthetic were the result of having become a wife. Of having submitted myself to my husband.

But finally I realized that I'd never submitted to him.

It was something else I'd submitted to, something bigger than him, something so big that Stan couldn't see it. Realizing that, I felt a surge of pity for Stan. Then I tried to be kinder.

"You'll have a great time without me," I said in a much gentler voice.

But poor Stan: he'd finally seen it.

The scales were falling away from his eyes. Then I was eighty-six pounds, and my coat was tattered, and my eyes were on fire and my hair was falling out of my head, and poor Stan finally saw me.

I stood there without moving. I let him see what I'd become. Once, I'd been a pretty girl. Once I was the sweet, pretty girl that he married. Now I was a revolting little reptile he hated.

"You're choosing your boss over me," Stan said.

His voice had finally changed. Suddenly it was clear to us both that he loathed me.

"He needs me," I said again.

"I need you," Stan said.

But in the end, he went alone, and I stayed with Robert in Princeton.

ON CHRISTMAS EVE, I REPORTED TO THE OFFICE, AND THERE WAS Robert, standing by the door with his hat on. I didn't take my own hat off, or my camel-hair coat. I just followed him out. All day, in the cold, we walked around campus. I had my pad and my pencil. I thought he'd start dictating a response. But he just walked around campus in silence.

Then we headed back to the office.

And for a few days, that was a pattern we kept: walking around campus, me with my pad, him leaning forward, smoking Chesterfields and facing the bare trees and the stone buildings in silence.

At night, when I got home, I tried to think what I could give him to help him. I went through all of Stan's favorite records. Then I went through my own books. Then I remembered that sampler.

For a moment, when I took it out, I wanted to keep it: my sister's blank sampler. The only artifact I had from her life.

But then I laughed to myself, thinking that wasn't the lesson my sister taught me.

So the next morning, I went to the office and gave Robert the sampler. I told him my sister made it during home economics at St. Stephen's, in the unit for decorating your shelter.

For a while, he looked at that sampler. Then, finally, he started laughing.

Then I started laughing as well.

I finally saw how funny it was, that sampler my sister made for decorating your atomic bomb shelter. A sampler without any thread. Nothing there. Nothing. And that's all we'd be left with, my sister was saying, all that would be worth depicting, all that would be worth saying, in the wake of such a disaster.

For a while, we both laughed. We laughed until tears came to my eyes, and I remembered those photographs in my sister's book, people walking away from the ruins, their faces in the waiting room, the weeds growing green over the ashes and the bones of their loved ones.

By then Robert had fallen silent. Both of us were quiet then, and the light was fading outside his window, and so I left him alone and went back to my office.

IT WAS ONLY A FEW MOMENTS LATER THAT ROBERT CAME IN. HE closed the door. Then he sat down.

"This is going to get very bad," he said, "but before it does, I want you to know the whole story."

POOR ROBERT. EVEN WITH THAT SAMPLER IN HIS HANDS, HE COULDN'T help it. He felt that there should be a whole story.

So he sat down in the chair and started to talk. After a few minutes I asked him if I should go get my pad, but he said, No: I just want to tell you.

Then he kept talking. He tried to start at the beginning. He told me his father emigrated from a German village called Hanau. When he arrived in New York, he began working his way up in men's clothing. By the time he turned thirty he was one of the wealthiest fabrics men in the city. He spent his free time reading history, visiting art museums, perfecting his English.

His mother was the daughter of German immigrants who settled down in Baltimore. She was beautiful, Robert told me. She was a painter. She had blue eyes and a congenitally unformed right hand, which she kept concealed by always wearing long sleeves and a pair of chamois gloves, even when she was inside. She went to Paris to study painting, and when she got back she had a career, but she gave it up to get married.

Both his parents were Jewish, he told me, though they'd turned from the religion by the time they were married. It was an anti-Semitic time in New York. Most of the best schools and the good clubs and the nicest hotels had closed their doors to Jews. In response, prominent Jewish immigrants—those who fled to this country imagining they might not face the same barriers to opportunity—began to search for new ways to assimilate.

Many of them joined a new group, the Society for Ethical Culture, which advertised itself as a modern replacement for ancient religions. The society took a stand, Robert told me, against any spirit of exclusion, or any impulse toward segregation.

It embraced a global intellectual culture. That spirit of universality was important to his parents, Robert told me, and also to him. Jews in the society were meant to give up their biblical identity, distinguishing themselves instead through social concern and good deeds.

And Robert's parents held themselves to those standards. His father spoke only English at home. He tried to better himself in all ways. His mother helped him. Nothing unpleasant was allowed to be mentioned at dinner. They collected art and they donated money. They lived in a sprawling, exemplary apartment on Riverside Drive, with windows facing the Hudson River, and an impressive collection of paintings, including a Cézanne and several Picassos.

A year after his parents were married, when his mother was thirty-four, Robert was born.

Four years after that, another son was born also, but he died several days later.

Then, for four more years, before his younger brother was born, Robert was all his mother had.

His childhood, Robert told me, was lonely.

He understood from the beginning that it was essential for him to be an exemplary child. His two major interests were playing with blocks and writing poems. His mother believed he would be an engineer or a poet. She watched him closely, and he was acutely aware of her loss.

To help compensate for the absence of that dead brother, and perhaps also for the loss of her career, he became a very good child.

He often painted with her in the apartment. He didn't play with other boys. If he got his hair cut, a barber was called into the house, so he didn't have to risk going out and exposing himself to some illness.

At some point, he told me, he started a collection of rocks. That was a great joy to him in his youth. He often persuaded his father to take him on expeditions to the Palisades, where he collected specimens, and labeled them, and carried them back to the apartment.

THAT'S WHAT HE TOLD ME. HE WENT ON AND ON: PROVIDING BACK-ground for his character, a good narrative arc, all those well-placed, salient details.

We tell our lives to other people like stories. We make characters out of ourselves. If we're skilled, we make ourselves seem almost lifelike.

Sitting there in that office, he told me that as a boy, he was prone to illness. The summer before he went to Harvard, he caught dysentery on a rock-collecting expedition. Then his father sent him to spend a summer in New Mexico, and for the first time he felt independent. He learned to ride horses. He learned to camp. He felt he was becoming himself, but then he went back to Harvard, and then he went to Cambridge, and once again he was unhappy.

He told me about the high standards he had for himself, and his fears that he couldn't meet them, and the nervous breakdown he'd nearly suffered.

Then he told me about Göttingen, and discovering theoretical physics, and an important experience reading Proust on an island, and how after that he'd come back to this country. He stopped in New York only briefly, then kept heading west. He traveled over the whole vast, wild country, all the way to California, and he told me that he sometimes wondered if the only really happy time in his life was during those years in Berkeley, when for a moment he let go of the idea that his life should be exemplary and simply lived, surrounded by friends, Jean, and Chevalier, and Bernard Peters, surrounded by his graduate students, in a small house on Shasta Road, with a redwood-paneled living room, and a eucalyptus in the backyard, and a view of the Pacific.

Sometimes, he said, he thought about his parents. Those were the years of the Depression, but his father had done well during the first war, and the fortune remained largely unscathed, and in those years of poverty it sometimes seemed somewhat grotesque.

In Berkeley, he said, he distanced himself from his parents. But then they died, one shortly after the other, and suddenly his loneliness almost overcame him.

Then he realized he'd never been really close to anyone but his parents, and now there was no longer anyone left to be good for, and he wondered if he'd ever had a real friend on the planet.

But then he remembered Jean. And he remembered Chevalier and Peters and those students who gathered around him, drinking cheap wine and sitting on the back porch, and in those days it was a great consolation. He taught them, he told me, to appreciate Bach. He showed them his collection of rocks, and Jean got him involved in the protests, and at night, Jean came and slept over if she didn't have to work, and if she did, he slept under the stars in that hammock.

And so on and so forth.

Robert told me his whole story, though of course sometimes there were holes. If a man told his life's story and didn't leave any holes, it would take him more than a lifetime to tell it.

It would take the person sitting beside him more than a whole lifetime to hear it.

So sometimes there were holes in the story, and it was always the holes that spoke to me loudest, the holes that called me back to their edges, the holes that I thought about later, and circled incessantly in my mind.

But in that moment, Robert kept going. He wanted to tell the whole story. He had the same bug I used to have back at Rosemont, wanting so badly to get everything in, wanting the whole mess down on paper.

Not realizing there are always holes in the story, that the holes are the most powerful part, that it's the holes people fall into, disappearing forever, dragging everyone and everything they love along with them.

But then Robert was sitting there at my desk, telling me that he'd been in love with Jean Tatlock, and they'd been close to marriage, but then they split up, and the next summer he and Kitty got married.

And by then, Robert told me, Hahn and Strassmann had produced fission, so they all knew the bombs could be made, and then Pearl Harbor was attacked, and General Groves chose him to lead the Manhattan Project.

And so on and so forth. On and on he kept talking: about the old school on the mesa and the mud roads, the Indian women who came up to clean, the hospital they built, the mountain lions you heard screaming at night, the way the pink cliffs looked bloodred when the sun set, how he learned about Jean in the winter, how he hadn't gone back for her funeral, how he still wasn't sure why she did it.

He talked all afternoon. He talked the way a river runs, with no sense of time, as if it could keep running forever.

By nighttime, he'd made us drinks, and I listened to him and knew that outside the cold stars were shining through the bare branches of the trees, and there was no one anymore for me to go home to.

And then I remembered again those days in Rosemont, staying up late, eating cereal, watching the leaves change on the trees, and feeling the press of my great ambitions, my desire to write a novel about the nuclear age.

And then I realized, with a private, terrible laugh, that Robert was describing himself as if presenting to me the central character of my Great American Novel.

There he was, the flawed but still noble hero, the figure fallen from myth.

And for a moment, I thought that perhaps I'd found my way to this office—perhaps Kathy and I had driven to Princeton and my sister had died and I'd married Stan all just to find my way to this office—so that Robert would sit down at my desk and give me the seed of my Great American Novel, teeming with immigrants and American cities and the hero who heads out west and the great violence and the secret shame and the bodies strewn and the guilty hero's belated confession.

It was as if he'd come to me like some angel God sent, to say here is your reward for keeping your eyes open in church.

Here is your recompense for your unhappy youth, for the time that you wasted, for those changing leaves, for your body that dried up under your husband and the nights you spent awake, longing for your lost sister.

And thinking that, I wanted to cry.

Then I did start crying a little.

Because by then, it was too late. I didn't care about writing a Great American Novel. I just didn't care. I was sick to death of my ambitions, and by then, if a Great American Novel had shown up on my desk, I'd have thrown it out for the pleasure of losing another thing I'd wanted to treasure.

By then I'd have thrown out everything left on this earth and the whole round planet as well, just to be lost along with my sister.

Just to be lost and come home again with my sister.

But of course the dead don't ever come back. The weeds just grow fat over the bones of their bodies.

So then I stopped crying, and Robert handed me a hand-kerchief and looked at me with his sad eyes and kept talking.

THAT WAS FEBRUARY. IN MARCH, THEY DETONATED THE SECOND hydrogen bomb, which was bigger than anyone thought.

The winds shifted, too, so fallout spread over the inhabited Rongelap and Rongerik atolls.

It spread as far as Australia, India, and Japan. A Japanese fishing boat was so badly exposed that all the crew members fell immediately ill with radiation sickness.

The Rongelap and Rongerik islanders were evacuated forty-eight hours after the test. Three years later, they were returned. Then they were evacuated again, and in the end, if I remember it right, something like twenty out of twenty-nine Rongelap children had cancer.

Needless to say, the test was conducted over Robert's objections.

But by then it didn't matter, because his security clearance had been temporarily revoked until the hearings were through, and nobody was listening to his opinions.

A month later, he and Kitty went to Washington, and the security hearings lasted three months. And that lawyer was right: everything did get leaked to the public. All his secrets came out, even the story about Jean, and all the lurid details about that trip to visit her, how he went to see her not because she was a member of the Communist Party but because he still cared for her very much, and the Mexican café where they danced, and the exact time at which they left, and drove back to her apartment, and spent the night together in her bedroom.

Several times in the course of the proceedings, Robert was forced to admit to all that again, while Kitty sat on a couch in the back of that windowless room, her eyes wide open and very dark, her leg in a cast because she fell down the stairs in those otherworldly weeks leading up to the hearings.

~

At three thirty, the rain stops. A new quiet settles outside the shelter. According to Frank, whom Oppenheimer has put in charge of the shelter, the only sound that can be heard is the croaking of the spadefoot toads that have emerged from their underground tunnels to gather in the puddles formed by the rainfall.

Outside, in the darkness, their pale throats extend and contract. Their webbed feet grip the wet stones.

And inside the shelter, Oppenheimer continues to wait.

I don't know what he does. I can't find any accounts.

Maybe he's drinking coffee. Maybe he stands and goes to the doorway. Maybe he looks out at the desert, where the clouds have finally dispersed, and ten thousand yards in the distance the shot tower is illuminated by starlight.

It looks like an oil derrick, or maybe a steeple. Does Oppenheimer consider that? Does he think of the mice? Does he think of Gruber's death? Does he remember the eight hundred Spanish settlers, or the millions dead in this war, or the hundreds of thousands whose deaths are still coming?

Does he look out at that steeple and think of the dead, or does he think of the living, or does he remember the name he chose for the test, and does he consider the reasons he chose it?

Trinity. *A strange, religious name for a bomb test. He'll never explain why he picked it. Nearly two decades later, General Groves will finally wonder, then write to ask if Oppenheimer chose that particular code name because it's common to rivers and peaks in that part of the country.*

Oppenheimer will reply:

Why I chose the name is not clear. There is a poem of John Donne, written just before his death, which I know and love. From it a quotation:

> As West and East
> In all flatt maps—and I am one—are one,
> So death doth touch the Resurrection.

That still does not make a Trinity; but in another, better-known devotional poem Donne opens, "Batter my heart, three person'd God; — ." Beyond this, I have no clues whatever.

Two decades after the test, that's all the explanation he'll manage: Why I chose the name is not clear. *That, and a couple of fragments of poems.* Beyond this, I have no clues whatever.

LÍA PEÓN

St. John, 1958

I CALLED HIM CHESTER, AND I ALWAYS LIKED HIM BECAUSE HE TREATED
me like a man. He was in the early stages of building his cottage, so we talked about pouring cement and choosing sawn
lumber, and he often asked my advice. By the end of our stay
there, he was my favorite of the sad clowns and exiles who
hid away on that island.

We only met him after we'd already spent eight months
on St. John. When we first arrived, in the summer of 1958,
we lived at the Caneel Bay Hotel, because Alice was coming
off a bad run. I liked her to have luxuries she wasn't used to.

In the mornings, we drank strong coffee on the tiled patio. We ate toast with butter and guava jam, surrounded by
potted palms and a wide view of the ocean.

We only read the local papers. I checked the headlines
before I handed them over to Alice. There were stories about
the sugarcane harvest, ferry repairs, and local art shows.

She read them and seemed unperturbed. Of course the

island had its own problems, but it was a relief to me at least to know that Alice wouldn't have to read any more news about "pervert purges," or "the homosexual menace," or see Roy Cohn on national television, saying that if you weren't with McCarthy, you were either a cocksucker or a Communist.

For a little while, at least, I wanted her to have peace over breakfast. Especially in those early months, when she was trying so hard to be better. All morning, she stuck with strong coffee. After breakfast, we went out walking, and in the afternoons she'd try to start painting.

Still, I felt the effort involved. The days went on forever, and we didn't have any friends. With each passing hour, surrounded on all sides by blue water, I was aware that it had been my idea to move out there. I watched her too closely for signs she was unhappy.

I was like Circe, watching Odysseus sneak down from the palace to the beach, planning new spells to keep him enchanted and hoping he wouldn't ready the ship. She tried to reassure me that she was content, but I could see she wasn't painting well. For months, she worked on one canvas of the anemic potted plant in our suite.

That plant was obviously dying. It had some secret disease. She'd set it on a marble table, and all summer, she painted its curled yellow fingers, making slow progress, then blotted it all out by the evening.

The whole suite smelled like turpentine. It smelled like mistakes getting rubbed out. We waited until dark to go down to dinner, but the sun never set.

And after dinner, at night, it was so quiet: the two of us alone in that hotel room together.

She tried to reassure me that I was enough, but Alice was used to being surrounded by people. Even in Washington, she had so many friends. In New York she had admirers. On St. John, I worried she'd lose her mind. She stuck to her word about drinking, but sometimes, in the evening, after she'd given up painting, I saw her striding in from the beach, holding her sandals, her eyes fixed on a point somewhere beyond the hotel and ignited by lights from the houseboats beyond her.

I DID WHAT I COULD TO HELP HER FEEL AT HOME. I TRIED TO FIND people who might entertain her. In July, for example, I remembered the Gibneys. We'd met them in New York, where Nancy was an editor. She'd worked at *Vogue,* but she quit when she married Bob, and they moved to St. John so he could finish his novel.

One day in July, I looked them up and invited them to the hotel to have dinner. We had a table on the patio, and I watched Alice the whole time, to see if she was enjoying herself. Nancy told stories that were funny and mean, and Bob laughed along with her, but when the check came, he became fascinated by a detail on the toe of his shoe. He remained entranced until I'd already paid, when he acted surprised and offended.

Later, when Alice was asleep and I'd gone down to the bar, the bartender told me that Bob sometimes did electrical repair work at the hotel. The novel, apparently, was not coming along. The longer the Gibneys stayed on the island, the less he actually wrote. Which probably at least partly explained why Nancy's anecdotes were honed to such a sharp point, as though the whole purpose was to show Bob how easy it is to bring a story to a satisfactory ending.

STILL, THEY WERE THE ONLY PEOPLE WE KNEW. AND EVERY SO OFTEN, if I thought Alice seemed particularly caged, I asked them to dinner. We learned how to get along with them well. It was best not to ask Bob about writing. Nancy was the more intelligent one, so we let her talk.

Once, while night fell on the patio, she entertained us with the story of the time Chester and Kitty stayed in their guest room. Two years before we came to the island, Bob and Nancy had sold a small piece of their beach to Chester and Kitty. They'd never intended to sell, but they'd used all of Bob's inheritance to buy the beach in the first place, and ten years later, Bob was still at work on that novel.

They needed the money. But they wanted to sell to people they liked, so they waited around a long time, and then they met Chester and Kitty at a luncheon at the Trunk Bay guesthouse.

According to Nancy, they were all dressed up in tourist gear: cotton from head to toe, and as pale as if they'd just stepped off the ferry. Right off the bat, Kitty made some rude comment about the heat and Nancy's thick hair. But Chester was polite, and Nancy and Bob—as Nancy made very clear—were good expatriate liberals.

They'd read about the security hearings. They were disgusted by McCarthy. They hated Roy Cohn. What was happening in Washington, Nancy said, giving me a meaningful look, was nothing if not a disgrace.

So when Chester and Kitty announced over lunch that they were looking to build a house on the island, Nancy and Bob decided to sell them the parcel. It was just after the sale that Kitty called to ask if they could come stay in the guest room while they were drawing up plans for the cottage. Nancy assumed that they wanted to stay for a weekend. But then they showed up with their daughter. And the daughter brought a school friend. As soon as they'd unpacked all their things, they announced that they couldn't possibly stay the whole summer, but they might be able to manage July.

While Nancy talked, occasionally taking a break to light another cigarette, darkness was creeping over the island. The lights of the houseboats were coming on in the harbor. Whenever Nancy came to a punch line, Alice laughed, politely, but she didn't draw her eyes away from the houseboats.

They stayed for *seven weeks,* Nancy said. The girls slept in a tent in the backyard. They were so quiet she often forgot they were there. But Robert and Kitty stayed in the guest room, and they were up every night until dawn, smoking and drinking in bed. Kitty would come out every five minutes to rattle around in the kitchen. Then, finally, when the roosters were just starting to crow, they'd go deathly quiet and sleep until noon, when they'd finally emerge, blinking in the bright light, wearing cotton shorts and big floppy sun hats.

While Nancy went on, I watched Alice light a cigarette. Her fingers weren't trembling so badly as they had in those last months in Washington. When she inhaled, she crossed one arm over her chest and looked out again over the darkening water.

No matter how much time they spent outside, Nancy said, Chester and Kitty were too pale and thin to be human. After a day on the beach, they'd come back paler than ever, and the first thing they did was pour a fresh drink. They never ate more than a few crackers for dinner. And then, all night, they'd be at it again, smoking and drinking in bed, knocking around for hours in the kitchen.

At that point in the story, the food finally came. Nancy paused her account. Bob assaulted his lobster croissant and when he finally came up for air, there was a fleck of mayonnaise on his chin.

Nancy gazed at it for a moment. Then she sighed and averted her eyes. Toward the end of July, she said, she'd had enough. The Oppenheimers had run the house for too long. Sometime after midnight, Kitty was at it again, rattling around, and Nancy got out of bed and marched out to the kitchen, where she found Kitty herself: pale as a ghost, dressed in nothing but a black negligee. Tail up, head down, her face shoved in the freezer like a skunk with its snout caught in a tin can.

She was using a flashlight, Nancy said, and fishing for ice at the back of the drawer. Then Nancy marched over and pulled her out of the freezer. Kitty, she said, no one who drinks all night needs ice in their whiskey.

When Nancy delivered this line, Bob laughed mechanically. He'd heard it before.

For a moment, Nancy examined him again. She was still beautiful, with that thick head of burnished gold hair. But Bob's hair had started receding, and the emerging dome of his forehead was sunburned. Nancy noted it, then went on with her story.

Apparently, interrupted in her foraging, Kitty drew herself out of the freezer. Then she took one look at Nancy, and swung the flashlight straight at her face.

Nancy had a bruise for two weeks. When she got back to bed, she told Bob she was going to visit her mother in Boston, at least until those lunatics had abandoned the guest room.

HAVING FINISHED HER STORY, NANCY TOOK A TRIUMPHANT SIP OF champagne.

Alice pointed out toward the horizon. "What are those lights?" she said.

Far off in the distance, there was a swarm of tiny globes of white light, bobbing up some invisible hillside.

Nancy glanced over her shoulder. She shrugged. No idea, she said.

Some ceremony or other, Bob guessed.

The dots of light kept swimming up. It looked as if a mob of angry villagers were storming the sky holding torches.

Of course Kitty's insane, Nancy went on, but given a choice, I'd take her over Robert.

I don't agree, Bob said, but Nancy ignored him.

It's him who's the real devil, Nancy said, leaning forward. He's what's driven her crazy. Once, you know, we asked him about Hiroshima. We assumed he'd be nearly mad with remorse. But he said he didn't regret what he'd done. He said he never had. And I said, but what about the radiation sickness? What about all the children dying of leukemia? What about the birth defects? What about the people who haven't been affected yet but still have to wait around, afraid of the day when they will be?

Then Nancy paused and took another sip of her champagne. Out in the darkness, those little globes of light were still climbing.

Anyway, Nancy said, he heard what I had to say. To his credit, he stayed there and listened. But even then he didn't say he was sorry. He just listened, and didn't respond, until finally he said something about how a scientist's job is to know, and how that's what he'd done. He'd set out to know the mystery of the atom. And I wanted to say, then how about you figure out the mystery of leukemia? Or how about, if you're so smart, you figure out the mystery of why people wage war? But I knew it wouldn't make any difference. You could tell how smug he was about the whole thing. He'd accomplished what he set out to accomplish.

Then Nancy finished. She took a bite of grilled shrimp. Alice was still gazing off at the far hillside. Those bobbing globes were reflected in her dark eyes, so that it seemed as if her pupils were giving off sparks.

Then the check came, and Bob disappeared under the table. Nancy watched him carefully. I took the check, and he surfaced again.

Your chin, Bob, Nancy said, at least ten or twenty minutes after she should have.

LATER, BACK IN OUR ROOM, ALICE LET DOWN HER HAIR AND SAT ON the edge of our bed. "I can't stand them," she said.

I started laughing. "We'll never see them again," I said.

She'd opened the shutters, and the moonlight shone on her hair. When she bent to rub lotion into her calves, she moved her hands in long, deliberate strokes, like someone washing clothes in a river.

AFTER THAT, IT WAS JUST US AGAIN IN THE HOTEL. ALICE DID HER best to make me think she was happy, but I know it wasn't easy for her.

It wasn't easy for me, either. What happened in New York was still so close behind us. I felt it breathing down the back of my neck.

To escape it, I hovered around her too much. She tried to pretend my hovering didn't bother her, but some days she'd startle when I walked into a room. Then I'd catch her absently fiddling with the ring I gave her in Washington, as though it irritated her finger. At night, she'd sleep on the far edge of the bed, and sometimes, when she came home from a walk, she'd knock around in the room for a while, stubbornly maintaining her distance, before finally giving in and coming over to kiss me.

Such little gestures. On their own, none of them meant much. But taken together, after what we'd left behind us, it was difficult for me not to transform them into signs of an impending departure.

I tried to keep myself busy, to avoid thinking such thoughts. I went out for long walks in the hills, keeping my back turned to the water. I moved uphill. That was a dry summer, and though the valleys were still dense and matted with green, as you climbed up the mountains, the hills that rose beyond you began to look like loaves of brown bread, studded with blue clumps of agave like spots of mold on the bread crust.

I walked until I was too tired to think. On bad days, that was my only relief. I'd walk until my thoughts had flattened out to nothing more than the sounds of my own footsteps crunching the stones. And I'd only start thinking again if I stopped, and sat down for a while on one of those rocks covered in suspended sea-green explosions of lichen.

Once I'd started thinking, I couldn't stop. Then, sometimes, I hated Alice. Sometimes I hated myself. I should have taken her away from Washington, I'd think to myself. I should have swept her off somewhere else.

Why didn't I see, earlier on, that we had to leave that despicable city?

I should have forced her to give up that job. We didn't need the money she made. She'd only taken it to prove I didn't have to support her. But trying to hang on to that job, when so many people were getting laid off: it made her start to go crazy. She became maniacal about keeping things between us a secret. She stopped wearing her ring. We stopped going out with our friends. If we went to a restaurant and ran into someone she knew, she'd introduce me as an old friend from college.

Then all through dinner she wouldn't touch me. She didn't hold my hand on the table. And if I reached underneath it to put my hand on her knee, she'd swat it away and her face would go stony.

After a while, we stopped going out to dinner together. It was easier just to see each other at home.

I wasn't working, so I wasted my days taking walks, or reading magazines in the park, but every second article was about some Hollywood star who'd been "exposed as a queer," or some politician who was "found out for a pervert."

At home, every time I turned on the TV a senator was getting interviewed about the secret menace of Communism in this country, about how you just couldn't tell: your neighbor might be a Red, your secretary might be a Red, your own mother might be a Commie.

Then the conversation would take a new turn, and the same senator, looking dignified in his dark suit, would say you couldn't separate homosexuals from subversives, because anyone who was keeping a secret was suspect.

So these senators said, as though they weren't the reason people were forced to keep secrets.

By then, more and more of our friends had been fired. And Alice wanted to hold on to that job, so we had no choice but to learn how to eat dinner like friends. We learned to never walk home together. We learned not to touch each other so often.

By then she was drinking so much her hands trembled when she held the paintbrush, but I was so preoccupied with my own anger that I didn't think to take her away. If I hadn't been so concerned with myself, I could have flown her down to Rio. I could have shown her the beach. I could have pointed out the billboard over my parents' apartment, with the black woman cooking alongside her white lover, two women smiling so brightly you knew they'd use that juicer forever.

But we didn't go. And Alice stopped painting, and then she felt so dull she started taking the train up to New York, where she could surround herself with old students and remember why they admired her.

Or that's the kind of reasoning I'd kick into gear if I ever got tired of walking. So then I'd get up from the rock. I'd move uphill, toward the blazing blue sky. I knew what was behind me. Somewhere in the depths of the valleys, under the canopies of the banana leaves, streams were babbling away. Wet black snakes were drawing signs in the mud of the stream banks, and ground doves in the thick ferns were murmuring innuendo.

I climbed up to the tops of the hills. I kept to the exposed parts of the island, the hillsides cleared to grow crops. Sometimes, I came across the ruins of the old sugar plantations. Hawks circled in the sky overhead, their shadows crossing the foundations of fallen plantation houses.

But I kept my eyes angled up. I tried not to think. And when I was too tired to walk anymore, I'd head back toward the hotel. Then I'd keep my eyes on the path until I'd reached the clipped hotel garden grounds, where the banana trees had been chopped down and the overgrowth had been contained, and every day the gardener was out mowing the lawn, or spraying the bougainvillea that cascaded over the walls, or lying on his back underneath the enormous king-sized agaves, pruning them down, lopping off big blue-green succulent fins and throwing them behind him onto a tarp heavy with the corpses of dolphins.

I WASN'T SURE ALICE AND I WOULD LAST THROUGH THAT SUMMER.

For weeks on end, she kept painting that dying plant, and I kept the sound of my footsteps in my ears, trying not to think about how I'd feel if she left.

Then one day I came back to the hotel and they'd pulled in the potted palms and rolled down the tin shutters over the windows.

For a moment I thought they'd decided to pack up the whole place, as though the hotel were a movie set they'd decided to strike, but then I realized we'd lasted the summer.

Somehow we'd made it to hurricane season. Then there was some comfort in the fact that the weather finally matched the mood Alice had been trying to hide. It almost seemed as though now, finally, we were approaching that time when everything would be out in the open.

For weeks, the sky was dark as a bruise, and I waited for the hammer to drop. The ocean was whitecapped and restless, and then Alice gave up that painting she'd been failing at all summer long.

A day later, the plant died. I put it in the corridor and someone took it away.

Then Alice started spending more time in bed. I tried not to hover. In that weather, I couldn't go out for walks in the hills, so sometimes I'd pace up and down the corridors of the hotel. Sometimes I went by myself to have a drink at the bar. I was reading a history of the island, and I'd sit by myself in the dim light of one of those little red lamps and read about the slave revolt.

After a bad drought and a worse hurricane season, Akwamu slaves began to escape and go into hiding. In November they emerged and took over the island, killing scores of Danish plantation owners.

For a few months, it was the first slave revolt in the New

World that succeeded. They were free until the following spring, when the Danes who escaped came back to the island with reinforcements from Martinique.

Seeing armed ships arriving in scores, many of the freed slaves shot themselves with the same guns they'd used to revolt. When the Danes stormed the island, they found dozens of dead former slaves. Those who hadn't killed themselves went into hiding, but by August, the militia had hunted them all down and killed them.

The slave trade continued for another hundred years after that. In 1848, the remaining slaves were finally set free. In the 1920s, the United States bought the island, and now the descendants of the freed slaves worked as gardeners, or clerks, or played in the scratchy band the hotel sometimes hired to keep us entertained through long afternoons while the tin shutters were rolled over the windows.

DURING THE FIRST REALLY VIOLENT STORM, A DOG FOUND ITS WAY to the hotel. He dragged his shivering gray body behind a potted palm and huddled there until the manager ordered the clerk to drive him back out. Two gardeners were pulling him over the marble when Alice happened to walk out of the restaurant.

She brought him up to the room. She toweled him off and named him Dog, and from then on, he followed her wherever she went. When she slept, he was a gray puddle by her side of the bed. When we stood in the corridor and talked about our plans for the day, he sat on one of her feet. When she took a shower, he placed himself on the bath mat to watch her.

At first, I felt annoyed by the intrusion of this new presence in our hotel room. But after a few days I was used to it, and watching the two of them walk off down the corridor, I felt relieved, as if Dog were doing my job.

It was as if I'd transformed the worst part of myself into a little gray creature, and sent it padding along after Alice.

Then I gave up on following her. I spent more time alone, reading at the bar, or exploring different wings of the hotel, and one day I came back to the room and Alice had flung open the shutters.

It was late afternoon, in a quiet hour between two blasts of a storm, and the air was the color of topaz. The storm hit again around nine, and Alice stayed up all night. In the morning, she'd covered a whole canvas with paint.

Throughout the rest of the season, she was painting all the time. She turned her attention to scenes outside the hotel room, and then we got along better. The little hotel room seemed to expand. By the time hurricane season had passed, and the clouds had broken apart and moved on, revealing a new beach, and a new ocean, that room could have been the whole island.

LATER WE EVEN MADE A FEW FRIENDS. IT WAS IVAN AND DORIS JADAN who introduced us to Chester and Kitty. We were at a dinner party on the patio outside their house, and as soon as I met them, I remembered the stories Nancy had told.

They were pale, that much was true. And Chester was extraordinarily thin. But all night, at that dinner, I watched them for evidence of the lunacy Nancy described, and I just couldn't see it.

We sat on the patio and watched the sun set over the

water. Doris made seafood soup from fish Ivan pulled in from his pot, and while we ate, Ivan went on one of his jags about the ignominy of life under the Soviet regime.

Then he mentioned that, during the war, the NKVD had an ongoing file on Chester. That's where the name Chester came from: it was the code name the NKVD gave him. We laughed about that, and I said he actually looked like a Chester, and suddenly, though she'd been silent before, Kitty emitted a hoarse, throaty laugh.

Then she tapped out her cigarette. She said she'd have liked to marry a person named Chester.

After that, all night, we were calling him Chester. He seemed to enjoy it. It was as if he was more at ease answering to a code name.

Still, every so often, when someone else was telling a story, I watched him for evidence of the cruel pride Nancy described. But he never talked about the bombs. He stayed away from politics. He was soft-spoken and polite, and only at Ivan's prodding did he start to recite one of the passages he'd memorized.

Ivan said he knew the whole *Odyssey* by heart, and later he stood up by the bonfire Ivan had built, with the shadows of the flames flickering over his face, and said, *Sing to me of the man, Muse, the man of twists and turns.*

He went on for a while, with the sound of the ocean washing behind him: *Many cities of men he saw and learned their minds, many pains he suffered, heartsick on the open sea.*

He knew pages and pages by heart. When he was finished, we all applauded. Ivan said he could recite any passage you requested, in any one of the eight languages he could fluently speak. We tried him for a while, and for the most part it was true. He had a genius for adopting other people's mother tongues. He did more from Homer, a few from Proust, and *The Tempest,* and a poem by Donne, always speaking somewhat quietly so that we had to lean forward to hear him, and Kitty smoked cigarette after cigarette, watching him perform, resting there on the patio, temporarily at ease, like a woman who's put aside what's left of her weaving.

Later, when the sun had almost disappeared below the horizon, Chester stopped reciting and looked over at Alice.

You're a painter, he said, or something like that.

She nodded, and he said, I'm going to show you something amazing.

He led the way, and she followed him over the edge of the hillside, heading down to the beach. They were gone for a while, and Kitty kept smoking and laughing with Doris and Ivan, but she never took her eyes off the place where they'd disappeared.

Later, when they came back, Alice was grinning. When she sat down beside me, she took my hand.

We sat there together all night, holding hands by the bonfire Ivan built to keep us warm, and when we got back to the hotel she couldn't even wait until the elevator doors had closed behind us before she started kissing me.

She was holding my face in her hands, pulling me closer. In the room, we took each other's clothes off as if we hadn't seen each other before. Afterward, I went to sleep, and Alice started a painting. It was the first of her green flashes, the first of that profitable series of paintings.

That's what Chester had shown her: the flash of green

light that spread over the horizon just before sunset. He'd explained to her why it happened. Where the atmosphere curved close to the earth, he said, it worked as a prism. And when the sun had nearly sunk behind that curved portion, the single sun as we perceive it was divided into many suns: a red sun, a yellow sun, purple and green suns.

In that moment, we could finally see that it had never been a single sun, but instead a cloud of merging, interpenetrating bodies of color, which had only appeared like one sun because all of them were sinking at the same speed. Only then, in that last second, when the other suns of other colors had sunk below the horizon, the slowest one—the green sun, the sun most loath to leave us—was the only sun left.

According to legend, Chester told Alice, anyone who saw that green flash would never again go wrong in any matter of the heart. They watched it go dark again, then turned and came back up to the fire to join us.

WHO KNOWS WHY HE FELT SHE NEEDED TO SEE THAT GREEN FLASH. Regardless, from that point on, we were friends with Chester and Kitty. For the most part our relationship was always open and easy, though there were some subjects we tried to avoid. We never talked, for instance, about his security hearings, though I'd read about them in Washington, in the same magazines where I read about exposed Hollywood stars, or all those "political perverts."

I could sympathize with what he'd been through. We'd stayed under the radar because we weren't as famous as Chester and Kitty. Alice was only the arts consultant for the Library of Congress, not the father of the atom bomb. But we'd been there, in that hateful city, in that hateful time, surrounded by those magazines and the gossip in all the restaurants, and sometimes, on the island, I wondered if Alice and I could have survived what he and Kitty endured: four months, in that little room, and all those secrets tumbling out.

Out of curiosity, once, I ordered the transcripts from the library on St. Thomas. I read them at an outdoor café in Cruz Bay. It was very early one morning. I'd had trouble sleeping, so I left Alice in bed and headed to that café when the sky was still transparent as a jellyfish and shot through with veins of bright color.

The transcripts went on for hundreds of pages. It was strange to read them on that island, while the roosters were still crowing and the ocean whispered somewhere nearby. They seemed to belong to another universe entirely, those records of the legal debate on whether or not Chester was a loyal citizen of his country.

The main question, the question the lawyers continually returned to, was whether or not, as a man, Chester was fit to be trusted.

The prosecutors emphasized that he had lied to his superiors in the army, just as he had lied to several friends, and to his wife, when he went back to spend that night with his girlfriend in San Francisco.

Could a man, the prosecutors wanted to know, who could not be trusted as a friend or a husband be trusted with his country's nuclear secrets?

Over and over again, his friends and colleagues attempted

to answer in the affirmative, but the prosecutors pressed further. How can you know? they asked. How can you be perfectly sure that you know him?

And over and over again, the witnesses—his friends; even his family—were forced to admit that they couldn't.

A Dr. Bradbury, for instance, who worked with him at Los Alamos, said: "I was not looking in his mind, and I cannot say this of course from definite knowledge. You can never say anything about a man's loyalty by looking at him, except what you feel."

Reading his answer, I felt a little creeping despair in my stomach. I began to feel as though my coffee might crawl back up my throat.

For some reason, it settled my stomach to start taking notes, so I wrote down Dr. Bradbury's answer on the paper napkin that came with my coffee. I wrote down what Edward Teller said, also: "In a great number of cases I have seen Dr. Oppenheimer act—I understood that Dr. Oppenheimer acted—in a way which for me was exceedingly hard to understand." And later: "To this extent, I feel that I would like to see the vital interests of this country in hands which I understand better, and therefore trust more."

I covered that napkin with lines, then went to the counter and picked up a fresh bundle of napkins, and as I continued to read, I kept taking notes. "How did you know him?" the defense lawyer asked a man named Dr. Latimer.

"Various things," he answered, "that go into a man's judgment are sometimes difficult to analyze."

"I am trying to figure out," the defense lawyer said, "to what extent objective facts—"

But Dr. Latimer interrupted. "I had studied this influence Dr. Oppenheimer had over men. It was a tremendous thing."

"When did you study this influence?" the defense lawyer asked.

"All during the war and after the war. He is such an amazing man that one couldn't help but try to put together some picture."

On and on, the interrogation continued. I covered the whole stack of napkins, while more and more probingly, the lawyers for both the prosecution and the defense questioned droves of witnesses about whether or not Chester's true nature could ever be known, and therefore trusted.

Chester, too, was called to account, and reading his answers—though I was so far away, sitting alone at that café while the roosters crowed under that jellyfish sky—I felt myself returning to those last months in Washington. I felt the suspicions that had caused me to stay awake all night, watching Alice, looking for signs.

In that spirit, I kept reading and copying notes, even though at some point I began to feel that I was prying unforgivably into the corners of another person's private life, such as when the prosecutors began to question him about the nature of his relationship with that girlfriend in San Francisco.

They quoted a letter he'd written in Princeton, answering each of their accusations, in which he'd explained that he and Jean Tatlock met in 1936. They'd grown very close, he said. Twice they were close enough to marriage to think of themselves as engaged. But between his marriage to Kitty in 1939 and her death in 1944, they only saw each other rarely. Her Communist beliefs had wavered by then. They never quite seemed to provide what she was seeking. Then he said that he did not believe she was a truly political person; rather, she was a person of deep religious feeling. She loved this country, its people, and its life.

Having read this account, the prosecutor looked at Chester over the table. Kitty was sitting behind him. The prosecutor asked whether, between 1939 and 1944, his relationship with Jean was casual.

Their meetings were rare, Chester said, but not casual. They had been deeply involved. There was still strong feeling when they saw each other.

How many times, the prosecutor wanted to know, did you see her between 1939 and 1944?

Chester guessed ten times in five years.

He had seen her, he said, socially with other people. He had seen her on New Year's of 1941, when he went to her house, and afterward they went out for a drink at the Top of the Mark. She had come more than once to visit his new home in Berkeley, and he had visited her at her father's house. And he had gone to see her in June of 1943, when he was directing the Manhattan Project.

Now the prosecutor was really licking his chops. "You said you had to see her," he said. "Why did you have to see her?"

Chester tried to answer well. She had wanted to see him before he left San Francisco to relocate to Los Alamos, but he hadn't gone then. He had felt, at that time, that he had to keep his destination a secret. But he'd wanted to go. He'd known she was unhappy.

"I felt," he said, "that she had to see me."

"Why did she have to see you?" the prosecutor asked.

"Because she was still in love with me," Chester said.

"Where did you see her?" the prosecutor asked.

"At her home, on Telegraph Hill."

"You spent the night with her, didn't you?"

"Yes."

"Did you see her again after that?"

"She took me to the airport," Chester said, "and I never saw her again."

And still the prosecutor wouldn't let up. Was it good security, he wanted to know, to spend the night with a woman who was loyal to the Communist Party?

"Oh, but she wasn't," Chester said.

How did you know? the prosecutor said.

"I knew her," Chester said.

I knew her.

That was the best answer he could come up with, in that room, surrounded by lawyers, with Kitty sitting immobile behind him.

BY THE TIME I'D FINISHED COPYING THAT, I FELT REALLY SICK. THEN I returned the transcripts to the library. I drove home in a strange mood, and the next time we saw Kitty and Chester, I couldn't help watching them a little more closely.

Nancy was probably right that they drank more than was healthy. And they never ate much. But they seemed to enjoy their life on the island. They chewed whelks like the natives. They went sailing together. They brought their daughter with them, and while the cottage was still getting built, they lived on the beach in two tents that they struck, sheltered in the back by a cluster of mangroves.

One night they came to have dinner with us at the hotel, and when Chester heard I'd built houses in Brazil before I met Alice, he asked my advice on tile work and cement.

He wasn't ashamed to ask for my help. When I talked, he listened carefully. He never interrupted. I felt he valued the opinions I gave, and sometimes, when they'd gone back to Princeton, he'd call and ask if I'd head out to their beach to oversee the contractor.

Even when he was on the island, he often asked for my help overseeing his workers. He didn't have the personality to manage construction. Sometimes I wondered how he managed that entire bomb project. One day, when I wasn't there, his workers laid the foundation wrong and started building too close to the water.

When Chester asked them what happened, the contractor just shrugged and said a donkey ate the surveyor's plans.

So then Chester gave up, and if he needed something changed or done better, he'd call me, and I'd drive over and order people around, or check on the quality of the tin they shipped in, or the terra-cotta tiles he'd ordered.

At night, when the workers had gone home, he and Kitty threw wonderful parties. They strung the mangrove trees with little white lights. They hired a scratchy band to play calypso, and they served good champagne, and Alice and I learned to eat dinner beforehand, because they never served enough food. Once they only served seaweed. Another time there was a thin vichyssoise. But by then, we knew what to expect, and Alice was doing so well that she didn't even look at the champagne as it was poured into people's glasses.

We sat together in the cold sand and held hands. Sometimes she got up to dance, but she always came back. She drank seltzer with lime, and afterward, we'd go back to the hotel, and even before the elevator had shut its doors behind us, we were already undressing each other.

When we got to the room, we didn't turn on any lights. I'd lie down and close my eyes and she'd kiss my eyelids and my cheekbones and the small oval pool of my throat, that place where rain could have been caught, where tide pools could have formed and minnows could have survived until the next tide rose to return them.

I kept my eyes closed, and I felt the touch of Alice's lips moving over my body, and it was as though we were both disappearing together, our edges melting, fading into the darkness, so that there was no before and no after, no other moment to think of, only that single small place on the island where her lips touched my skin in the darkened hotel room.

Afterward, we lay in bed, and Alice said, "Let's never leave."

"What about New York?" I said. I had a sudden pain in my throat.

But Alice kissed the shell of my ear, and I smelled the salt on her shoulder.

"What about it?" she said.

Then I thought maybe there's a version of the old story in which Odysseus never readies his ship.

In which he stays on the island, contented in the sorceress's palace.

THAT YEAR, CHESTER AND KITTY WERE IN PRINCETON THROUGH THE hurricane season. But they came back in the winter, and they'd finished construction by the end of December.

To celebrate, they threw a New Year's Eve party, and Chester gave us a tour of the cottage. He'd done a good job. It was a nice spot they had, under Peace Hill. They called it Easter Rock, and the whole cottage was a single, big room, with one open wall facing the ocean.

There we stood—Alice and Chester and I, with Dog at our feet—facing the water. For a little while we stood there in silence, listening to the sounds of the ocean lapping the shore, and the scratchy band they'd brought in for the party.

Then Alice looked at me and said, "Let's build a house here," and I don't think I've ever been quite so sure of having arrived at the place I was meant to.

AFTER WE FINISHED THE TOUR, CHESTER TOOK US OUT TO THE EDGE of the water and pointed out constellations: the huntress, and the warrior, and the warrior's dogs. Behind him, we could see the lights in the mangrove trees, people dancing on the beach, the orange tips of cigarettes.

It looked as if we'd arrived on the shore of Never Never Land. Chester led us back to the party. They were serving lobster and champagne, and Alice and I sat at a round table with Chester and Kitty. Alice held my hand. She even had a sip of champagne, but then she pressed the glass away and put her head on my shoulder.

After a while, Ivan showed up, holding a turtle he'd caught. He was laughing, and holding it up, saying he planned to eat it for dinner.

I happened to be looking at Chester. His face looked awful. Then he took a big swig of champagne. And finally, in that quiet voice, he said that after the test, they'd gone back to check on the site and found thousands of turtles belly up on the sand, burned to death inside their shells.

For a moment, everyone else at the party was quiet. The band had taken a break, so you could hear the sound of the water washing up on the beach. Then the girl—their daughter—got up from her chair and headed out toward the water. I hadn't even realized she was there at the party.

In silence, we all watched her move over the beach: a girl in a white dress. Then Ivan made a joke about how Chester had granted the turtle a pardon. We all laughed, even Chester, and Ivan carved his initials in the turtle's soft shell. Then he released it onto the sand, and we watched it trundle off toward the water.

After that, the music started playing again. The girl came back to the party. She slipped in so quietly it was almost as if she were her own shadow.

Later, Alice danced a calypso with Chester. She was so beautiful, in her silver dress, with her blond hair falling over her shoulders.

For a while, Kitty watched them. Then, for the first time in months, I remembered those transcripts. I felt for her, I really did. But Alice never liked sleeping with men, and when she came back to me she slipped her fingers through mine and leaned her heavy head on my shoulder.

AFTER WE RANG IN THE NEW YEAR, IVAN TOLD THE BAND TO TAKE A break. Then he stood out in the sand, under the stars, and started singing.

He'd been a premier Bolshoi tenor before he escaped Russia. He'd surrendered to German forces during the war.

When he got out of prison in Berlin, he went to America. From there, he and Doris found their way to the island, and when they got off the ferry, Ivan said, "Here we stay."

By then his singing career was long over. But on that New Year's Eve, ringing in the new decade, we sat at that round table and listened while he sang so beautifully I remembered when I was a little girl and my father took me to the opera in Rio.

I was sitting there with my eyes closed, holding Alice's hand, remembering my childhood and listening while Ivan sang, and then suddenly we all heard a stirring in the mangrove trees. I opened my eyes in time to see Bob storm out with a pistol.

"Too much noise!" he was shouting, waving his pistol around. "There's too much damn noise on this island!"

Then he started firing into the sky.

I looked at Chester, and for the first time since I'd met him, I saw him look angry. Then I remembered what Nancy said—It's *him* who's the devil—because when he stood, and started moving toward Bob, his eyes were darker than blackness.

For a moment, I thought that maybe, after all, I knew nothing about him. I'd never even spoken with him about those bombs, or the security hearings, or that woman he'd loved, and whom he'd come so close to marrying, who killed herself in 1944.

Did he blame himself for that death? I wondered for the first time. Did he blame himself for the others?

Or were those deaths in other lives, lives that had slipped beyond the horizon, leaving behind only this one: this single life on this beach, the lights strung up in the mangroves, the turtle saved, the girl in the white dress returned to the table.

As soon as Chester started approaching with that black look on his face, Bob stopped shooting.

For a moment, he stood there with his mouth nervously twitching. Still pointing that pistol up into the mangroves.

Then Chester pulled himself up to his fullest height. "Get off my property," he said.

Bob ran off into the trees. Then Chester sat down.

Kitty watched the whole thing with her big, fathomless eyes, and, after a short pause, during which the ocean sounded quite loud, Ivan Jadan kept singing.

In the absence of a conclusive account, some biographers have suggested that, in naming the test, Oppenheimer must have been thinking of Jean, who—according to Oppenheimer's own descriptions of their relationship—nearly married him at several points, and influenced him a great deal, and introduced him to the Donne poems he quoted, and killed herself a year and a half before he scheduled the test.

But Oppenheimer never said, at least in any public accounts, that it was Jean he was thinking of. And other biographers have concluded that in fact it wasn't Donne he had in mind, but instead the Hindu Trimurti.

In the end, however, they can't say they're certain. They've made their best guesses, based on evidence they've assembled. They've tried to piece together a motive, as we often do, when we're faced with a violence we didn't foresee and find that we can't quite comprehend fully.

In such dangerous times, when the order of the world seems to shift, it becomes essential to understand people's motives. We gather our facts: the books he read, the lovers he took, the answers he gave to questions asked later. We arrange them into reliable orders.

But two decades after the test, in his public accounts, not even Oppenheimer seems to understand fully.

Why I chose the name is not clear, *he wrote to Groves.* Beyond this, I have no clues whatever. *And in the absence of any clarity on what he might have been thinking, all I can say for certain is that at 3:30 A.M. on July 16, the date scheduled for the Trinity Test, Oppenheimer is waiting inside South Shelter, ten thousand yards away from the tower.*

TIM SCHMIDT

Massachusetts, 1963

IT WAS MY SENIOR YEAR, LATE IN THE SPRING OF 1963, WHEN HE CAME
to Sudbury to speak. He must have been invited as part of
the political rehabilitation his friends and allies undertook
when Kennedy was elected.

To prepare for his coming, we spent a few weeks in
Mr. Rosenberg's history class learning about his security hearings. By then, the McCarthy era had come to be seen as a
shameful episode. Mr. Rosenberg told us how, during the
hearings, they'd turned his life inside out.

But still, Mr. Rosenberg said, despite their defamations,
he carried himself with dignity.

He refused to resign. He stood up and faced each of the
charges.

By then, it was spring, and Mr. Rosenberg sometimes held
classes outside. The elms were in full leaf. The new grass on
the lawns was that color of green that defied all attempts at
description.

I always loved the grass on those lawns: its neatness, and its health. Out of respect for the care the groundskeepers so obviously took, I was always conscientious about using the walkways on my way between buildings. I never cut corners, as some of the other boys did, especially when they were running late for their classes.

Secretly, I looked down on the boys who ran over the lawns. Of course most people did, and there was nothing I could say without seeming unacceptably square. But I had my own established rituals. By then, I was a senior. I wasn't so nervous about fitting in. I wasn't so afraid my mother would show up and behave in some unpredictable manner.

I'd been at Sudbury four years, and she hadn't done it so far, at least not in any way I couldn't manage.

So I'd begun to feel safe. By then, I'd taken up squash, and that fall I'd been accepted to college, so I was starting to feel confident that things would work out.

And it wasn't only my personal life that seemed to have been set in better order. The state of the world seemed more hopeful as well. Kennedy had averted the missile crisis in Cuba. He'd opened diplomatic channels with Khrushchev. It seemed possible that a larger-scale nuclear disarmament might be pursued.

You could have been forgiven, that spring, for thinking the nuclear threat had receded.

ON THE DAY THAT HE CAME TO SPEAK, I MUST HAVE BEEN SITTING IN the senior class transept. I was in the front pew. I remember that while we sang the opening hymn, he processed behind the chaplain and the headmaster.

He walked with his head down, carrying the hymnal, but I don't think he was singing.

Our headmaster, Mr. Pritchard, introduced him. Mr. Pritchard had been a military historian at West Point before he came to Sudbury, so his opinion carried weight. When he walked up to the lectern, he carried himself with military correctness, and he stood very tall when he praised the unique contributions Dr. Oppenheimer had made to the war.

Even more than his military accomplishments, Mr. Pritchard said, it was his sense of restraint—the willingness to embrace limits—that placed him so squarely in that class of men we call great.

That's what he said: "the willingness to embrace limits." I remember it clearly. And I remember that, throughout the whole introduction, Dr. Oppenheimer sat with his head down. His long hands were clasped on his lap. He wore a suit with a vest, a style I liked, and he looked up only once, to survey us with an expression that was impossible to interpret.

Later, he rose and crossed the chancel. Then he climbed up to the lectern. His theme was the connection between power and privilege. He said—and I remember this well—that responsibility comes only with power.

I remember I wasn't sure if I understood him correctly. Was he saying that we have no responsibility if we've been rendered powerless? That didn't seem to me to be right, but he spoke with such quiet wisdom that I was sure I'd misinterpreted his theme.

He spoke so quietly and with so little bombast that even those of us in the front pew had to lean forward to hear him. At one point, he even trailed off into silence. He seemed to lose his train of thought. For a moment, he stared out the far door of the chapel, and in that moment my heart stopped.

At the eighth-grade graduation for the boarding school I'd managed to attend as a child, my mother showed up unannounced. She stormed in through the back door of the chapel, in the middle of the ceremony. The headmaster, who was delivering the graduation address, abruptly fell silent as she marched up to my pew and dragged me out down the aisle.

It would have been in protest against something having to do with Russian agents. But what I recall thinking, even as she pushed me out the same door she'd come in through, is that she'd clearly tried to look dignified for the occasion. She was wearing a white hat and white gloves, and carrying a nice purse, and she walked very straight, with her chin up. She ignored the fact that the students and even some of the teachers were nervously laughing, and whispering among one another.

Now it makes me sorry, to think of the effort she must have made to look dignified on my behalf. And how embarrassed I was, nonetheless, by everything about her behavior.

Later, in the car, on our way back to my grandmother's house, I realized her gloves didn't match. One was white, the other was cream, and for some reason, it was that fact that always made my face burn again when I remembered her dragging me out of the chapel.

BUT NOW I'M GETTING DISTRACTED. SHE DIDN'T COME TO THE CHAPEL that day. When he looked out the back door, he'd only lost his train of thought for a moment. Then he finished the talk, and it sounded so noble and wise that at the end, we stood and applauded.

The whole thing went off very well. Only afterward, when I'd headed to my next class, I realized I'd forgotten my blazer.

It was the only blazer I had, a hand-me-down from the financial aid office, so I had to run back to chapel to get it. I was annoyed at myself for my predictable vagueness. I could never seem to remember that blazer, and I hated nothing more than arriving late for my classes.

For a moment, on my way back, I stopped to wonder whether I should take the paths and run late, or cross over the lawn, and it was then that I happened to see him.

He was walking alone, heading away from me, moving toward the parking lot at the back of the chapel. Forgetting where I was and the dilemma I faced, I watched him go: the man who had created the atom bombs that were dropped on Hiroshima and Nagasaki; the inventor of the opening move of the Cold War, the move all the others had followed.

It seemed to me that someone should have accompanied him to his car. I thought he was the kind of man who should be followed by a whole cloud of admiring people, so it was strange to see him alone, moving through the shadows cast by the elm trees.

OF COURSE NOW IT'S DOUBLY STRANGE TO THINK HOW HOPEFUL I was as I watched him. The following fall, in my first semester of college, Kennedy was assassinated in Dallas. On the day he assumed office, Johnson made the commitment to escalate the war in Vietnam.

By the time I'd graduated from college, the draft was in place. Operation Rolling Thunder had nearly come to a close. We'd dropped more tons of explosives and incendiaries on Vietnam in three years than were dropped in the whole Korean War, and meanwhile, Johnson had modernized the nuclear arsenal and authorized dispersal of our nuclear weapons to countries abroad.

On a more personal note, moreover, my mother's condition had deteriorated. I'd been made her legal guardian, which meant that it was my responsibility when she escaped from one of the halfway houses where I managed to place her. For weeks, after one of her many escapes, I'd live in a state of awful suspense until the police found her again, living somewhere on the streets, muttering about Soviet spies and Communist persecution.

You can imagine the relief I felt when, after graduating from college, I was offered the opportunity to return to Sudbury to teach. There, temporarily safe from the draft, earning enough money to place my mother in a private institution, I moved along the same walkways again, surrounded by the same fresh, healthful grass, and it seemed to me that the Sudbury campus was the one place on earth that had been untouched by all the recent political tumult.

Back on the campus of my alma mater, everything seemed to be in order. In June, for instance, as they always did, the tiger lilies around the chapel came into bloom. Walking by them, pausing for a moment to notice again the freckled throats of their flowers, I felt for the first time in several years that I knew where I was, and who I was in that instant.

It was just after I saw those lilies again, when I was moving away from the chapel, that I remembered Oppenheimer, walking alone, heading out from under the shade of the elms and off into the sunlight.

For a moment, I was transported back to that time again. I was running back to chapel, in search of my blazer, choosing between the grass and inevitable lateness.

Then I shook my head. I remembered that four years had passed since that afternoon. It must have been a scent in the air, I thought to myself, that caught me and plunged me back to that time. Then, out of curiosity, I looked around for the bloom that had caused it.

For a few minutes, like a lunatic, I walked in circles, smelling various flowers and bushes, and only when I'd given up hope and was heading off toward the main building did I happen to look up and see bees moving between the greenish-gold blossoms of the tree overhead, which wasn't an elm, in fact, but a linden.

LATER, I LEARNED FROM MR. ROSENBERG THAT THE ELMS FOR WHICH Sudbury was famous—and under which Oppenheimer and I had crossed paths four years before—had been struck down one by one, until every last elm on that campus had rotted.

They were victims, Mr. Rosenberg told me, of Dutch elm disease, a fungus native to Asia. It was introduced to America in 1928, when beetles carrying the disease arrived on a shipment of logs. Sanitation and quarantine measures were taken, and they contained the disease until 1941, at which time wartime demands meant that those initial measures were abandoned.

At that point, from New York, the disease spread to New

England, and since I'd been at Sudbury last, more than half of the seventy-seven million elms in North America had been destroyed, and all the elms on Sudbury's campus had quickly rotted and succumbed to the fungus.

By the time I returned, the elms had been replaced by other trees, such as that linden, whose shadows I moved through, imagining they were the same shadows that danced over the grass on that other, earlier afternoon, when Dr. Oppenheimer walked off alone, heading out of the frame of a moment that would never be summoned again, changed as it was by what followed, so that the original almost seemed to have been dreamed: those still-healthy trees, that indescribable grass, those dappled shadows, and the man I only saw at a distance, when he was already moving away, heading off into the afternoon sunlight.

WATCHING HIM GO, I FELT A CERTAIN STRANGE SORROW GROWING within me. Over my head, the leaves of the elms were rustling in the wind, as if whispering some revelation I couldn't quite comprehend, and as soon as he stepped out from under the branches, the light—which I remember as having that softened, gold quality of late afternoons on our campus—enveloped his body.

It slipped around him, blurring his edges, so for a moment, he almost seemed to be disappearing before me, and I felt a strange, inexplicable desire to run after him and detain him. To ask him what I'd missed. What the elms were trying to say. What I hadn't yet quite comprehended.

An hour goes by. The weather holds. By 4:30 A.M., the winds have slowed down. In the new still of the desert spreading out from the tower, the scrap wood and metal rest where they were dropped in the snakeweed. The corpses of the white mice remain tied to the electrical wires. The only sound outside the shelter is the pleated croaking of toads, and by 4:45, it's clear to everyone that the test will proceed at 5:30.

At 5:10, a voice from the loudspeaker outside announces zero minus twenty minutes.

At 5:20, zero minus ten minutes.

A siren wails, and Oppenheimer goes outside with the others. They lie facedown in a trench, to protect their eyes from the bomb flash, and at some point, according to a witness standing farther away, a herd of antelope begins crossing the desert several hundred yards from the tower.

But Oppenheimer himself doesn't see it. He's lying facedown in the trench, along with his brother, Frank, and a handful of officers and technicians, all of them waiting with their heads down for something they've never seen, an impact the force of which they can't predict, a violence that's never been known on this planet.

The minutes tick past. According to a witness nearby, Oppenheimer grows more and more tense. At the announcement of zero minus two minutes, he mutters, "Lord, these affairs are hard on the heart."

At zero minus one minute, he scarcely breathes.

As the last seconds tick by, in a still more awful than any sea, he's lying facedown in the dirt, and the antelope are still crossing.

HELEN CHILDS
Princeton, 1966

THE LAST TIME I SAW OPPENHEIMER WAS DECEMBER OF 1966.

By then he was dying. He'd suffered the trauma of his security hearings. He'd weathered the fanfare of his symbolic rehabilitation, which occurred just before he fell ill. When I saw him in Princeton, he was only sixty-two, but he had inoperable cancer. He was frail and defeated and perhaps I should have been more sympathetic.

I startled him when I knocked on the door. When he rose to come forward and greet me, he was as courteous as I'd remembered him, from that time he and Kitty came to my parents' house. He kissed me on the cheek. Then he sat at his desk. I pulled out my tape recorder, and while I untangled the cords, he watched me with his gray eyes, and I thought that his face seemed like a dog's face.

Maybe it was because of his eyebrows, which had always been heavy. But it was also his wary expression when he watched me set the tape recorder down on the oddly bare desk in his new office. It was as if he knew I'd come there with the intention to harm him.

SINCE THAT DAY, I'VE SOMETIMES WONDERED WHY I COULDN'T JUST let him be. But as soon as I crossed the threshold and moved into his office, I knew I'd make myself his enemy.

I felt he should have to tell the whole story. After the violence he'd unleashed and failed to control, after the guilt that he'd involved us in, after all the lies that he'd told: I felt that he should make himself clear, and he watched me with those dog's eyes as if he knew my intentions.

As if he accepted the fact that I'd come to force him to reveal the secrets he'd previously kept. As if he knew that I'd insist on the whole truth and nothing but, and that he would refuse, but that in his desire to remain courteous, in his awareness of the responsibilities that came with his position, he would stop short of sending me out of his office, and that therefore the interrogation would continue, and the arrangement would only become more and more brutal, until it seemed that only one of us could emerge alive from that office.

And still, he allowed me to come in. In fact, he invited me.

FROM THE BEGINNING, I'D DISLIKED THE ASSIGNMENT: A FINAL PRO-file on Oppenheimer, looking back on the course of his life.

It seemed to me somewhat brutal, since he hadn't died yet. But still, I accepted, mostly because I needed the work. Over the course of the last two or three years, I'd become a less reliable writer. The stream of work I'd once taken for granted had steadily slowed. When my editor called to offer me the Oppenheimer profile, I hadn't heard from him for over a year.

So I accepted, but it was with none of the enthusiasm I used to feel for the project of interviewing a subject.

Though I was only thirty-two at the time, it seemed to me that decades had passed since my early days as a journalist, when I still believed in my own special talent for interviewing a subject. In place of that old confidence, there was a dreadful, dull blankness, like a single empty room in an otherwise well-furnished house.

Still, I needed the work, so I accepted the assignment. That afternoon, I called Oppenheimer to schedule an interview. I explained the profile, and mentioned that, when I was a girl, my family had lived down the street from Olden Manor. When they first moved to Princeton from California, he and Kitty had come to a Christmas party at my parents' house. Kitty wore a lovely mink coat.

He laughed, and said he remembered my parents and that mink coat, then invited me to his new office at the institute. He explained that it was a smaller office, on the second floor, to which he'd moved when he'd resigned the directorship. Then we scheduled the interview for a date in December, and once I'd hung up the phone, I arranged for my son to spend that night with our neighbor. Then I booked a flight to New York, and a local train ticket to Princeton.

Several weeks later, when I arrived at the new institute building, I found it deserted. Strangely, he'd invited me to come on a Sunday. So I let myself in, passed all the empty offices on the first floor, climbed the echoing stairway, and found his new office at the end of a dark hallway.

It was small and out of the way, unprotected by a secretary. There was no one there to protect him. And because he hadn't heard my approach, I was able to stand in the doorway for a few moments, watching him before he became aware of my presence.

He was turned away from the desk, looking out toward the window, and I wondered if he'd posed himself in that contemplative position, anticipating my arrival, or whether I'd really caught him in an unguarded moment.

The window faced out toward the bare trees and the frozen pond where my sister and I used to ice-skate. Inside his office, there was no furniture except that big metal desk, which was bare, and a file cabinet in the corner. The only photograph on the wall was a single, framed picture of Kitty, which I observed with detachment.

When I saw her last, as a child in my parents' house, I was sitting with my sister on the landing of the carpeted staircase, where we sat to observe our parents' parties. Oppenheimer and Kitty came late. They'd only recently moved. She was beautiful, in her gleaming mink coat and her pearl necklace, and he was still the celebrity scientist he remained for several years after the war.

As the party progressed, however, it was clear that she'd had too much to drink. I watched her carefully from the stairwell. By then, I'd learned to immediately locate any potential sources of conflict. So I saw that, no matter where she stood in my parents' living room, she was always watching her husband, and she was often alone, while he was generally surrounded by women.

He had a way of listening to them very intently, leaning

forward with his silver cigarette lighter whenever they needed a light. He was courteous and attentive, and from wherever Kitty stood in that party, she watched him with her ravenous little face, occasionally touching the pearls at her throat.

At some point, as he occasionally did when he'd been drinking, our father called our mother to play the piano. Then she sat, and played with her head down, her dark hair drawn up so the vulnerable back of her neck was revealed.

Kitty stood alone in the corner, sucking down the last of her drink. She was swaying lightly in her black pumps. Throughout the whole piece, she watched her husband, and in the silence that opened when the music had stopped, she suddenly lurched forward and said, "Robert, I love you."

Everyone froze. On the landing, I reached for my sister's hand. In her forward lurch, Kitty had wanted to reach him, but her heel caught on the carpet, so instead of finding his arm, she fell into one of the women who'd gathered around him.

And even so, she didn't take her eyes off her husband. Getting set straight by that woman, she was still looking up at her husband, and finally he turned his attention to her.

For a moment, he watched her struggle in that woman's arms with the same courteous intensity he'd formerly turned on the women who gathered around him.

A moment passed before he himself took her.

Then, patiently, he gathered her up from that other woman, offered his general regrets, helped her into her coat, and guided her gently out of the party.

AND THERE SHE WAS AGAIN, WHEN I CAME BACK TO PRINCETON IN December of 1966: the only photograph on a blank wall.

In the picture, she was riding a horse, heading off toward a jump. Her body was lifted slightly out of the saddle and leaning in toward the upcoming fence. She was wearing jodhpurs and boots, and her riding hat covered most of her face.

For some reason, I was glad for her that this was the only image he'd kept: not her falling forward, her heel caught on the carpet, but her riding off, away from us all, most of her expression kept secret.

OPPENHEIMER STILL HADN'T NOTICED MY PRESENCE. HE FACED THE frozen pond and the stripped trees that huddled unhappily around its circumference, and from behind, his neck looked very frail. The collar of his shirt circled it loosely. His hair was a white mist over his skull, and his hand, resting on his knee, was a collection of bones, numbered and arranged on the dark wool of his trousers.

I wondered, then, why he'd invited me to come on a Sunday, when the building was otherwise empty. When there would be no witnesses if I made an interrogation room of that office.

I looked at him more closely. He was dying; that much I could see. I knew that he deserved mercy, but when he finally noticed me and invited me in, I crossed the threshold with brutality in my heart, and as he watched me pull out my tape recorder and unravel its cords, his eyes—gray and intent under those disheveled white eyebrows—reminded me of a dog's eyes.

They also reminded me of my husband's.

ONCE WE STARTED TALKING, IT TOOK LITTLE TO PROMPT HIM TO continue. One question led to many answers. Often he returned to the subject of physics. He stressed what that new science had meant to him as a young man: the great shift in his mind-set that it had produced, to understand that any given entity can only be defined as a function of its observer. To come to the realization that the very aim of understanding an individual unit might be inherently impossible.

It had alleviated, he told me, his loneliness. It had caused him to understand that he could only ever know himself as part of a system.

As a young man, he was saying, he'd immediately understood the new physics to be less in line with Western religion than it was with philosophies from the East, in which the immeasurable was regarded as the primary reality.

In Sanskrit, he said, the root for the verb *to measure* was the same as the root for *illusion*. The truth of this relation, he said, had been demonstrated by quantum theory. To measure any aspect of the world, he said, was to pull an individual unit apart from the whole flow of a system, a flow of which that individual unit was an integral part, and which defined that individual unit as integrally as its own characteristics.

Explaining this, he spoke very quietly, but he continued to engage me with his gray, doglike eyes, keeping them fixed on my face, so that I couldn't help but acknowledge them. Even if I looked away, I eventually felt compelled to return my gaze to meet his.

My husband's eyes were the same. They were just as insistent, although his, unlike Oppenheimer's, were brown. But at that time of my life, even when I wasn't with him, they were always perfectly clear in my mind, so that my thoughts returned to them often, in the grocery store, or while driving, or while interviewing Oppenheimer in his new office.

Sitting opposite Oppenheimer, I thought of the adage everyone knows, about how the eyes are the windows to a person's soul. I wasn't sure that expression was right. Of all the people I'd tried to know in my life, I knew my husband least, and he was the one whose eyes I'd most determinedly studied.

It was a painful thought, which occurred to me while Oppenheimer was talking about the impossibility of knowing everything about any particle in isolation, and in order to distract myself, I glanced up again at that picture of Kitty.

Then I remembered a photograph I'd seen as a child, of several Japanese women searching the rubble in the days after the bomb was dropped on Hiroshima. Their faces had been bandaged, to keep the skin from falling away, and their eyes were gaps in the fabric.

It was frightening to me when I first saw that photograph: those gaps they had for eyes. I found it unacceptable not to be able to read their expressions, to know what they might be thinking, or feeling, wandering through the ruin of their former city.

Up until that explosion, they'd lived in apartments and houses, with plants they'd watered, books they'd read, windows they'd stood beside and looked out from onto the treetops. But when that bomb was dropped, the city wasn't only partially damaged. The entire reality of the place was destroyed in the course of a day, first by the explosion, then by the firestorm that raged through the city, and, as a child, having never experienced such total destruction, I had no way of knowing what those women with no eyes could have been thinking while they searched through what remained of the rubble.

And now Oppenheimer was sitting in his bare office, compelling me to notice his eyes, which, like my husband's, seemed to tell a whole story, but perhaps did just the reverse.

Because what, I thought, did I really know about Oppenheimer, who made those bombs in secret though he believed in transparency and had been a pacifist at one point? And what, for that matter, did I know about my husband?

And meanwhile, across from me, Oppenheimer hadn't stopped speaking. He was talking about how, for all intents and purposes, an individual unit only exists at the moment it collides with and absorbs some other unit. It only exists, he was saying, when it's becoming something new.

His words issued from him as smoothly as breath, as if to survive he had to keep talking, as a fish can only breathe when it's swimming. He was only safe, I thought, as long as he was still uttering words.

Then I interrupted him. Why, I asked, had he felt compelled to lie about going back to visit Jean Tatlock?

In an instant, his expression became wary. Behind his paused face, he crouched very still, waiting for the blow of my next question.

And why, I said, warming to the brutality of my approach, did you also lie about informing on Bernard Peters?

How many lies did you tell, I asked, while you were advocating transparency about nuclear secrets?

By then he'd turned away from me.

He was looking out the window again, and it was a long

time before he turned back. It seemed to me then that the sun dropped while I waited. It seemed that we both grew several years older.

Outside the window, the trees had changed in the waning light. Their bare branches were no longer gray. Now they were burnished and almost soft, as if covered by a rust-colored velvet. As the light drained from the sky, the reddish hue of their branches intensified to the point that when Oppenheimer finally decided to speak, they almost seemed to be burning.

"To tell the whole story," he said, fixing me with those eyes that reminded me so much of my husband's, "you'd have to go back to the beginning."

"Go, then," I said.

"But of course," he said, "you can't ever go back to the very beginning. And how, then, do you ever tell the whole story?"

WHEN I FIRST INTERVIEWED MY HUSBAND, OR THE STRANGER HE WAS to me at that point, I had no intention of getting involved. I was twenty-eight, which at that time was old for a woman not to be married. But then I'd already been divorced. It seemed to me that the choice was between marriage and work. I'd chosen work, which, for me, was choosing survival. And I'd never regretted that choice. By the time of that first interview with my husband, I was rising rapidly in the ranks of the magazine where I was a staff writer.

When I met my husband, therefore, I had no intention of risking my position. I only wanted to complete the profile I'd been assigned.

That, however, proved to be an unusually challenging task. From the beginning, I felt that the personality my subject had constructed—and was trying to force me to describe in my profile—was obviously false.

It struck me as silly. It seemed to be a childish costume, some Davy Crockett routine he'd carried over into adulthood.

I'm not sure I need to go into detail. I don't want to depict him as absurd. But by way of example, though it was 1963 and he was born in Manhattan—and, with the exception of a brief stint at Oak Ridge, had lived in the city for most of his life—he wore cowboy boots and a big belt with an enormous, engraved silver buckle. The sculptures that had brought him renown were reminiscent of American Indian totems, and his apartment was full of bear heads and flint weapons.

Now that's enough. I don't want to mock him. I only mean to suggest that my husband—or the stranger he was to me at the time—seemed to have employed more contrivance than most in his manner of self-presentation, and I felt that it should be my task as a writer to work my way past the imposture and understand him in a subtler fashion.

He, however, was skilled at avoiding my strategies for eliciting authentic responses. If he couldn't answer a query with one of his practiced anecdotes about living in the Tennessee wilds, he was capable of simply not hearing the question.

Alternatively, he'd simply go blank. He'd look off into the distance, blinking blindly and scratching the side of his nose with one finger.

Other times, after I asked a question he wasn't expecting, he'd tilt his head at me and smile, as if I'd said something endearing and he'd been distracted by the desire to lean forward and kiss me.

IN MY DESIRE TO AVOID THAT POSSIBILITY, I HAD TO BE STRATEGIC about meeting him in public places, where I'd have an easy excuse for not wanting to kiss him. But his own strategies conflicted with mine, and we often engaged in complicated negotiations over the locations of our interviews.

He'd suggest his apartment in the Village, and I'd suggest a restaurant down the street from my office in midtown. Then he'd counter with the bar underneath his apartment, a place with sawdust on the floor and big barrels of peanuts.

When we met there, and drank pints of beer in a banquette toward the back, he often grabbed for my hand on the table.

SOMETIMES, IF I CLOSE MY EYES, I CAN STILL SMELL THE SAWDUST, WET with spilled beer. I can taste the salt of the peanuts on my dry lips.

I know that I'm not, but when I remember that taste, it almost seems as if I'm still the same woman who sat there with him and tried to remove my hand from his grasp, without allowing him to suspect how much I disliked him.

Over time, as you can imagine, these complicated strategies for avoiding his advances became somewhat draining, and meanwhile none of my questions seemed to scratch the surface of his outsized personality.

Our interviews were frustrating. I felt I was failing. Afterward, on warm evenings, I'd walk home to my own apartment on the other side of Washington Square Park, watching, as

I often did in those days, the lights coming on in people's apartments. And though that experience usually brought me a reliable pleasure, a kind of warmth at a remove, on such evenings I walked with the nagging sensation that I still knew nothing about him.

I wasn't even sure where he'd grown up. Though he'd lived most of his life in Manhattan, there were several years in his childhood that he didn't ever account for, and I didn't know if they'd been spent in some western state.

I didn't know, in other words, whether his western routine was a souvenir of those lost years in his youth, or whether, spontaneously, as an adult, he'd started to affect that routine precisely because it had nothing to do with a youth he hoped to forget.

Though I suspected this was the case, I had no real way of knowing if he'd chosen his western persona for no better reason than that it made him feel like an adult out of an American myth, like an adult who was never a child, but instead emerged fully formed from a god's skull, carrying a quiver of Indian arrows.

FOR SOME TIME, USING MY USUAL TACTICS, I TRIED TO KNOW HIM. And when I found those tactics thwarted, I resorted to others.

During one of our meetings, for instance, I began to tell him stories from my own life in the attempt to make him comfortable with telling his own.

At first, I was clumsy in my approach. I had little practice in such self-revelations. Afterward, as a result, I often walked home through the park regretting the ways that I'd stumbled, by telling the anecdotes poorly, or misrepresenting the truth in an effort to make him feel that I understood or might understand him.

I told him, for instance, about a joke my father kept up throughout my childhood in Princeton. Because we all knew my mother hated the sound of knives being sharpened on flint, he always took care to sharpen the kitchen set near where she sat at the table. Grinning, goading her to a reaction, he'd swipe the blades closer and closer to the crescent of her cheek until he was so close we feared he'd slice her ear off.

When I told that story, in the back of that bar, I focused on my mother's reaction. Staying true to her role in the joke, she never stood up. She never moved. Despite the fact that she knew her two daughters were watching, she stayed still as a statue, pretending to ignore him while he honed closer and closer.

But later, after I'd told the story, when I was walking home under the fringed canopies of the locusts, past the lights in people's ground-level kitchens, I'd realize that, in focusing on my mother's reaction, I'd neglected the expression on my father's face, which always started exuberantly amused, and then began to shift, changing farther and farther away from itself the longer my mother remained at the table.

It was as though he, also, hated the joke. As though only her impenetrable stillness had forced him to continue, as though he was now the only active partner in the exchange. Grimly, forced to push the joke through to the punch line, he did so, but despised her the whole time for having coerced him to finish.

Instead of taking any pleasure in what had at first delighted him, he always finished that joke with a baffled expression. Just short of her ear, he'd simply stop and return to the kitchen, and maybe it was he who was more hurt and belittled than she was, bound in the position of finishing a joke he knew was a failure, a failure he might have been saved from if she'd simply stood up from the table and left him.

IF I TOLD SUCH STORIES IN AN ATTEMPT TO MAKE MY HUSBAND FEEL more at ease, and therefore more capable of making his own revelations, the strategy was a failure.

He only listened with that expression of deepening sympathy and attention that I recognized in Oppenheimer's eyes when I sat down in his office.

And noticing the way that my husband—or the stranger he was then—was listening, I was sometimes overtaken with the realization that my childhood had in fact been quite sad.

That realization, hitting me by surprise, made me occasionally worry I might cry at that booth, in that bar that smelled like wet sawdust. And after completing such interviews with my husband, walking home through the park, I'd realize that, absorbed as I'd been in self-pity, I'd failed once again to find a doorway into my subject.

PERHAPS IT WAS THE FEELING OF EMBARRASSMENT AT MY SELF- absorption, or embarrassment at my ongoing failure, that caused me to give up my parrying efforts and finally allow my subject to kiss me.

From there, the involvement escalated rapidly. By the end of the month, I rarely went home to my own apartment. I spent most of my nights sleeping beside him in his, so that in almost no time at all, my discomfort with him had started to ebb, replaced with the thrill of practicing a new kind of knowledge.

Then, finally, I felt that I was coming to know him. Slowly, and without any sense that his story was taking any one final shape, I felt I was coming to an understanding of him that was far superior to the way I'd known my previous subjects: by attending to the facts of their lives, and organizing their plots in chronological sequence.

With my former subjects, I realized, I had been tyrannical. I had arranged their stories according to my own desire for a neatly developing plot.

With my husband, however, the process was different. I stood before him and allowed him to arrange me, and the glimpses of him that I received as a result were—or so I believed at the time—less forced, more authentic.

I allowed him, in other words, to remain a mystery. I allowed him to be incomprehensibly different from me. And in doing so, I felt I was coming to know him in the way you might know the center of a lake when you approach its farthest reaches at night: when you hear the sound of its edges lapping the shore but haven't yet touched the skin of the water and don't allow yourself to wade in yet.

In other words, I was careful. I didn't intrude. I let him into me instead, and afterward, if I couldn't sleep, I'd sometimes get out of bed and move through his apartment, observing his records, or the liquor he stored in the cabinet, or the rock collection he kept on a bookshelf.

I noted his fingerprints on the mirror in the bathroom, and the warped ring from his glass on a magazine he left accidentally open.

THIS NEW KIND OF KNOWLEDGE FASCINATED ME MORE THAN ANY
other kind I'd acquired. During the day, when I was at work,
or on the rare nights I spent in my own apartment, I began
to experience the sensation of waiting to get back to the main
project.

I lived my life, therefore, with a new feeling of anticipation, a feeling that built throughout the day, and became as
distracting as something like hunger, so that when I walked
into my husband's apartment, I reached for him immediately.

From that point on, rather than listening to his somewhat
ridiculous stories in that bar with the wet sawdust, I listened
to him in the darkness of his bedroom after we'd slept together, while I was lying beside him, my body changed by the
way that he'd touched me.

Outside, on the streets, the wails of sirens rose and fell,
and red taillights passed their light over the back side of the
curtains. People laughed on their way home from the bar.
And inside, in the darkness, his fingertips ran the pearled
length of my backbone, and my lips brushed his skin when I
asked him my questions.

WE SEEMED TO BE DEPARTING THE CITY OUTSIDE. SOMETIMES, IN THE
luxurious darkness of that apartment, set farther and farther
away from the noises that filtered up from the street, I felt as
if I'd followed him into the wood at the edge of the village.

Then I stopped asking questions. I simply followed, waiting to come to what he wanted to show me.

THEN THERE WAS LESS NEED FOR ACTUAL WORDS. SOMETIMES, IN
fact, when my husband spoke, I stopped listening to what

he was saying. I only heard the rising and falling notes of his voice, or watched his mouth move, or touched his teeth with the tips of my fingers.

Or I'd close my eyes and wait for his hand on my back, a touch that was startlingly light when contrasted with the blunt personality he'd cultivated in public.

And it was that contrast, more than anything else, that allowed me to believe I'd finally stepped past the contrivance of his persona, and that in the privacy of the wood I'd followed him into, I was finally coming to know him.

IT MUST HAVE BEEN A STRANGE WOOD WE'D WANDERED INTO, BE-cause when I learned I was pregnant, I wasn't afraid.

It was as if I'd stepped into the body of some other woman, a woman without my anxieties about work and surviving and losing my right to a separate existence. Though the idea of becoming a mother had always frightened me, and was, in fact, one of the reasons for my early divorce, when I learned I was pregnant, I felt strangely serene. And when I told my husband, he was delighted. He started building a crib that afternoon. By evening, the floor of his studio was covered in sweet curls of wood.

That night, in bed, we laughed about the names we'd give our daughter, or the names we'd give to our son. So we forged deeper into the forest. He led the way, and I let myself follow, both of us children in the fairy tale he was telling, a fairy tale that only made sense in that forest.

The fast pace of the story, its strange devotions, the sweet curls of wood and the distant, meaningless sounds filtering up from the street: all of that would have alarmed me if I was still living in the old city, where I was a journalist who arranged the facts of people's lives in meaningful order.

But in my new life, I allowed the story he was telling to move me. We were married only three months after we started sleeping together, and it was just the two of us there, alone at the courthouse, him in his boots and his absurd silver belt, me in a bright yellow shift dress we'd bought on a whim when we passed it in a window the previous evening.

I'd tried it on in the dressing room while he watched. He approved, and I wore it the next day at our wedding, and several weeks after that, he accepted a job in the Fine Arts Department at the University of Texas, a decision that surprised me, because he'd told me he didn't like teaching.

But he'd enjoyed his visit there. And he liked the idea of moving to Texas, and raising a child in a house with a yard and trees for the child to climb in.

Once he'd proposed the idea, I found I liked it as well. I'd be able to write there, I thought, better than I could in the din of a city.

And in a new place, where we lived alone, we could be closer. We could raise our child together.

THAT SPRING, WHILE WE WAITED TO MOVE, I FELT MYSELF SINKING into an interesting new kind of aloneness. I drifted farther away from my friends and colleagues.

I began to cancel the dinners I'd formerly scheduled, and I avoided the work events I'd always attended, and the meetings for causes I'd once been involved in.

I even read the newspaper less. I began disengaging from the external world, and once I'd started cutting those ties, it seemed to me I could finally focus on what was really important.

My eyesight seemed to be improving. When I looked out the window of his apartment that March, I saw the dusting of chartreuse on the gray branches, and then the little forked tongues of the new leaves on the maple trees lining his street. In April, the cherry trees were in bloom, and after a windy afternoon, the gutters ran pink with their petals. By the end of the month, the maple leaves had grown so they were no longer chartreuse but silvery green, rising up from their stems like partially opened umbrellas.

When my husband went out for drinks with his friends, I waited for him to come home, sitting in the quiet of his apartment. I sat still, not daring to move, my vision sharpened so I saw each shadow on the underside of each bobbing leaf, each serrated edge, and all night I could think or feel nothing but warm anticipation in the pit of my stomach that began to spread out through my body when I heard the tread of his feet ascending the staircase.

WE MOVED TO TEXAS THAT SUMMER, AND IT WAS TRUE THAT IN THE quiet of our new home, I was more able to focus on my husband's nature.

I didn't have any friends or colleagues to distract me. When we first arrived, a group of wives in the Fine Arts Department invited me out to have lunch, but that was my last invitation.

Maybe, as some people do, they found me somewhat distant or cold. Perhaps they hadn't realized in advance that I would appear foreign, a fact that surprised me as well.

In New York, I often forgot I was the daughter of an immigrant, my mother having come to America from Japan several years before the war to perform a series of concerts, and having stayed when she met and married my father.

On the East Coast, I often forgot that my face was marked by her features. In Austin, however, I felt a certain strangeness about me. It's possible that it was only because I was from the East Coast. Or perhaps it was because of my mother, though she only ever spoke English with us, and never told us any details about the family she'd left in Japan.

In Austin, though I didn't share my mother's tongue, I also didn't feel fully native, as my father—who came from an old Southern family, so that he always seemed to feel entirely at home in the pillared white house where he raised us— would have felt in a new American city.

Sometimes, in Austin, I felt I'd come to exist somewhere unclaimed between my two parents. My mother had died when I was in college. My father hadn't approved of my divorce, so by the time I went to Austin, we rarely spoke.

A distance, in other words, was widening between myself as I had been on the East Coast—the daughter of my two parents—and myself as I was in Austin. Relocated, I sometimes had the vague sense that I'd lost all guarantees of my existence, and I wondered if my mother had felt the same way, though clearly she would have felt it much more intensely, when, during the war, her Japanese passport was declared no longer valid.

At that point, though she was already married, her American passport hadn't come through yet, so for a short window of time, which happened to be the precise window when

Japanese citizens on the West Coast were being removed to those camps, there was no place where my mother could claim the rights of citizenship, no place for her to return in the event of a disaster.

There were no available authorities, in other words, for her to appeal to. And I often considered that unsheltered state when I was first living in Austin. In Austin, as the weeks of my pregnancy passed, instead of feeling heavier, I sometimes felt as if I were floating.

I had always been quiet, but I grew even more so, which probably contributed to people's assumption that I was either foreign or snobbish. More and more, I kept to myself, when I wasn't spending time with my husband.

THE ISOLATION DIDN'T PERTURB ME. I LIKED OUR NEW HOUSE. THE front yard was surrounded by a high fence, and we had a porch that faced the back alley, shaded by the leaves of an overgrown loquat.

Sitting in the porch swing, swatting mosquitoes, I read or worked on various projects. Though I'd agreed with my editor that he should send me assignments in Texas, I began to find such assignments annoying.

If they required me to fly to other places, I found reasons for turning them down. And sometime that summer, I realized with a flicker of concern that I found writing less pleasurable than I once had. Or perhaps I should say that the thrill I had once felt in understanding the lives of my subjects now seemed childish when compared to the pleasure with which I studied my husband.

The way I'd written before seemed to me very similar to a

girl playing with dolls, pushing people around and asserting her will over their lives, temporarily escaping her own life in order to insert herself into somebody else's.

The work I did now with my husband—trying to remain very still while he came toward me and touched me—felt like something else entirely. Trying to keep my beating heart calm, I watched him when he came in from the car. I watched the way he started to smile, and, if I stayed very still, in my own throat I felt his desire.

I felt how it built as he climbed the back steps, then took my face in his hand, then cut off my breath when he kissed me.

IN AUSTIN, NOW HEAVILY PREGNANT, I TOOK LONG WALKS AROUND our neighborhood, past small houses with wide lawns, along streets that were shaded by pecan trees and the glossy leaves of magnolias. I folded the laundry, or prepared lunch, or headed to the grocery store, and as I did so I developed intricate theories about the personality of my husband.

I examined him closely, and what interested me most of all were the ways in which his sweetness inside our house contrasted with the increasing roughness he advertised when we were in public.

In Texas, as if overnight, his opinions on civil rights and the feminist movement had been touched with obstinate contrarianism, which then began to shade into downright objection. At the same time, he'd begun to carry a hunting knife in his pocket. And at some point, several weeks into our time there, he bought a pistol that he kept in his nightstand.

He did so without telling me, so that one afternoon, by

accident, I opened the drawer and discovered it there, squat and blunt and entirely unexpected.

Instantly, I felt accused. It was as if I'd riffled through his personal papers. As if I'd spied on him, or done something illicit.

Why, I wondered, had I gone through his drawer in the first place? There hadn't been a good reason. I'd simply opened it out of some overly curious impulse, and found not what I was expecting or feared that I'd find, but that pistol, with its efficient body and the round O of its muzzle, squatting angrily in the drawer beside the bed that we slept in.

IT ALARMED ME, OF COURSE, BUT IN THE END I DIDN'T MENTION IT. Maybe I imagined that to ask him directly would have been cheating: a shortcut to the knowledge I was slowly collecting.

To ask a question like that would have delivered a blow to the delicate line of research I was following deeper into my husband, navigating the widening space between his interior sweetness and the roughness he demonstrated in public.

With a devotional attention to detail, after I heard him, for instance, express more and more brutal opinions to our friends and neighbors, or when I discovered that pistol, I remembered again the sweetness in his smile when he bounded up the back steps, returning to the secret place we'd created.

In our bedroom, after we'd slept together, he stroked my hair back from my face. He kissed each one of the freckles over my nose. With wonder, he touched the expanding curve of my stomach, and he laughed like a boy at the stories I told him.

I weighed such evidence against the fact of that squat

little pistol, or the way he'd taken to wearing his knife so that other people could see it. And while it's true that I found those developments disconcerting, I also hypothesized that a man of genuine brutality would have no motivation to advertise it in such an overt and obvious fashion.

A man of real brutality, I thought, would do what he could to conceal it.

PERHAPS THE FACT THAT I WAS PREGNANT INCREASED MY DESIRE TO believe in the fidelity of the sketch I'd drawn of my husband's sweet nature.

It was to him that I turned, after all, in those somewhat uneasy days, while in the isolation of our new home my body changed and a new person grew slowly inside me.

When he was with me in the house, I often touched him for reassurance. At night, even when I lay on my side, facing the wall, I fell asleep with one arm flung backward to reach him.

And if he was away—because almost immediately, as I should have predicted, he remembered he didn't like teaching, and began to fly to New York and Chicago to take meetings for new public commissions—I lay awake in the dark, and turned for reassurance to the story I was telling about him, the portrait I was so carefully painting.

I retouched the lines. I added shades of new color. I treasured it, treating it gently, though sometimes, it's true, my husband provided evidence that his nature was more complicated than I was allowing myself to imagine. Once, for instance, we had dinner with our neighbor—a young, widowed woman with a four-year-old daughter, who sometimes shyly came over for coffee—and the man she'd begun dating, a somewhat pompous little English professor.

She was the only woman in Austin with whom I'd managed to build something resembling a friendship, and my husband liked the man she was dating, or liked him enough, at least, to want to impress him. And maybe my husband had too much to drink, because over the spaghetti and meatballs my new friend had cooked, he made several brash comments about other women he'd slept with.

He made those comments in a light, joking voice, and while he did so, he slung his arm around my neck and pulled me in toward him, laughing over my head with the English professor.

Pulled in, I felt my face getting hot. I avoided making eye contact with my new friend. It was an embarrassing moment, but then it passed, and I managed to forget it completely until another dinner with the same friends.

This time, we were out at a Mexican restaurant. I found myself absorbed by a print on the wall, one of those paintings you see on the walls of old Spanish missions, depicting a train of those mournful, one-dimensional American Indian women, following Christ toward his crucifixion.

Their faces were flat, as were their hands, which were held up in the air, forming incomprehensible signs signaling the approach of an awful disaster.

There was something disturbing to me in that painting, so that while I examined it, the story my husband was telling faded somewhat into the background. I was surprised, then, when I felt him grab the back of my neck and shake me until I managed to look up in confusion.

It was nothing extreme, but it startled me. Again, it caused me to feel somewhat embarrassed in the eyes of our new friends. Not terribly so, but enough that I began to avoid them, and the woman and I met less often for coffee.

ON MOST OTHER OCCASIONS, MY HUSBAND PROVIDED A GREAT DEAL of evidence of his sweet nature, so it was easy for me to feel that I was succeeding in the portrait I'd started painting. When he came home from his trips to New York or Chicago, he often got in late at night. He came to bed while I was sleeping. Then he woke me sweetly, his fingertips brushing my cheek, and when we slept together he was always almost unbearably gentle, almost apologetically tender, though I came at him with increasing roughness, having missed him as I did in his absence.

In such moments, looking at me with that expression of almost painful sympathy—an expression of sympathy so intense it almost resembled repentance felt in advance for a crime not yet committed, or for a crime I hadn't yet apprehended—he kindly assisted me in the portrait I'd undertaken of his secret nature.

That September, we often sat on the back porch under the thick, glossy leaves of the loquat, eating fruit he pulled from the branches. He held my hand in his own. He kissed my temple. In our bed, he touched me gently, and afterward I fell asleep with my arm flung backward to reach him.

AS WE APPROACHED OUR CHILD'S DUE DATE, THE LENGTH OF MY HUS-band's trips to New York and Chicago began to grow longer. He wanted to finish lining up work before the child was born, and it was then, in the last several weeks leading up to the due date, after months of an oddly placid pregnancy, that I began to worry about the grave responsibilities involved with caring for a new child.

I worried about whether or not the child would be born healthy. I worried about whether something I'd done during the pregnancy had harmed him in some way, and whether I could care for him if he was terribly sick.

It helped, then, to consider my husband. The puzzle of my husband's nature soothed me in such moments. It seemed to me to be a puzzle that it was possible to complete, or at least a puzzle approaching completion.

Some nights, from New York or Chicago, he called me sounding exuberant and excited, and I laughed at the stories he told of meetings with gallery owners and interested buyers.

Other nights, however, he sounded tired and somewhat removed, as if speaking through a cloth that muffled the receiver.

Other nights still, he didn't call me at all. Then he'd call early in the morning, sometimes waking me up, apologizing profusely and providing the reasons why it hadn't been possible for him to call the previous evening, though it hadn't occurred to me to ask for a reason, and when I picked up I hadn't been angry.

THERE WERE SIGNS, IN OTHER WORDS, THAT THE PUZZLE I WAS WORK-ing on was far from complete. And yet I persisted in ignoring those signs, and took comfort in the exercise, imagining I was making slow but ineluctable progress, so when he called me from Chicago sometime in early October, sounding shaken, and saying in a weird tone of voice that he wanted to come home the next morning, that he missed me and didn't feel like himself and couldn't stay away any longer, I accepted his rushed return with a kind of placid, presumptuous pride, and felt a shock that embarrasses me still when, several days later, I picked up the phone and listened while a woman from Chicago related to me the story of her relationship with my husband.

ONCE SHE FINISHED OUTLINING THE STORY, SHE APOLOGIZED FOR disturbing me.

Her voice sounded odd, as if it were slipping over a smooth, icy surface, attempting and failing to find any traction. It had obviously been difficult for her to tell me the details. She said she'd thought very hard about whether to call me, and for a while she'd tried to convince herself that it wasn't her business, but in the end she felt I should know.

If she'd had any idea, she said, that he had a wife, or that his wife was pregnant, she'd never have gotten involved with him.

But he hadn't told her. And when he did, she'd ended the relationship.

STANDING IN THE KITCHEN, HOLDING THE RECEIVER, MY FACE FELT very cold. It seems to me now that I must have encouraged her to keep talking, because why else would she have done so. But I don't remember actually offering encouragement, and it's hard for me to believe that I could have spoken clearly during that phone call.

Nevertheless, with or without my encouragement, she told

me that she was staying in a hotel downtown. She'd flown to Austin, she said, because she felt it was her responsibility to tell me in person. But once she'd arrived, she'd realized I might not want to see her, and she didn't want to upset me.

She knew I was pregnant. So she'd decided to call. And if I didn't want her to keep talking she wouldn't.

THAT'S HOW IT WENT. SHE WAS VERY POLITE.

It might have been simpler, I think, if she'd been rude or aggressive. If there had been any way for me to channel my anger at my husband toward this woman I didn't know, a woman who had no real role in my life, I would have happily done it.

But she was so polite on the phone, and so thoughtful. And really, his behavior had given her no choice in the matter of whether or not to intervene in my life, because by the time she learned about my existence and the existence of our still-unborn child, she had already intruded.

Because of my husband's behavior, in other words, the two of us were already connected. We were already related, whether we wanted to be or not.

And she, too, had been betrayed by my husband. He'd lied to her about having a wife. So by the time she was sitting in a hotel room in Austin, telling me on the phone about how their relationship had developed so quickly and so intensely over the course of the last seven weeks, she was already crying.

It upset her to recall, from this new position, the hopeful moments of their relationship. She'd been so hopeless, she said, since her brother died in Vietnam, but then she met him, and she told me about how she thought they'd get married.

They'd already talked about children. They'd made jokes

266

about the old age they'd spend together. And even outside explicit conversations about a more solid future, a future that was crystallizing before her very eyes, she'd been given hope simply by the fact of his presence. By the hours she spent lying with him in her bed, imagining she'd found a way to be happy, and never suspecting that such hours would be recast so drastically when she discovered that he was already married.

Now, she told me, she could no longer remember those moments as happy. She understood that those happy moments had been invented. Though they had actually happened, her recollection of them had been rendered unreliable by her new understanding that those moments weren't the early expressions of a still-simple love, but a complicated betrayal that she'd been dragged into.

And now, too late to go back and fix it, she realized she'd participated in the act of turning my happiness into a fiction, just as my existence in Austin had turned her happiness into a fiction, and not even a good fiction, but an embarrassing and tasteless cliché.

STANDING THERE IN THE KITCHEN, I REALIZED THAT HER VOICE BE-came more confident as she described these realizations.

She tracked the switchbacks of her thought with that sickening attention to detail that a novelist might provide in a book, detail we rarely note while we're living real moments and tend to only add later, when we're belatedly telling the story, when the actual events have passed by and we're left trying to piece them faithfully back together.

It's then, when we're left with nothing more than the shadows of events that have already dematerialized, that we're compelled to add layers of detail, as if we might give substance to shadows, converting them into the status of objects.

Then I felt my stomach turning to ice. That phone call, that woman, that relationship in Chicago: those weren't the dangers I'd prepared myself to expect.

OBVIOUSLY I SHOULD HAVE SEEN IT. I KNOW THAT'S WHAT PEOPLE think. I myself have thought it so often. We imagine people should have foreseen such events when they happen. We judge them for having been blind to the foreshadowing. It comforts us to think that, in their place, we wouldn't have been so naïve. We would have expected the obvious ending.

But it wasn't as if I hadn't considered the potential for danger when I diligently worked at my sketch of my husband. Why work so diligently at such a sketch if you don't suspect that person might someday evade you?

I'd known, in other words, that something was coming. Only the danger I'd been so strenuously leaving out of the portrait wasn't that kind of banal betrayal, some sad woman my husband was lying to in Chicago.

No. I'd been distracted from that possibility by my husband's well-advertised brutality: the pistol he kept in the nightstand, his new reactionary politics, his hand shaking the nape of my neck.

It had been violence I was attempting to cut out of the picture, not this deceit. Not the cultivation of some other life in some other city, into which my husband had occasionally stepped without acknowledging the transition, as if our life in Austin had been temporarily suspended.

As if it had been paused, as you might pause between

chapters of a book, setting it aside, leaving it behind for a while. As though I wasn't fully alive, but existed as a character only as long as he was animating me with his attention, and could be suspended in midsentence as soon as he wasn't.

Or as though I hadn't really existed before he opened the book, and would cease to exist when he shut it.

CALMLY, THOUGH MY STOMACH HAD GONE VERY COLD, I LISTENED while the woman from Chicago finished her story.

She told me in detail about the last conversation she'd had with my husband. He'd told her about my existence and admitted we were expecting a baby. He'd apologized for having deceived her, and went on to say that he hoped they could continue their relationship.

He only asked that she be discreet. He asked her not to tell her friends or anyone else about the relationship they were starting, because if I were to find out, it would hurt me.

THEN, HAVING REACHED THE CULMINATING PAIN OF HER STORY, THE woman started crying again. But even so, she didn't stop talking. After a pause, while she caught her breath, she then almost frantically returned to the beginning of the whole story, going back to relate certain details she'd missed, details she'd clearly saved up over the days since their relationship ended, when she didn't know if she should call me and felt she couldn't talk to her friends or her family, the relationship now having transformed in such a way that she feared they would judge her.

She was reluctant, she said, to bring the pain of her fictional relationship—her fictional pain—to her family, each member of which was still suffering real pain at the real loss of her brother.

As a result, in the days since that conversation, she'd slept doubly alone, set apart not only from the man she'd imagined she was falling in love with, but also from the family she couldn't talk to, and the friends who she believed would no longer understand or trust her side of the story, her perspective having been rendered unreliable by the fact that she'd believed him so completely, up to that moment when he finally told her the truth and she ended the relationship, after which point, when he was alone again in his hotel room, he called me and told me he didn't feel like himself and wanted to come home the next morning to see me.

NOW THE WOMAN WAS CRYING MORE FREELY. IT WAS CLEARLY PAIN-ful for her to talk about those days of isolation.

Then, finally stirring myself to speak, I apologized for the distress she was obviously feeling.

Then I thanked her for letting me know. I told her it wasn't her fault. I took down the name of her hotel, where she said she'd stay for several more days, in case I decided I wanted to see her. Then I thanked her, again, for letting me know.

Oddly, I wished her all the best in her future endeavors.

Then I hung up and went to the bathroom, and vomited until the off-hook tone started ringing.

LATER THAT NIGHT, WHEN MY HUSBAND CAME HOME, IT WAS AL-ready dark. I was sitting on the back porch. Though it was October, it was still very hot, and while I waited, mosquitoes landed on my ankles, inserting their needles into the bare skin between the hem of my jeans and my sneakers.

His car pulled up to the driveway around nine o'clock, and when he came toward the porch, he was still smiling in that sweet, childish way he always smiled on his way up to greet me.

When he'd climbed the steps—still smiling, unaware of what was lying in wait—he sat next to me on the porch swing. He reached for my hand and leaned over to kiss me.

IT WAS HIS CHILDISH HAPPINESS, HIS NAÏVE LACK OF AWARENESS OF what I already knew, that made me feel somewhat ashamed as I started relating the story.

I related it, I noticed, in the same somewhat slippery voice that woman had used when she called me: a voice that wasn't at all steady or strong, a voice that wasn't sure the story it was telling was either believable or convincing.

And suddenly, as I related those details, I did indeed wonder whether they were correct.

I wondered whether, in fact, the woman on the phone had been lying.

That afternoon, when I was listening to her for the first time, I'd believed every word that she said. But now I wondered whether in fact she might have some reason I didn't know for hating my husband, and whether, for that reason, she had therefore plotted an ingenious attack on his most personal life, a vicious attack in which I was now participating, ambushing him in that precise moment—coming up the stairs to his house, sitting beside his pregnant wife—when he'd allowed himself to feel safe.

THAT POSSIBILITY TEMPTED ME TO FEEL HOPE. PERHAPS, I TOLD MY-self, as I related her story in a less and less certain voice, it wasn't my husband but that woman in her hotel room who had lied, and who had so abruptly altered the foundation of the life I was leading.

Then, in order to convince myself of this possibility, I changed the tone I was using.

Now, as I imparted the same details, I punctuated them every so often with an odd breathless laugh: communicating, or attempting to communicate, my growing belief that this was a fantastical story.

And as I related it in this new tone, the story did begin to seem almost silly. How could they have planned to have children together, when our son was due in two weeks? And how could the thing have continued so long without her having any idea he was married?

I felt almost foolish, repeating that part back to him. By then, I was prepared to believe him completely when he told me that this woman had fabricated the story. But as I continued to relate that fantastical tale, I couldn't help but notice that the story was affecting him not as something absurd, but as a blow he felt in the deepest part of his body.

The color had drained from his face. Then his hand became very hot. Then he jerked it away from my hand, as if I'd said something vicious.

AFTER THAT, HE NO LONGER TOUCHED ME. EVER SO SLIGHTLY, HE moved away from me on the porch swing, and I realized that I wasn't telling him a fantastical tale. I was repeating for him, instead, a series of unbearable facts, unbearable not because they struck him as false, but because he hadn't expected to hear them in this context.

Now, hearing the facts of that other case repeated out loud in this context, realizing the two cases had invaded each other, his lips had become visibly dry. His hunting knife peeked out of his pocket, pointless and irrelevant, and when I finished talking, he didn't speak.

There remained between us a sickening silence.

WHEN HE DID FINALLY STIR HIMSELF TO ANSWER, HIS VOICE WAS almost inaudibly low.

"I only saw her once," he said.

He glanced at me quickly, then looked away.

"Twice," he corrected himself. Then: "Three times."

Then he put his face in his hands.

IT WAS THEN, FINALLY, AS IF RELEASED BY THAT GESTURE, THAT THE vague forces of destruction that had hovered around me since I picked up the phone in the kitchen finally gathered their fury and pooled in the belly of those eight words.

"I only saw her once," my husband said. Then, "Twice. Three times."

And with each hapless, belated lunge he made toward the truth, I felt my stomach go cold again, as if at the sudden retreat of a knife.

AFTER THAT, THE WORDS WE EXCHANGED BECAME USELESS AGAIN. That conversation between me and my husband continued well into the morning, and yet, when I look back on it now, it seems that almost nothing was said.

Though he admitted he'd slept with the woman in Chicago on three separate occasions, he was adamant that it had never been a relationship. He said that he hadn't loved her. He said that he'd ended whatever it was that existed between them because it was me that he was in love with.

I asked him why he'd had to end whatever it was that existed between them if it wasn't a relationship in the first place.

He said that, though it wasn't a relationship, he felt he owed her a clear explanation.

Then I asked him why he suddenly felt he owed her a clear explanation. I'm not sure how he answered. Then I asked him again whether in fact he'd really ended the relationship.

Yes, he told me, with the full force of conviction: he'd ended the relationship.

But by then, though I'd have liked to believe him over her, it was impossible for me to dismiss what she'd said. Perhaps it was because I'd heard her story first. Or because my husband had already admitted that he'd lied to me for some time. Regardless, it was impossible for me to fully believe him when he said that he'd ended the relationship, and therefore it was impossible for me to believe anything else that he said throughout that long and entirely useless first conversation.

LATER, WHEN I WENT INTO THE BEDROOM TO SLEEP, AND MY HUSband was outside on the couch, I began to reflect in the darkness.

I reminded myself that, freely and from the start, he'd admitted that he'd slept with her. With my unsure tone of voice and that odd slippery laughter, I'd basically encouraged him to keep me in the dark, but he'd felt compelled to admit that he'd slept with her not only once, but three different times.

I thought that perhaps that admission should give me reason to accept the rest of his story.

But then I reminded myself, lying there in the darkness, that what I wasn't taking into account in this version was the fact that experienced liars often deliver their fabrications in a coating of truth that serves to protect the softer, more vulnerable lies underneath, allowing them to get past your defenses, like the shell around the DNA of a virus, which protects it while it enters your body and begins infecting your cells, so that by the time you realize you've been infected, it's already in you, and you've already been altered by it, and even in some ways become it.

THERE WAS ALSO THE DETAIL OF THE WOMAN'S STORY THAT I HAD TO contend with, while I lay there in the darkness of the bedroom.

Such exquisite detail she'd given: the names they'd planned to give to their children, the jokes he'd made about their old age. She'd repeated exactly what he'd said to her, word for word, how he'd asked her to be "discreet," how he'd said that we were "expecting a baby."

I could imagine him saying those words. That's the power of a story with detail. And my husband's story, by contrast, was vague. The story he told had many holes. There were many points he didn't recall.

He couldn't, for instance, remember precisely how he'd ended things. He couldn't tell me what he'd said exactly.

Her contrastingly impressive level of detail—that clipped word, "discreet," or that strange expression, "expecting a baby," as though we believed a baby was coming but felt that it was possible it might be something else on the way—inclined me to believe her.

But then I remembered, lying there in the dark, trying to calm myself so the baby we were expecting wouldn't be scared by the wild way my heart was behaving, that an impressive level of detail is also a strategy employed by many experienced liars.

Many liars, I reminded myself in the dark, add extraneous detail to the stories they tell, in order to make them resemble the truth.

In fact, we rarely recollect so many detailed impressions of the conversations we have. We so often forget exactly what was said by the people we talk to. Perhaps, then, I said to myself, a certain vagueness and inability to recall all the details is the best guarantee of the truth.

In that way, all night, I continued to balance the two stories I'd been given that day: two incompatible tales that came up against each other, making it impossible for me to believe either one, or to feel any certainty about the new, altered life I'd been given, so that in the end my heart beat even faster, and I couldn't find a way of soothing myself.

I began to worry I'd vomit again. Then I worried that all the adrenaline and the vomiting and the wild beating of my heart would damage the baby within me, which was how I persuaded myself, in the end, to go get my husband up from the couch and to bring him into the bedroom, and let him lie down behind me, and hold me, and temporarily calm me.

SEVERAL DAYS AFTER THAT, OUR SON WAS BORN.

It was a difficult time. Though, as I've said, I'd felt oddly placid through most of the pregnancy, those last days before his birth were not calm.

And after his birth, because he was a difficult baby, or perhaps more accurately an unhappy baby, I feared that my anxiety had affected him badly.

As soon as we'd gotten him home, I was almost immediately overwhelmed by the responsibility of caring for such a small creature, a creature I'd brought into a world that seemed only to shock and alarm him.

He cried all the time. Often, inconsolable, he cried until his throat was hoarse, and still he didn't stop crying.

Though I did my best to soothe him, caressing him, changing his diaper, giving him my nipple to suck, he wouldn't be soothed. He seemed to feel that something was definitively wrong, but what that something was I couldn't place, and therefore couldn't prevent, and the awareness of this constant failure, my inability to protect this creature I'd introduced to the world, caused me to move through my day in a state of steady decay, so that by nighttime my mind was no longer coherent.

In the time between when I put my son down in his crib and when I myself went to sleep, I wandered around the house strangely, picking up items that someone else had at some point misplaced or forgotten.

BETWEEN MY EXHAUSTION AND THE IMMEDIATE REQUIREMENTS OF raising our child, I was distracted for several months, through the winter and the short spring. I only emerged from that state when the weather was hot again and I'd gotten more of a handle on how to put our son to sleep, and how to organize the hours of his day so that he was less often unhappy.

It was June when I woke from the daze I'd slipped into and returned to the work of understanding my husband.

By then, I was still absorbed in our son, but because he and I were so often together, there was less of a requirement for me to puzzle over his nature. Our son revealed himself to me entirely. He wore his emotions openly. There was no way for me to escape them, or for him to escape me.

My husband was different. He traveled less often now— he'd made an effort to spend more time at home—but still, during the week, he spent his days in his studio or in the classroom, and he came home quite late at night, so in his absence I was free to consider him from a distance.

I saw, for instance, that though for our child's sake we had attempted to piece back together the reality of our life, nothing was real. When he told me he loved me, for instance, it was with a heightened gravity that made me feel, again, the original slight. His words were a narrow bridge over the awful knowledge I'd acquired when I picked up that phone call, a thin fiction of security, and all I had to do was look down to see the true depths of the chaos beneath them.

And when he helped me with taking care of our child, he did so with an almost religious expression, smashing pears or changing diapers with a devotional intensity that only caused me to remember how lightly he'd once taken the requirements of his position, how easily he'd set them aside, how coolly he'd closed the book of our lives and charged headlong into another.

FOR MY PART, I WOKE EACH MORNING SICK TO MY STOMACH. I FELT nauseated enough that it was difficult for me to drag my body out of bed, and in fact I began to worry that I'd gotten pregnant again, but it was only a kind of seasickness on land, my own life having begun to feel permanently unstable.

To fix that nauseating liquidity, and to get back to my usual capable self, so that I could better take care of our child, I attempted to reconstruct the solidity of our previous life.

To that end, once summer had arrived, I returned to examining what happened between my husband and that woman who'd called me, but whom I'd never gone to see in her hotel room. It seemed to me that I had to figure out exactly what happened, in order to return to my normal existence.

I had to see it clearly and completely, to know what I was putting behind me.

As a first task, therefore, I worked to weigh out and correctly distribute the blame. This, however, proved to be a trickier business than I'd originally expected. Some mornings, I felt that my husband was entirely to blame, he having chosen to lie in the first place. Other mornings, however, I felt that it was the disproportionate violence of my initial reaction that had caused such an irreparable rift in our marriage.

It seemed to me then that it was the brutality of that first response—confronting him so directly on the back porch; attacking him with my prying questions—that had dissolved the structure of our life together, changing him, and changing me, and altering the life we'd constructed.

I shouldn't, I told myself, have treated that lie as such a disaster. In the scheme of things, I said to myself, what did some careless fling really matter?

I rebuked myself for dramatizing such a small thing, which wasn't, after all, an offense on the same scale as something like murder. He'd only, I told myself, slept in some other bed, beside some other body, and if he lied about it, he only did so to protect me.

THESE WERE THE STRUCTURES OF LOGIC I BUILT, IN THE ATTEMPT TO shore up our life together. And for his part, my husband did what he could to help. He took more responsibility for our child. He woke before me, so that I could sleep later. He walked, holding our baby, up and down the block outside our house, trying to persuade him to cease crying.

At parties, with friends, my husband no longer reached for my neck. He stood beside me, somehow disarmed, and somehow smaller, blinking around the room in confusion.

He had been altered, in other words, but he did what he could to help me reconstruct the old sketch. And I tried to devote myself also. In some ways, I tried more determinedly than before. But the truth is, I no longer had faith that the portrait was coming together. No matter which details I added, no matter which techniques I employed, his face never quite came to life.

This blankness in the portrait I'd drawn of my husband was compounded by the fact that I also couldn't picture the woman he'd loved—or simply slept with—in Chicago.

I knew she had a brother who died, but I didn't know anything else. I'd never gone to her hotel room, so I didn't know what she looked like, and in the absence of recognizable features, she haunted me more than she otherwise might have.

What was she like? I wondered, when I was nursing our son, sitting with the small weight of him in the darkness.

Was she tall, or short? Was her hair dark, like mine, or was it light, and did she have a hard face, or was it soft, and if I saw her would I feel for her and wish I could help her?

THE FACT THAT I KNEW SO LITTLE ABOUT HER BEGAN TO BE GALLING. I realized that she knew far more about me than I knew about her. She'd found, for instance, the phone number of my house. She'd known my name. She must have known, therefore, my address. And perhaps she'd driven by on her way to that hotel, where she waited for several days to see if I'd come.

Perhaps she'd driven down the back alley. Perhaps she'd seen me on the back porch.

The inequity of that situation—that her featurelessness should be so haunting for me, while for her I was a simple collection of facts—struck me as cruel. That basic unfairness began, in fact, to seem like the root of the whole problem, and so with my husband, I began a new system of interrogation, one that moved beyond blame assignation and attempted to pin down the features of his relationship in Chicago.

I felt that once I could imagine the scene, the mystery would no longer haunt me.

Then, I thought, I'd finally put it aside, as you might put down an interesting book, having turned the last page, and having closed the back cover, giving it the brief moment of silence you'd give a good book before returning it to its rightful place on the bookshelf.

TO THAT END, SHYLY AT FIRST, THEN MORE AND MORE BOLDLY, I IN-terrogated my husband. With each new series of questions, I tried to collect all the facts that I'd missed in previous sessions, which, upon reconsideration in the light of the next day, when my husband was at work and I was pacing around with our child over my shoulder, always seemed full of holes, and oddly uninformative: less like the transcripts of interrogations, and more like stories told without endings, more haunting and insistent because they weren't ever finished.

To correct this, I tried to develop better interrogation techniques.

Sometimes, at night, when he'd come home from work and we'd put our son to bed, I asked my husband to repeat the story of his infidelity in Chicago. Then, immediately after he'd finished, I'd ask him to repeat the same story, looking for discrepancies in the second retelling.

I've heard, since then, that this is a technique employed by prison interrogators in totalitarian states. It's the same technique that was used on Oppenheimer in the months and years after that fatal trip to San Francisco, when he was asked by his handlers at Los Alamos, and Lieutenant Pash, who led the San Francisco G-2 office, and General Groves, who was the general in charge of the Manhattan Project, and the prosecutors handling his security hearings, to repeat again the same story of that visit to San Francisco, when he spent the night with Jean Tatlock, or to repeat again the same story of that conversation about espionage with Haakon Chevalier.

That summer, when our son was nearly a year, when I was attempting to put together the full picture of my husband's infidelity, I used that strategy freely.

Sometimes, I kept dinner waiting until he'd told the story again, allowing him to grow hungry. Perhaps I believed that a certain desperation on his part might make him more honest. Or perhaps I believed that a taste of desperation would allow him to understand why I needed him to tell me the whole story over. Regardless, I often kept my husband hungry, and sometimes I kept him awake until the early hours of morning, touching his face to revive him if it seemed as if his eyelids were drooping.

Sometimes I switched the lamp on. And sometimes I kept him with me by asking new, startling questions: what had motivated him to seek this other woman, what had drawn him to her in particular, why hadn't he chosen to tell me, whether or not he regretted that choice.

Under the pressures of these interrogation techniques, my husband tried to stay calm. But often, in response to my prompts, he became confused.

"I don't know," he often said, looking at me with that dog's expression. "I wish I could explain. You might understand it better than I do."

Or he'd give me several contradictory responses. Then, eventually, he'd simply trail off, as if even he understood that the explanation wasn't cohering.

Then, once again, he'd look up at me like an old dog whose owner has taken it into the woods, and is now holding the muzzle of a gun to its temple.

LATER, LOOKING BACK, I WISHED I'D BETTER UNDERSTOOD THAT EX-
pression.

In that moment, when I was busy conducting my interrogations, it only confused me.

It seemed to indicate that he was unable to answer. But
it was he, after all, or so I told myself, who had initiated this
new story in which we were now living. Shouldn't he, therefore, be capable of clarifying the logic by which it functioned?

I expected him to have a method, a strategy planned in
advance, some way of guiding this new, sickening story toward resolution.

So I continued to interrogate, but the more evidence I
compiled, the more holes I discovered in the case I was building. Or perhaps I should say that with each newly acquired
piece of evidence, new questions came up. And by the time
July had bled into August, the case had expanded.

By then, I wasn't only interested in what was true and
what wasn't, or what my husband did and didn't do in Chicago. I was also interested in what he'd been feeling while he
was acting: his intentions, his desires, the degrees of pleasure
and shame he'd experienced concomitant with the crime that
he was committing.

NOW, LOOKING BACK, MY INVESTMENT IN UNDERSTANDING EVERY
aspect of his state of mind seems ill founded.

But, then again, the questions I was asking myself were
the same questions that are asked every day in murder trials,
which don't only involve litigating whether or not a murder
was done, but also whether the murderer was sane when he
did it, whether he imagined the crime in advance, whether,

while performing the crime, he felt pleasure, or whether he was plagued with remorse even as he pulled the knife out of his victim.

It's never enough, for any of us, simply to know that a murder occurred. We always want to know why it was committed.

If we want to condemn the person who committed the murder, we want to know that he's different from us: a person capable of committing a murder.

If we want to forgive him, we want to know that his feelings ran the same gamut as ours, and that he experienced the same horror and remorse we'd have felt in the same situation. We want to know that the action of murdering gave him no pleasure, and that we and the murderer, therefore, both exist on the same acceptable emotional spectrum.

That summer, before our child turned one, I desperately wanted to forgive my husband. How could I build a life with a man I didn't forgive? How could I raise a child alongside him?

I wanted to forgive him, quickly and efficiently, because I felt my son and I could no longer continue in a world made so turbulent by my own confusion. As a result, I believed, I needed to experience what he felt when he went to Chicago. I needed to walk in his shoes, to go with him when he went to visit that woman.

How else, I thought, could I reliably understand, and therefore forgive, what he had chosen to do when he saw her?

But how could I feel, from the impossible distance of Austin a year after the fact, the exact pitch of excitement he felt when he waited behind her, while she unlocked the door to her apartment?

Or whether, rather than feeling excitement, he in fact felt a moment's compunction, a fleeting desire to escape the web he himself had been weaving?

I tried to picture the front door of her apartment. I tried to hear the sound of her self-conscious laughter when she fumbled with the key in the lock.

Standing behind her, did he notice the trouble she had? Did he realize she was nervous? And did it make him feel slightly triumphant, or did he reach out to reassure her? Did he touch her elbow? Did he smile gently?

And, once she did finally succeed in opening the door, when they entered the darkened living room, did he immediately move to undress her, as he often immediately moved to undress me when I walked over the threshold into our house? Or did he give her time to turn on the light before he leaned forward to kiss her?

Closing my eyes, I tried to feel his first kiss. On her cheek, perhaps. Or perhaps on her lips. I tried to feel his hand on the small of her back, moving upward, lifting her sweater. But even then, even if I did feel his hand on her back, the picture remained incomplete, because, from that moment on, there were so many other possible moments, and each of those branched into so many other possible moments, until the options were countless.

Did he guide her immediately to the bedroom, or did they sit for some time, talking, in her living room? And where in her living room did they sit? It was important to me, in those days, to picture that room. Was it a separate room, or did she live in a studio, and was it only a portion of the room set off from the bedroom?

An enclosure, perhaps, with a TV and a couch. A couch, perhaps, where before she met my husband, she spent too many evenings alone, eating dinner by herself after work, wishing for the right man to come join her.

And even if the room could be settled, there were so many other possible choices. Did they drink wine, for instance, or did they drink beer? And did they sit close on the couch, with their knees lightly touching, or, tempting her to move forward, did he leave a small space open between them?

I tried to see what he saw from where he sat on the couch. I tried to feel the touch of her hand on my knee. I tried to feel the wool of her sweater. Perhaps it's insanity that I'm describing. Maybe it's empathy, *Einfühlung,* feeling into a person's muscles and nerves: his skin when her nails traced his bare shoulder, her neck when he leaned forward and kissed it.

Perhaps. But more likely it was insanity. A sane person knows that you never know.

You never know, absolutely, what another person was feeling, just as we never know the velocity and the position of a particle at any one moment, all knowledge being by nature incomplete, all studies missing an aspect at least of the object they study.

And that was the worst part of those months: that it should have become my job in our marriage to picture a scene that I couldn't picture, a scene that only my husband could help me piece back together, but that he found himself incapable of describing, his own mind having become oddly foggy, so that he responded to my questions with the same stunned and incapable blankness, that weird dog's expression, that sometimes made me trust him more and sometimes made me trust him less, but always placed the full burden on me alone—then and later, while filling the gas tank, or mopping the soggy cereal at the foot of the high chair—to reconstruct a scene I was incapable of reconstructing, even as I continued to try, so that no matter how often I thought it over, no matter how often I closed my eyes and tried to feel what he'd been feeling, I couldn't ever know fully whether he'd thought of our son when he lifted that woman's sweater over her head, whether he'd thought of me when he drew her skirt up to her waist, whether he'd only thought of the woman before him, or whether he'd only thought of himself when he pulled her underwear down and pushed himself inside her.

So that was the worst part. Knowing, as I knew, even while I couldn't stop trying, that I had no way of reliably reconstructing the entirety of that moment in Chicago, or any of the other moments leading up to it and in its wake, my uncertainty stretching from that point outward to every other moment my husband spent in cities other than Austin, and equally to every moment in our life together, in the uncertain and therefore unreliable existence we'd built for ourselves and for our child to dwell in.

I REALIZE I'M DRAMATIZING THIS INCIDENT SOMEWHAT. I KNOW I sound hysterical. I've conflated concepts like unkindness and cruelty, violence and deceit.

But murder isn't infidelity. Lying is not the same thing as knifing a person you love in the gut, much less dropping a bomb on a city.

As a writer, particularly, I have always imagined that

detail and precision are important, so this blurring of lines makes me wary. After all, wasn't it my initial mistake to focus too hard on the feint of my husband's brutality—that gun in the drawer, the knife in his pocket—and therefore fail to detect that the real danger was different?

But if I am trying to represent those months precisely, it's important to capture my frame of mind at the time.

During those months, when I was trying to piece back together the reality that we'd lived in, my husband and I were still sleeping together. In fact, the minutes while we were sleeping together were the only minutes of the day in which I could persuade myself that everything had been patched up again, because as soon as he removed himself from my body, I remembered again the feeling I'd experienced when we were sitting on the back porch, when, with each failed attempt he made at telling the truth, it had seemed that a knife had been swiftly drawn from my stomach.

And so each time we slept together felt like a murder, and afterward my murderer lay beside me and kissed me and tried to hold me so the death at least wouldn't hurt. In his arms, I lay in our bed, slowly but inevitably dying, knowing I would continue to do so until he began to run his hand up my back once again, until he cupped my breast in his palm, until he spread my legs with his knee and did that which seemed to be in his power alone to fill the hole that he'd opened.

PERHAPS IT'S INCORRECT TO SAY THAT AN INFIDELITY FEELS LIKE A murder. But some people feel things correctly. Some other people, unfortunately, don't. In early August, for instance, while I was dropping our son at day care, I heard strange popping sounds coming from the direction of campus, and then for nearly an hour I heard the sound of wailing sirens.

When my husband came home that night, he told me there had been a shooting on campus.

The news barely penetrated the fog of my own obsessions. I was feeding our son, he had to be put to sleep, and afterward there was a life to put back together.

But in the morning, I opened the paper and learned that Charles Whitman had killed his mother and his wife, and had then gone to the UT Tower, from which vantage point he had used a rifle and an array of other firearms to kill thirteen people and injure thirty-two others.

It was a terrible, violent story, horrid enough to distract me for a few minutes from my own much smaller but still entirely preoccupying disaster. Then—because, when we're afraid or panicked or lost, as so many of us so often are throughout the course of our lives, it's impossible to sustain for any extended period our sense that strangers, the victims of violence far away, are as real as we are, as frightened as we are, as sensitive to pain or disaster as we feel ourselves to be—I focused on my own life, and dropped my son off at day care, and tried to shake the sound of his crying while I walked back to our house.

When I'd arrived, I sat down on the same swing where I'd confronted my husband, and read about the events leading up to the shooting.

On the afternoon of July 31, Charles and his wife, Kathy, had visited friends. They left early enough in the evening so that Kathy could get to her night shift, and while she was there, Charles wrote a suicide note that read—and I remember this, because later I often took the article out and reread it—"I do not understand what it is that compels me to leave this letter. Perhaps it is to leave some vague reason for the actions I have recently performed. I do not really understand myself these days. I am supposed to be an average reasonable and intelligent young man. However, lately (I cannot recall when it started) I have been a victim of many unusual and irrational thoughts."

Then he drove to his mother's apartment on Guadalupe. After killing her, he left a note by her body: "To Whom It May Concern, I have just taken my mother's life. I am very upset over having done it. I am truly sorry. Let there be no doubt in your mind that I loved this woman with all my heart."

After that, he returned to his home on Jewell Street. His wife had gotten home from her shift, and he killed her by stabbing her three times in the heart. Then he finished his suicide note: "I imagine it appears that I brutally killed both of my loved ones. I was only trying to do a thorough job."

The next morning, he rented a truck. Then he drove to the hardware store, where he purchased a Universal M1 carbine, two ammunition magazines, and eight boxes of ammunition. After that, he drove to Chuck's Gun Shop, where he purchased four further carbine magazines, six additional boxes of ammunition, and a can of gun-cleaning solvent. From there he drove to Sears, where he purchased a twelve-gauge semiautomatic before returning home, where he sawed off his shotgun and packed it in a bag, along with a Remington hunting rifle, a .30-caliber carbine M1, a Luger pistol, a Galesi-Brescia pistol, a Smith & Wesson Magnum revolver, over seven hundred rounds of ammunition, food, coffee, vitamins, Dexedrine, Excedrin, earplugs, jugs of water, matches, lighter fluid, rope, binoculars, a machete, three knives, a transistor radio, toilet paper, a razor, and a bottle of deodorant. Then he headed off to the tower.

THESE WERE THE DETAILS I READ ABOUT IN THE PAPER. WHEN I'D finished reading, I neatly clipped the article and folded it in the drawer where I kept my stockings.

Still, I couldn't stop thinking about it. Though it was difficult for me to comprehend—or to even try to comprehend—the pain of the victims, it seemed essential to me to understand the mind-set of the perpetrator.

Later that day, while I picked up milk at the grocery store, and while I vacuumed the rug, and later while I nursed our child on the green chair by his crib, I found I was incapable of shaking those words from my head: "I do not understand what it is that compels me . . . Perhaps it is to leave some vague reason for the actions I have recently performed."

In my mind, those words repeated themselves, over and over, like some kind of dangerous spell. It occurred to me that, in this case, as in so many others, a basic mental cloudiness had permitted extraordinary violence.

Most often, I said to myself, the worst brutality occurs not as a result of pure evil, if such a thing even exists, but because of a person's frustrating inability to explain his motivations either to himself or to others.

So many of us, I thought, when I was nursing my child, go through our lives making little real effort to understand why we behave as we do, and are therefore forced to act abruptly and with more force, simply to cover up our lack of any good explanation, so that we fly around through the world like so many dull knives, more dangerous to cut with than sharp ones.

That's what I was thinking about, while I nursed our son the night after I clipped that article out. And it was that night, after I sang to him about ash trees and the lost friends of a childhood, after I'd placed him in the crib and lightly rocked the small of his back until it seemed he'd released whatever frustration and fear had kept him crying all day and finally settled into sleep, that I walked back out of the warm darkness of his bedroom, into the light of our living room, and my husband met me and guided me to the couch.

HE SAT BESIDE ME. THEN HE TOOK MY HAND.

For a moment, he couldn't draw his eyes away from my hand, with the result that I, too, stared at it for a moment and realized that it didn't look like my own hand.

Then my husband started to speak. He told me he'd come to understand that his presence in our house was a mistake. He could see it was causing me too much distress, and could only continue to do so, whether I wanted to admit it or not.

You're not happy, he said. You're not yourself anymore.

Then he said, you're not even writing.

I THINK I TRIED TO PROTEST, BUT HE SHOOK HIS HEAD AND PULLED me up short. We were both still staring at that strange hand.

Then he said that he cared for me too much to continue to hurt me. He said it had become absolutely clear to him that no matter how he tried to explain his actions, or apologize for having behaved in the manner he did, his presence in the house could only continue to hurt me.

He had become, he said, nothing more than a visitation of a past pain. He had become a walking reminder of a fatal mistake that couldn't ever be fixed. And anything he did now, any attempts he might make to redefine himself once again, were bound to be failures.

Listen, he said. What I did is in me now. It's a disease that can't be cured, and if I stay here, I'll only infect you.

I'll only infect him, he said, gesturing at our son's room.

The only hope, he said, is to remove myself. You'll be better off in my absence.

I REMAINED THERE BESIDE HIM, STARING AT THAT AWFUL HAND, AND what I wanted to tell him was that he'd already infected me, and that he'd already infected our son.

He'd already irrevocably changed us. The violence of cutting himself out of our lives would only change us more awfully.

But while I was still formulating the words I wanted to use, my husband was already saying that he'd found a house south of town, a small place out in the country.

He planned, he said, to move out that night.

He was still looking down at my hand, which was for some reason swollen, so that when I looked at my fingers I thought they looked like the fingers of a corpse, the fingers on a severed hand my husband had brought home for me to examine.

Luckily, he said, our son was too young to notice the difference. For now, I was the one he really needed, and there would be no requirement for some awful, torturous explanation. That could come later, when the pain of the thing had eased down, and he could at least partially understand it.

I must have protested, because the next thing my husband said was in contradiction: No, he said. It's my fault, I recognize that. Now it's my responsibility to mitigate the damages.

Then I started crying. My husband leaned forward and kissed my forehead. Then he moved as if to kiss my mouth, but, cruelly, I turned my face from the gesture.

Hurt, he pulled himself back. He looked at me with that awful, doglike expression, but suddenly I realized that it wasn't the dog's expression at all. It was the expression, instead, of a man who's carried his dog into the woods, a man who is now looking down at the dead dog in its grave, baffled by his own pain at the sight.

Then he stood to leave.

Sitting there on the couch, I was flooded with panic. He was leaving me, I realized, in the grave. Believing that I'd lie peacefully in the hole, he was leaving me to tend his own pain, and all I could do to signal the fact that I wasn't at peace, that I was still living, that even now I was watching him leave, was to reach for him and clutch him.

It was horrible—my strange, swollen hand shooting out of the earth—but it was all I could think to do to signal the fact that I was still living. So I clutched his wrist, and pulled him back toward my body, and when I leaned forward and kissed him, with a quickness that surprised me, because he'd been so firm about leaving, his hand had already drawn up the skirt of my dress, and then he was inside me and I was biting his neck, clawing his back, trying to hold on to his body and keep him.

WHEN WE WERE FINISHED, HE LAY WITH ME FOR A WHILE, HIS BODY behind mine on the couch, and though I couldn't see his expression, I could feel him counting the minutes as they reached toward the hour.

Realizing that, I also kept my eyes on the clock over the mantel. I, too, watched each minute pass.

He hoped, I think, that I'd fall asleep. But I stayed awake. I watched the second hand of the clock. As a result, I was able to see that it was before the hour was finished that my husband stood up.

I kept my back to him while he dressed. I listened while he buckled his big, ridiculous belt. Then I felt him standing over me, hovering somewhat awkwardly, like the last person remaining after the end of a funeral.

He stood there like someone who can't bring himself to leave the cemetery just yet, a man looking down at that hole in the ground and trying to think of something to say, worrying he hasn't yet felt the appropriate sorrow.

After a moment of silence, he kneeled beside me. "I love you," he said.

I didn't answer.

A few minutes later, the back door clicked shut and his truck sighed and slid off down the alley, and in such an efficient if inelegant manner, my husband ended the story we'd started when I first interviewed him in that bar in New York, with the beer-soaked wood shavings on the floor, and his hand grabbing mine over the table.

IT WAS AUGUST WHEN HE LEFT, AND I MOVED THROUGH THAT month in a strange state, having strange recollections.

Once, for instance, when we were still living together, my husband told me the story of a friend of his who died early. It was a man my husband had considered a mentor, in the early days of his career, when he was still living in Tennessee. This man had died abruptly of cancer, only suffering for two or three months, and dying before his wife had time to find out that through most of their marriage, he'd been having an affair.

The wife arranged the funeral with no suspicion at all, and when her husband's friends and family members had settled into their places, another woman also showed up: a stranger at the funeral, a woman nobody knew, younger than the man's wife, and dressed very differently from everyone else, so differently she almost seemed to have shown up at the wrong funeral.

Still, she stayed, and grieved in such a proprietary fashion that the man's wife—and everyone else at the funeral—immediately understood that she'd been the man's mistress.

And in the weeks after my husband left, I remembered thinking—when he first told me that story—how cruel it was that the man died before his wife had time to find out.

Or that he died before he told her the truth, before he confessed everything to her completely, so that, having lost a husband already, she lost him again in a new way at the funeral.

Such a discovery might make anyone angry, but now—finding out in the particular moment she did—the wife no longer had any right to her anger. What could her anger do, after all, now that he'd already been drastically punished?

In the same way, after my husband quarantined himself in the country, exiling himself from our house, I lived alone with my no-longer-justified anger. All I could do, now that he was already punished, if not punished by me, was to try to understand him in the light of the new information I'd gathered.

As a result, in the wake of his departure, I became more alert than I'd ever been to the details of his personality. I felt his absence as an ongoing and intensifying presence, like the pressure in the air before a storm hits. Everywhere I went—walking my son to day care, having coffee with my neighbor, driving to the grocery store—he hovered around me, following in my wake, making his presence known but never quite materializing fully.

THAT FALL, THE SUMMER HEAT HELD THROUGH OCTOBER. IN NOVEM-ber, it dropped off abruptly.

Suddenly, as if overnight, it was bitterly cold. In the mornings, each blade of grass in our front yard was furred with new frost. The sidewalk in front of our house was strewn with magnolia seed pods that looked like the severed paws of gray rabbits.

Everywhere I went in Austin, I saw signs of such brutality. I remembered Charles Whitman, or I thought of Kennedy's recent assassination in Dallas, or the civil rights worker killings that happened the previous year, or the insane number of bombs we were dropping in Vietnam, all the incomprehensible numbers of deaths, and in the air all throughout Austin, I felt a closer violence coming.

In Austin, as the days became shorter, evening arrived with outrageous force. At that time of day, I pushed my son in his stroller down the side streets in our neighborhood, toward the state hospital on Guadalupe. On our way home, for those few minutes before the last light was sucked from the sky, I was almost always overcome with that nameless dread that was growing within me. Then the blank sky over the roads was streaked with alarming new color, electric tangerine and neon pink, the sun's last, desperate light caught and magnified by the low clouds, and the telephone wires that lined Guadalupe were beaded with innumerable grackles, hunched shoulder to shoulder along the sagging lengths of the wires, as if strung together on the necklace of some demented boy chief.

Occasionally, warned by a shriek I couldn't detect, they lifted all on one wing and waved against the sky like a black flag at the head of an army. Then, just as suddenly, they landed again, and the crazed color drained out of the sky, and in the new darkness the dried husks of pecan leaves scuttled nervously off down the sidewalks.

SOMETIMES, IN SUCH A DIRE ATMOSPHERE, I WISHED FOR MY HUS-band to come home and protect us.

Other times I was more realistic. What could he do, with his little pistol, his mere pocketknife, to ward off that bloody sky, or the waving black flags of the grackles?

Nothing. In my more realistic moments, I knew that. In the end, I didn't attribute to him the power to protect me against the forces of destruction that hovered around me that winter. I only attributed to him the power to kill me.

And perhaps, in the end, that was the only power he'd ever had, and the only power I'd ever relied on. With his knife and the gun that he'd bought and the way he'd grabbed my neck and shaken it roughly, he'd advertised himself as a man who possessed the power to end a life swiftly.

And yet even that, I realized, had been a mere feint. Because rather than putting me out of my suffering swiftly, he'd simply walked out. He couldn't even stand to see me feel sorrow. In the end, he left me wounded on that couch, and though he might have easily bludgeoned me to death with the buckle of that ridiculous belt, he didn't even have the courage to kill me.

He was not, I realized, like a man who takes his old dog out to the woods in order to shoot it.

He was a man who takes his old dog out to the woods, then can't summon the will. Though he knows the dog is in pain, he can't kill it. He doesn't want the blood on his hands. He's too afraid of the guilt he'll feel after.

So instead, he leaves the old dog to suffer in agony through a cold season, dying alone in the forest, blood seeping into the fallen pecan leaves, still lifting its muzzle at any stray sound, imagining with a surge of joy that will soon plunge in the other direction that the sound might signal the approach of its master, the one man who could come and explain the sudden change in the dog's situation, or who, if he can't explain it, if he can't find the right words, will at least have the decency to simply and regrettably kill it.

THESE, OF COURSE, ARE HYSTERICAL THOUGHTS. I KNEW IT, EVEN back then. I realized that it was essential for me to stop thinking in such an uncontrolled way.

Such hysterical thoughts, as I well understood, are un-

300

forgivable thoughts in a mother. I had a child to look after. I had no right to drive myself insane for no reason. Diligently, therefore, every day, I reminded myself of the pertinent facts. Your husband only had an affair, I told myself. Many people have affairs at some point.

Who cares if he lied, I said to myself. Who cares if he left you. You're still alive, you have a son, you have a floundering career to restart.

IN MY EFFORT TO CEASE FEELING SUCH UNTOWARD EMOTIONS, I RE- doubled my efforts to understand the situation correctly. I could see no other way out than to understand the person who had caused the situation to start with.

By then, however, I no longer had the subject at hand. I couldn't question him further.

Then it seemed to me that my major mistake had been to allow my subject to escape before I'd finished the portrait. I should have managed to keep him, I thought, at least until I'd written the ending. Then I rebuked myself for all the insufferable questions I'd asked. I chastised myself for conducting those endless interrogations.

At night, trying to fall asleep while the branches of the loquat clicked their fingernails on the window, I accused myself of having presided over a brutal inquisition. I'd set up, I realized, a McCarthyan trial, adjudicating my husband's personal life. Ever since that woman called, I'd approached my husband like a prosecutor with no sense of restraint, prying into his most intimate secrets.

Standing above him and his flaws, I'd been like a cruel judge, condemning him with no sense of restraint.

Then, abhorring myself for that role in the trial, I'd find myself switching sides.

Your Honor, I often said to myself, while walking our son to day care, and arguing like a lawyer for the defense: it was only one little betrayal.

It was a little betrayal, I said to myself, that was, in the end, only a test of your capacity to understand and forgive.

It was a test of your ability to be a fair judge, to see a man's nature wholly—complicated and fallen, as all our natures are—and embrace it despite its slight imperfections.

THEN, ON MY WAY HOME FROM DAY CARE, THOUGH I'D ONCE BEEN the judge, I now found that it was I who was on trial for the crime of failing to love a man despite his imperfections.

By leaving our house, therefore, my husband hadn't punished himself, he'd punished me, and rightly, for imagining I loved him as a woman should love her husband, when in fact I was only capable of a puritanical, trite kind of judicious affection: the prudish love of a woman who won't watch violent movies, or tolerate curse words, or keep her eyes open while fucking.

ONE MORNING, IN THE SECOND WEEK OF NOVEMBER—THE MORNING before I received the call from my editor to give me the Oppenheimer assignment—I was on my way out of the grocery store, holding a bag on one hip and my son on the other, when I was stung by a bee.

It came out of nowhere. I hadn't been stung by a bee since I was a child in Princeton. Now it seemed almost funny, an absurd little slight, that in the face of everything else that had happened in the last year, some quixotic bee should think to attack me.

Swiftly, decisively, I brushed the bee off my hand. I buckled my son in his car seat. I loaded the groceries into the trunk. And only then did I notice that the bee was writhing in agony on the concrete.

I stood over it, looking down from above.

I realized that I must have brushed it off with more force than I'd thought. It was moving in circles, dragging one of its wings.

I watched it writhe for a while, wondering whether or not I should kill it. The sting on my hand had started to hurt, but that wasn't what bothered me most. What bothered me was watching its little performance. Standing there, looking down from above, and watching its flamboyant, useless suffering, and feeling within myself a surge of guilt for my part in its demise, which was a much more uncomfortable sensation than hurt or even anger.

I'd have preferred, in that moment, to feel anger at the fact that it stung me, or hurt at having been stung, rather than guilt for my part in its pain.

But there it was, dragging its wing, moving in circles, aware perhaps that it had acted stupidly, that it had stung a woman who had no intention of bringing it harm, and that in its absurd act of aggression it had caused me—taken by surprise as I was—to retaliate with equally ludicrous force.

The problem, I saw now, too late to change my reaction, was not that the bee had attacked me—the sting itself was a manageable pain—but that I hadn't foreseen the attack. Like a bad reader who fails to pick up on obvious foreshadowing, I'd failed to know that the painful moment was coming, and to prepare myself for its arrival, perhaps to plan a less brutal retaliatory attack.

Then, in the parking lot of the grocery store, I felt a rush of weariness. I had to lean against the car for a moment. We only ever know things too late, I thought. Knowledge only comes when we've obliterated the need to possess it.

WHEN I'D RECOVERED MYSELF ENOUGH TO STAND UP AGAIN, I crushed the bee under the toe of my sneaker. Afterward, it was nothing more than a smudge of black ash on the sidewalk, glamoured by faint iridescence.

People lie all the time, I thought, while starting the car and driving out of the lot. Behind me, in his car seat, my son blinked out at the world while it passed.

My husband lied to me for a long time. That wasn't unforgivable. What was unforgivable was that I failed to foresee it.

THE FOLLOWING DAY, MY EDITOR CALLED ME AND ASKED ME IF I'D write a piece on Robert Oppenheimer.

A kind of farewell, my editor said. A piece covering the span of his life, anticipating his final departure.

His death, I thought. Not his departure.

Why, I wondered, standing in the kitchen, talking on the phone, just as I had when I received that call from the woman who'd flown in from Chicago, do people insist on confusing deaths and departures?

ONCE I'D ACCEPTED THE ASSIGNMENT AND ARRANGED THE INTER-
view with Oppenheimer, I had three weeks to research his
career before I met with him in his new office.

I had three weeks, in other words, to plan the questions
I wanted to ask him: three weeks to prepare the right words,
the phrases that would elicit the answers I needed, if I was
going to get him to tell the whole story.

And of course that should have been plenty of time, but I
was operating at something less than my usual capacity. Each
time I began to prepare, I was overwhelmed by the prospect
of attempting to speak with any real authority on the life of
a man I'd never met, when—as I was beginning to realize
more and more clearly—with each effort I made to know the
man I'd chosen to marry, I only knew him less, as though my
very attempts at knowledge were to blame for my dwindling
certainty about the character of my husband. It seemed to
me that any attempts at knowledge made in a state of fear or
uncertainty—a state I'd lived in since I spoke to that woman
from Chicago—were doomed to fail, and not only to fail but
to further obscure the original subject.

And how, I thought, could I try to know a man like
Oppenheimer—who created the weapons he did, who, though
he probably didn't intend to, ushered us into an era of anxiety
unlike any era before ours—in any state other than fear and
uncertainty?

By then, I was taking care of our son on my own, and
having a hard time falling asleep. I moved through a fog. I
had trouble working. Still, however, on a few ambitious afternoons, when our son was at day care, I headed to the library

and unloaded myself onto one of the smooth plastic chairs in front of the microfiche.

Then, in a state of mesmerized detachment, I'd stare at images of mushroom clouds in various countries: the Trinity Test in the Jornada del Muerto desert, followed by explosions in Hiroshima and Nagasaki, followed by the Soviet tests of Joe 1, Joe 2, and Joe 3. And then the first real United States thermonuclear test, Ivy Mike, which incinerated an island in Eniwetok Atoll, followed by the Soviet test of the Sloika, followed by the U.S. test of Castle Bravo, which spread nuclear fallout over the Rongelap and Rongerik atolls, and poisoned the crew of a Japanese fishing boat, and polluted waters as far as Australia.

And those were only just a few of the tests. There were tests underwater, tests in outer space, submarine-launched tests, tests buried in craters.

Crime and retribution, over and over again, leading to the Soviet test of the Tsar Bomba, in 1961, the biggest bomb ever exploded, with a mushroom cloud seven times the height of Mount Everest, which destroyed all the buildings in a village thirty-four miles away from ground zero, could have caused third-degree burns sixty-two miles away, and shattered windows in Norway and Finland.

SITTING IN THE LIBRARY, I PERUSED PHOTOGRAPH UPON PHOTO-graph of mushroom clouds in various sizes and I felt no more or less nausea than I felt on a regular morning when I woke up and realized again that my husband was no longer with us.

Fear is a blind, selfish state. One morning, for instance,

sitting in the library, I found again that photograph of those women in Hiroshima, their faces bandaged so that their eyes became gaps, absences I couldn't begin to comprehend, sifting through the rubble of their former lives.

It was a photograph that had haunted me in my youth. It had given me years of nightmares, perhaps, in part, because of what I didn't know about my mother's family, about the people she'd left behind, and where they were, and what they'd suffered. But also simply because I couldn't understand what those women were feeling, what they could possibly be feeling, in the wake of such an incomprehensible stroke of destruction, and to not understand them felt to me as a child to be an unforgivable thing, such incomprehension, as I knew even then, being the only possible explanation for how the decision could be made to destroy them.

But this time, in the library, when I saw that photograph again, I felt no more spark of kinship with the women in their bandages, no more desire to feel what they might have been feeling, than I would have if the photograph had been taken of dolls.

I looked at it flatly.

That's just the truth. I don't, of course, admit it with pride. It revolted me, even then, to sit there in the library and look at that picture so flatly.

Even then, I tried to force myself to feel it. I zoomed in on the images of those women. I examined them from all angles, trying to feel some spark of desire to know them.

But in the end, I could summon little real feeling for the catastrophe that they suffered. Their existence remained unforgivably distant.

AT NIGHT, AFTER SUCH DAYS OF INEFFECTUAL RESEARCH, MY SON AND I ate dinner together. I arranged a variety of options for him on the tray of his high chair, but he never ate them. He was appalled by the foods young children usually like. He rejected whatever I tried. He drank milk, and sometimes I could induce him to eat some mashed pears, but he was horrified by everything else.

I, too, often found that I was disgusted by the food on my plate. I felt if we both managed a few bites we'd done well. Afterward, I allowed him to sit in front of the TV, something he seemed to find soothing, though probably it was bad for his brain.

But then I found it soothing as well, watching him while he watched the TV, his pale face rapt in the gloom of the dark room, the television flashing, lozenges of colored light floating over his forehead.

DURING THE DAY, IN MY RESEARCH, I TRIED TO FOCUS ON WHAT WAS important in understanding Oppenheimer.

I learned that he'd named the Trinity Test for a Donne poem. I read that, after the test, radioactive clouds drifted over towns as far as 120 miles from the test site, raining poisonous ash on cattle ranches along the Chupadera Mesa. I learned that the workers who were sent in to examine the site found thousands of dead turtles in the cracked sand, burned to death inside their shells.

I discovered, also, that the two plutonium hemispheres at the core of Oppenheimer's bomb were originally plated with silver. This blistered as a result of the heat, and in the final test, the hemispheres were plated with gold.

These are the kinds of incidental anecdotes I collected. I knew, of course, that in my research I should be focusing on the bombings of Hiroshima and Nagasaki, but it was hard for me to effectively do so.

It's difficult to focus on enormous tragedies: 129,000 dead, or approximately 129,000 dead, because the chaos in those cities was such that no one will ever know exactly how many lives were affected.

What does that number mean? In those days of research, my mind couldn't contain a number like that. It's hard enough, I thought, to focus on the facts surrounding one death. It's hard enough to make sense of the repercussions of a single betrayal.

Of course I knew, even then, that the two acts can't be compared. A betrayal is only a betrayal, even if it feels like a murder.

Even if, perhaps, it's the only possible way to ever really feel what it is to be murdered, because if we were actually murdered, we wouldn't feel it, at least not at length, and probably not with the attention to detail that we're able to register in the wake of betrayal.

In other words, or so I thought while I researched the effects of Oppenheimer's work, there's no way to obsessively ruminate over the facts of our own murder. Only a betrayal really feels—over time, in a way that can last, in a way we hold on to forever—like a murder.

And in some ways, I told myself, if you think about it too much, a betrayal *is* a kind of murder, because no man or woman is ever the same after he or she's been betrayed, and no woman or man—except, perhaps, the most craven sociopath—is ever the same after she or he's committed an act of betrayal.

So a betrayal—or so I told myself, sitting at the microfiche—*is* a murder in some ways, a murder of the betrayed as she was, and the betrayer as he was. A murder of who they were together, as a couple, or a pair, an interlocking, undifferentiable system in which the two parts depend on each other.

All of which explains, perhaps, I told myself while sitting in the library, why we never tried Oppenheimer, or anyone else involved in the Manhattan Project, or General Groves, or President Truman, or the country that voted for President Truman, for their decision to take part in a program that killed 129,000 people when, according to most historians, the war had already essentially been won, Germany having already surrendered, Japan no longer even rousing itself to defend its cities from airborne attacks, and the Soviets having already agreed to join the fight in the Pacific.

But we didn't hold any trials for that. Instead, we tried Oppenheimer for lying. We tried him for betraying his friends, his wife, and his country.

IN THOSE DAYS LEADING UP TO MY TRIP TO PRINCETON, THOUGH I knew I was focusing on the wrong thing, it was to his security hearings—in which friends and companions and enemies of Oppenheimer were asked, over and over again, how well they knew him, if he'd deceived them, whether or not they felt he could be trusted—that my attention was drawn.

Over and over again, I found myself returning to the transcripts of that unofficial trial that was held in a secret room with no windows, with two long tables organized in the shape of a T, the judges sitting along the top branch, Oppenheimer alone at the base, and Kitty sitting behind him on a sofa they dragged into the room, her leg immobilized in a cast.

At length, for days on end, Kitty sat on that sofa, and Oppenheimer sat alone at the base, and the prosecutors along one side of the T questioned him on the documented falsehoods he'd told.

From the beginning of the trial, his answers are completely unhelpful. Though he admits from the start that he lied about his trip to visit Jean Tatlock, and also about the conversations he had with Haakon Chevalier, he provides entirely unsatisfactory reasons. The prosecutors press him for more detail, but he simply can't rise to the level they want. "When you ask," he says at one point, "for a more persuasive argument as to why I did this than that I was an idiot, I am going to have more trouble being understandable."

Later, he tries again: "Whether I embroidered the story in order to underline the seriousness, or whether I embroidered it to make it more tolerable that I would not tell the simple facts . . . I don't know."

And later: "I think I need to say that it was essential that I tell this story, that I should have told it at once and should have told it completely accurately, but that it was a matter of conflict for me and I found myself, I believe, trying to give a tip to the intelligence people without realizing that when you give a tip you must tell the whole story. When I was asked to elaborate, I started off on a false pattern."

Later, growing frustrated with his attempts to explain why he lied in the first place, the prosecutors ask why, having started on a false pattern, he failed to correct it. And again, in his answer, he comes up short.

"I wish I could explain," he concludes—and as I read his response I remembered the doglike expression on my husband's face, that animal look, the expression of a creature who has no way of explaining to himself or to others why he has behaved in such a manner—"I wish I could explain to you better why I falsified and fabricated."

IN DECEMBER, HAVING RUN OUT OF TIME TO FINISH MY RESEARCH, I left my son with my neighbor and flew to New York. Then, on the train down to Princeton, while the world of winter colors rushed by, I remembered how I'd admired Oppenheimer when I was a girl, when he stood in my parents' living room with such melancholy forbearance when Kitty lurched toward him and told him she loved him. I thought of how he'd looked down at her in that woman's arms, then reached to collect her, and wrap her in her mink, and guide her gently out of the party.

From the station, I could have taken a taxi, but I decided to walk. It was a cold, unpleasant day, one of those winter afternoons when the sky hangs low overhead, gray as an old rag. Under that sky, I walked along the same streets I'd walked along so many centuries ago when I was a child: picking up candy from the store with my sister, collecting horse chestnuts alone, watching mallards swim in the pond.

For a moment, I paused on the corner of the street I grew up on. I could have walked to our old house. I could have rung the bell. I could have stepped into that same living room where my sister and I watched that Christmas party from the landing of the carpeted stairs, where my father sometimes called my mother to play the piano in front of his guests, where he used to sharpen the knives so close to her face and once, when he was goading her into a response and she wouldn't give in, he pushed her into the hearth so that she knocked her head on the stone and slid slowly down to the ground, and afterward—when she wasn't responding—he leaned down in remorse and picked her up so tenderly, like a child, and carried her gently upstairs to the bedroom.

Now my mother was dead, not because of the violence we waited for and expected, but because of an illness, which slipped in and took her when we weren't paying attention, and I hadn't spoken to my father in over a year.

On the corner, I stopped for a moment, as if to turn and walk down the street. As if I planned to go in again through that door, and call out in the foyer, as I used to call for my mother.

But then I kept walking. As I headed toward campus, I thought about the kindness that so often comes in the wake of some cruelty: My father, stooping to tenderly pick up my mother. Or Oppenheimer, gently guiding Kitty out of the party. Or even my husband, kneeling and saying I love you, when of course by then he was already leaving.

I thought that such kindness, which we produce in order to ameliorate our own guilt, was in fact an extraordinarily self-absorbed impulse, a way of decreasing the weight of our burden while also removing someone else's right to feel anger.

And by then, in the angry, unforgiving state I was in, I thought: What was wrong with the impulse to try Oppenheimer for his betrayals?

Why should we hold tribunals for war crimes and not more minute, personal errors? Such smaller crimes, I thought to myself, are in some ways even worse than the grand crimes, because they're not committed out of obedience, or in the name of higher ideals, but because we simply forget our responsibility to a person who loves us.

Or because we feel an irresistible impulse. Or because we allow ourselves to believe that it is excusable to commit some small, personal crime because we are not committing a more grandiose form of violence, like mass murder in warfare, or one of those other outsized forms of human carnage that we all enjoy protesting against because they distract us momentarily from our minute errors, the endless cascades of smaller but more pointless and cowardly little betrayals.

Why, I thought, striding down the sidewalks of Princeton—a smallish woman, dark eyed and foreign-feeling and never quite at home in any place I arrived—why should a man in this uncertain, violent world be permitted to hide behind vagueness, behind claims about the mystery of his internal existence?

Shouldn't we all live our lives knowing it's our responsibility to account for ourselves with precision?

Those were the bitter thoughts that had lodged themselves in my heart by the time I crossed campus in the ugliness of that winter afternoon, the lawns brown, the trees stripped, the fallen leaves scuttling off. And by the time I arrived at Oppenheimer's new office, at the end of that dark hallway, and he'd turned in from the window and seen me standing there on the threshold, it was clear to me as it must have been clear to him, also, that I'd come to question him so brutally that only one of us would emerge living. And when I'd taken my seat opposite him and he'd begun talking about our inability to know all the aspects of any given particle, I interrupted him rudely and began to ask questions about why he'd lied so much in those years leading up to the trial.

Then, as I've said, he turned to the window, and we both waited a long time, while the light began to drain out of the sky, and the bare trees became rust red rather than gray.

And finally he turned back from the window, and uttered that hazy answer about "the whole story of a man's life," and even then, I continued to interrogate him, and he continued evading my questions, until finally he turned and looked out the window again, toward the pond where I used to watch those pairs of mallards, and where in the winter my sister and I used to ice-skate.

His profile was emaciated: a beak of a nose, those shaggy eyebrows. I noticed that his mouth twitched at one corner. The skin sagged from his cheekbones.

Then, suddenly, I remembered that bee. I remembered that wounded bee, dragging its wing on the pavement, the bee I'd destroyed with such outlandish retaliation because I was startled.

And I realized I was watching Oppenheimer with the same sad, tired curiosity with which I'd watched that bee, dragging itself in those awful circles. I'd treated him, I realized, too harshly. I realized I'd felt, for a moment, as if all the new uncertainty in my life—the forces of destruction that had started to gather around me in the kitchen when that woman called; or perhaps the forces of destruction that had been gathering around me since I was a child in that house in

Princeton, waiting on the carpeted stairs to witness the violence that was sure to take place; or perhaps indeed the forces of destruction that had gathered around me everywhere I went in this world, in which people I didn't know in positions of power possessed such weapons as I could barely bring myself to imagine—as if all the uncertainty in the world had been caused by this one man, and that therefore he should be punished.

And yet, watching him now, I realized how small and how weak he really was. I realized that he, too, lived in the same uncertain world, and that he had always lived in that world, even when he was making those weapons, imagining he was in control of their outcome, not yet knowing that he in fact had no say over when and how the army would use them, indeed over when and how the army and the president had already decided to use them, and for what reasons, and to what end. I had imagined—he had imagined—that he had some power over those forces, but in fact he was only a small, helpless part of a process that was bigger than him and that he hadn't yet comprehended.

His major mistake, I realized, had been to believe that he understood. That he could set himself apart from history and see his role in it, and therefore act well, and with full comprehension.

But in the end he, too, had lived caught up in the incomprehensible tumult, caught in the same uncertainty I'd always hated, and why he'd done what he did to take control of that chaos didn't matter as much anymore. I was sorry for what he'd suffered, as a result of the suffering he'd caused other people.

THEN, FOR SOME TIME, WHILE HE LOOKED OUT THE WINDOW, WE SAT together in that silence that rose up around us. Outside, the light had fallen to the point that the edges of things were lined with thin brightness, so that solid objects like trees and buildings seemed flat and insubstantial, like cardboard illuminated from behind.

In that light, nothing seemed real. Everything seemed to be shifting into the new order of evening, taking new shape, becoming less solid. Even the objects inside, the desk, the file cabinet, even Oppenheimer himself seemed to be growing flimsy and thin, as though, if I'd tried to reach out to touch him, my hand might have moved through him.

For a while I watched him, sitting there at his desk, with the same unsteady feeling I'd lived with since that woman called and informed me that the idea I'd had of my husband was false, or at least no more true than the idea she'd had of my husband, so that the original became confused with its shadow, and neither one was really solid, neither one could be grasped fully.

In the same way, Oppenheimer had lost his definite shape. As if, in his office, sitting in silence, we sat together in the chaos of a kaleidoscope that's turned between slides, before the blurred geometries have resolved themselves once again into crystals.

For a moment, he'd become insubstantial, as though my hand might have passed through him. As though he could have passed through me, into me, infecting me, becoming more real inside me than he was in the real world.

"You'll have to forgive me," he said finally. "I'm in some pain. My hearing and speech are quite poor at this point."

I CAN'T REMEMBER WHICH QUESTIONS I INVENTED TO FINISH THE interview after that. I tried, to whatever extent I was able, to be easy on him when I could. I realized I'd been a bully, so I was careful to assist him in the work of picking himself up and brushing himself off after that embarrassing silence.

And slowly—though never completely—he assembled himself into a person again. He told me his anecdotes, crystallized over a lifetime. He demonstrated several points about theoretical physics. He explained the picture of Kitty. He told me a story about a friend of his on St. John and a turtle he and his daughter had released back to the ocean. He told me about a dinner party he and Kitty had gone to in Paris, thrown by an old friend from Berkeley.

He told me about that awful night on the mesa, after they'd exploded the Nagasaki bomb, a bomb he hadn't known would be dropped, and how the GIs threw a party he'd felt obligated to attend.

He told me about a talk he gave at a school called Sudbury once, on the subject of responsibility and privilege, and he told me about a secretary he had in Princeton, who gave him a blank sampler her sister embroidered.

He told me about a house he'd loved once, on Shasta Road. He told me he'd often listened to Bach in difficult moments. He told me it was Jean who introduced him to the metaphysical poets, and that the last time he'd seen her, they'd danced at the Xochimilco Café.

He said he'd begun collecting rocks when he was a child and his father took him back to Germany, where he met his grandfather for the first and only time in his life.

He told me that his mother could have been a great

painter, but she'd gotten married. He told me that he'd really believed it was the right thing to do to go back and see Jean, though six months later she drowned herself in the bathtub. And he told me that even despite everything he'd learned about the dreadful politics of the thing, the fact that it might have done nothing to speed up the end of the war, and the new facts revealed every day about the extent of the suffering they caused in Japan, he didn't regret building the bomb, because he felt it was a scientist's duty to know, and he'd acted as a scientist.

And I listened to him while he spoke, attempting to assemble himself once again, trying to describe himself in a way that would cohere, and when the interview had concluded, I stood and shook his hand and moved to the door, and as I crossed the room, I saw a pack of cigarettes underfoot.

I looked down at them for a moment. Somehow I'd missed them on my way in. I'd imagined I'd seen everything in that clean, oddly bare office. But I'd missed that open pack.

It was a strange piece of evidence, because Oppenheimer had only smoked pipes since he learned that he was dying of cancer. But there it was, its top tilted open, revealing the foil and a few loose cigarettes falling out.

Stiffly, as if I'd been sitting longer than I really had, I leaned over and picked them up, and by the time I'd stood again, Oppenheimer was already there by my side, offering me his silver lighter.

How seamlessly, in that single gesture, he slipped again into the charm of his youth.

With such practiced style, he gave the kaleidoscope a quick turn. With the same elegance that was his when those women congregated around him in the living room of my parents' house, he offered me that silver lighter, holding it before him like a torch, like an invaluable clue, a discovery I'd nearly missed.

Here I am, he seemed to be saying. Remember me: a boy who learned to ride over the mountains.

Who came home to his parents, who later went west again and felt free, who loved a girl and didn't save her, who noted the sky, who noted the mountains, who did harm he never intended and didn't ever forgive himself simply.

I am he, Oppenheimer seemed to be saying. A scientist. A man who helps his wife into her coat. A man who will always swoop in with his lighter.

THOUGH I DON'T SMOKE, I LET HIM LIGHT THE CIGARETTE.

I thanked him, and when I left his new office, the cigarette was still lighted. I walked with it down the empty staircase, along the empty front hall, and out the front doors of the new institute building. I only stubbed it out when I'd reached the sidewalk.

Then, standing alone, in my thin coat, I looked down at the smudge of ash on the concrete and thought about that bee I killed, and the article I'd have to write.

I felt strangely rooted in place, staring down at that smudge of ash, wondering about how I'd ever get started. Where could I begin, I thought, in telling the story of such a man's life? Looking down at that glistening smudge, I thought of the anecdotes he'd relied on: the secretary with her blank sampler; the Berkeley friend he'd seen in Paris; the song he and Jean danced to at the Xochimilco Café. What could they tell me, I wondered, about such a man? How could they help me to know him?

Lost in such thoughts, I had to tear myself away and force myself to move toward the station, and as I walked away from campus, past the street where I grew up, where my mother never explained to me why she stayed with my father, or what she left behind when she came here, I thought that perhaps it's only in those moments between the slides of the kaleidoscope, those moments of a life that never crystallize into practiced anecdote or reliable knowledge, that we close our eyes and people pass through us, or over us and around us, as a wave sweeps us off our feet and makes us another part of its motion.

Then, I thought, in that moment of unknowing, there's no difference between us. And I thought again about that bee I'd crushed in the weeks after that woman called me, and the love I'd felt for it after, when it was dragging itself in circles, both of us stunned by the violence that had escalated so abruptly. I thought about my husband, and the love I'd felt for him when he sat on the rug with our son, looking up at me with that lost expression, befuddled by the unhappiness he'd set into motion. I thought about my father, stung by the stupidity of his own joke, and my mother, with her frozen face, playing the piano while we watched from the landing, all of us caught up in that wave of cruelty we couldn't quite grasp, all of us swept off our feet and tumbled over by that force so much larger than any one of us could be: trying, in that tumult, to find something solid to keep, a person to know, a rock to hold on to.

And then I thought again of those women in the photograph of Hiroshima, their faces bandaged, their eyes holes in the white cloth, moving through the charred rubble.

I thought of those women who, in the days after the bombings, seemed to be scouring the ruins, looking for some artifact of their former lives, which—in one instant after that single plane passed over a sky described by everyone who survived as irreproachably, perfectly blue—had been so thoroughly and absolutely demolished.

Walking back toward the train, in that strange and wavering light, I thought about what I didn't know of those women in that photograph.

They'd lost so much more than I'd ever lost, searching in the rubble that was the result of one plane crossing a clear blue sky and a single flash of white light, obliterating their city in an inexplicable instant, so that later, in the wake of that instantaneous and total destruction, they were left to search the rubble for some piece of proof that their former lives had ever existed.

Or that's what I imagined. Maybe, I thought, though I'd never know, they were searching for some little thing—an old scrap of fabric, a rock, a page torn from a book—something that could be held, something that could be felt as evidence of those days before the destruction, days that passed in relative peace, searching for something solid to hold so they wouldn't be forced to carry the entirety of the world as it once was—the seasons as they'd once developed, the trees as they'd come to leaf, the people they'd fallen in love with under the canopies of those branches—inside their own minds, a world purely imagined, the real world having flashed white and then tilted and passed thinly shuddering through them.

Acknowledgments

I am beyond grateful to Megan Lynch, Susanna Lea, and Kerry Glencorse, for guiding this book through every stage of existence; to Emma Dries, Ashley Garland, and everyone at Ecco, as well as Mark Kessler and everyone at Susanna Lea Associates, for all their support; and to Marie-Pierre Gracedieu at Gallimard, for helping me understand what it was I was writing.

Thanks also to everyone at Yaddo, Macdowell, and La Maison de la Poésie, for precious time to finish this; and to the nonfiction writers—especially Kai Bird and Martin J. Sherwin, Michihiko Hachiya, M.D., John Hershey, A. C. Grayling, and the contributors to Women of Wartime Los Alamos—whose research and testimony provided the backbone of this novel.

And, finally, thanks to William Callahan, Matthew Hall, Louisa Thomas, Ben Heller, and Daniel Thomas Davis, who read drafts and offered wise counsel, and who are also people

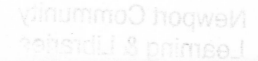

I love and am so deeply grateful to have in my life; and to all the friends and family members without whose support I couldn't have finished, especially my mother and sister, Carlin Wing, Anna Margaret Hollyman, Rachel Reilich, and Ivy Pochoda.

Also by Louisa Hall

SPEAK
THE CARRIAGE HOUSE

Louisa Hall grew up in Philadelphia. After graduating from Harvard, she played squash professionally while finishing her premedical coursework and working in a research lab at the Albert Einstein Hospital. She holds a PhD in literature from the University of Texas at Austin. She is the author of *The Carriage House* and *Speak* and lives in New York.